Goblin King

Also by Kara Barbieri

White Stag

Goblin King

KARA BARBIERI

WEDNESDAY BOOKS
NEW YORK

First published in the United States by Wednesday Books, an imprint of St. Martin's Publishing Group

GOBLIN KING. Copyright © 2020 by Kara Barbieri. All rights reserved. Printed in the United States of America. For information, address St. Martin's Publishing Group, 120 Broadway, New York, NY 10271.

www.wednesdaybooks.com

Designed by Devan Norman

Library of Congress Cataloging-in-Publication Data

Names: Barbieri, Kara, author.
Title: Goblin king / Kara Barbieri.
Description: First edition. | New York : Wednesday Books, 2020. | Series: Permafrost ; Book 2 | Summary: As Janneke struggles with her new powers and Soren adapts to being Erlking, the world they know is on the brink of ending, and freeing Janneke's tormentor's spirit from Hel may be the only way to prevent Ragnarök.
Identifiers: LCCN 2020030037 | ISBN 9781250247605 (hardcover) | ISBN 9781250149619 (ebook)
Subjects: CYAC: Goblins—Fiction. | End of the world—Fiction. | Hell—Fiction. | Fantasy.
Classification: LCC PZ7.1.B3705 Go 2020 | DDC [Fic]—dc23
LC record available at https://lccn.loc.gov/2020030037

Our books may be purchased in bulk for promotional, educational, or business use. Please contact your local bookseller or the Macmillan Corporate and Premium Sales Department at 1-800-221-7945, extension 5442, or by email at MacmillanSpecialMarkets@macmillan.com.

First Edition: 2020

10 9 8 7 6 5 4 3 2 1

To Erika, my first friend and biggest fan. I love that you're cool talking about Permafrost at two in the morning.

To Katherine, who is one of the best people in my life. Your support, strength, and resilience inspire and empower me every day.

I was angry with my friend;
I told my wrath, my wrath did end.
I was angry with my foe:
I told it not, my wrath did grow.
And I waterd it in fears,
Night & morning with my tears:
And I sunned it with smiles,
And with soft deceitful wiles.
And it grew both day and night.
Till it bore an apple bright.
And my foe beheld it shine,
And he knew that it was mine.
And into my garden stole,
When the night had veild the pole;
In the morning glad I see;
My foe outstretched beneath the tree.

—WILLIAM BLAKE,
"A POISON TREE"

Prologue

FEAR

THE STAG HAS never been afraid. Never had a reason to be afraid. He's the lifebringer to the Permafrost; he is the reason the Permafrost exists. And even when he is hunted, he feels no fear, only the thrill of a challenge. That was how it had always been and would always be. Because those hunting him want *his* favor, not his flesh.

At least that is how it used to be.

Now he is stuck in the void that is time and space, death but not death.

He doesn't blame the girl who took the mantle of his power, his abilities, away from him. In fact, he encouraged her, knowing well that he was dying and would not receive a second life.

But even in the void, he felt her desperately reach out to him, begging for his help. But the once-stag ignored it. She would have to figure it out on her own. No more did he exist on her level. She must learn to exist as he did. He fears she will never learn.

She has survived so much. A sadistic goblin who tried to destroy her body, the slow acceptance of another goblin in her life, the Hunt where she found much of what she missed about herself, and the brutal fights along the way. She is strong. She will continue to survive.

The once-stag hopes, at least. Because the towers of the worlds are falling down, and the current stag needs to be ready.

PART ONE

THE STAG

1

VISIONS

THE EYES STARING back at me in the mirror weren't
my own. Sure, they were green, but a different kind
of green. Not like mine. Not the color of moss and ivy
but an unnaturally bright color.

They were mocking eyes with a cruel mouth and a harsh
nose. Freshly made scars littered the intruder's once-pretty
face.

Lydian stared back at me from the mirror with a slow,
taunting smile growing on his face.

From beside me, Soren was still heavily asleep, and for
that, I was glad. Perhaps if he looked in the mirror, all he
would see was our own reflections, but I didn't want to risk it.
Not with my worst nightmare staring back at me.

"Leave me alone," I said, knowing full well that he
wouldn't.

But you haven't answered my question. He didn't open his
mouth to speak, but I heard the words in my head all the same.
What happens when the serpent stops eating its tail?

"What happens if I smash this mirror? Will you leave?"

Oh, you should know by now I'll never leave, Janneka. Not when there's so much work to be done.

That was it. With a flash of hot fury, I slammed the heel of my palm into the glass, causing it to shatter on the floor. The specter of Lydian disappeared with the broken glass, but his voice still lingered in my head.

You cannot get rid of me. Not when there's still so much to do.

"Janneke?" I whirled around, prepared to see Lydian somehow staring behind me, but it was only Soren. His long hair was disheveled and his lilac eyes blinked sleepily. "Are you okay?"

"I—I'm fine," I stammered. "Sorry for waking you."

He sniffed the air. "You're bleeding."

I was silent. What was I supposed to say? That I kept seeing the apparition of his dead uncle who gave me cryptic advice, and I got tired of it so I smashed the mirror? That would go over well.

Soren sighed and took my bleeding hand, gently nipping the broken skin until it knit itself back together. "I'm not going to ask you why you smashed the mirror," he said. "I know you'll tell me in your own time."

"I keep having nightmares," I said. It was true. Maybe not the reason I smashed the mirror, but it definitely was true. They plagued me every time I closed my eyes. A serpent twined around the world, waiting to devour it whole; a ship manned by the dead, made of fingernails, sailing ever closer to us; the earth crumbling in on itself and falling into oblivion; people riddled with holes and pockmarks and wounds so terrible that all they could do was lie there and wish for the sweet release of death.

The nightmares came from stories I'd grown up on. The serpent that stretched around the world forced to bite its own tail to keep it from devouring the world was the world serpent, Jörmungandr. My father delighted in scaring all of his daughters with tales of the jaws of the great beast. And the ship made of fingernails . . . the *Naglafar*. Too terrifying to put into words, almost; I would hide under my blankets whenever he told that tale—something unbecoming of a young warrior. If you didn't die in battle, and your life wasn't bad enough solely for Hel, then the *Naglafar* is where you went. To work bone-chilling labor as your fingernails grew faster and faster, painful and debilitating, until they fell off thick as wood and long as branches. They crafted a ship with them; a ship where they would travel to fight in Ragnarök, on the side of those who'd end the world.

My father used to hold me and say they were just stories. But, considering all I'd been through, considering I'd even talked with a goddess, my faith that the horrific remained in stories was starting to waver.

But I was no longer a child. Yes, I had nightmares. But until now, they never were like this.

Part of me believed I would always have nightmares. There was so much in my past that continued to haunt me. I was safe. But I would always be haunted. My mind couldn't simply forget the horrors I'd been through. But at least those nightmares had a root, a cause. At least those nightmares made some sort of sense. I *knew* why I was having them. With these, I didn't even know where to begin. None of it made sense. It was horror after horror flashing in my mind.

"Lydian?" Soren asked, wrapping one strong arm around me.

I leaned into the embrace. "Yes," I said. "Among other things."

Soren kissed the top of my head. "He's dead. He can't hurt you anymore. I know it takes . . . time, and you might never get over what he did to you. But you have to keep repeating that he can't hurt you anymore."

I glanced to the shattered mirror; a sliver of blond hair flickered in the glass before disappearing once again. *Oh, how I wished that were true.* But I couldn't tell Soren that. I didn't know how I'd do so without convincing him I'd gone certifiably mad, and to be honest, I was embarrassed to admit what had been going on after keeping the secret for half a year. So, instead, I continued to press into his embrace, cherishing the warmth of his body and the sound of his beating heart.

"Come back to bed," he said, and I let him guide me back to the sleeping platform we shared, and we climbed under the furs. His arm was still around my shoulders as I curled up close to him, my head resting on his chest. His heart beat calmly, slower than a human's and quieter, but it beat all the same. I let it lull me to sleep.

Thankfully, the nightmares didn't come back.

———

THE COLD SUNLIGHT was filtering in through the glass panes of the window by the time I woke, and I immediately swore. It had to be nearing noon and we'd *drastically* overslept.

Usually I woke up with the sun and then spent the next hour rousing Soren until he finally got up, but obviously I'd been too exhausted from my ordeal last night to do so.

Continuing to swear under my breath, I nudged Soren. He groaned a little and threw an arm over his face.

"Soren, get up." I nudged a little harder, not wanting to startle him and risk the possibility of a bloody nose. Goblin fast reflexes were not always a blessing.

"Five more minutes," he moaned and tried to pull the furs over his head.

I yanked them back down. "It's nearly noon, Soren. We're late. We're *incredibly* late. You've got a meeting with the svartelves today. Do you want Donnar to get mad?"

At the word "svartelves," his eyes shot open and I quickly got out of the way as he sprung to a sitting position. "Fuck," he said. "Shit." He looked at the sunlight gleaming through the window. "Fuck," he said again. "Shit."

"Your vocabulary continues to astound me," I deadpanned, already up and dressing for the day. The room we shared in the Erlking's palace was much bigger than either of our rooms had been back at Soren's manor, though it was as sparsely furnished. Soren and I decided to get rid of most of the decorations and trappings when we moved in. Soren's statement long ago about the Erlking's palace sorely needing redecoration had not been wrong.

"Someone's cheeky this morning," he said as he joined me in the rush to get ready. He turned toward the mirror as he raked his hair with his hands before swearing when he realized it was broken. "How's my hair look?"

I gave him a withering look. "Soren, your hair always looks perfect." The white locks were shorter now after they'd been burned during the final fight with Lydian, reaching a little bit past his ears. Too short for traditional long braids, he wore it all in a single braid atop his scalp. To my great ire, he never woke up with bedhead, no matter how disheveled the rest of his appearance was in the morning. In comparison, it took me at least a half hour to be presentable.

"The day it doesn't," I continued, "I will declare a national holiday."

That gave him pause. "You know, maybe I should go in looking sloppy. Just in case Tibra is there." He scowled. "That little menace cannot keep her hands to herself."

"Try not to kill them," I said. "It would really put a damper on the whole diplomacy thing."

Soren cracked a smile. "It'd be so much easier not to kill them if you were with me."

"You know I have training," I said. "If I ever want to fully learn how to use the stag's power, then I need to train my abilities. I've not even reached a quarter of their capabilities. Besides, Satu will definitely keep you from killing anyone."

"I know, I know," Soren said. "Go train, little stag. I'll hold down the fort and try not to kill anyone. But first." He swept me up into a kiss. What was probably only meant to last a second lasted even longer as I twined my fingers in his hair, pulling him against my body. His heat, his smell, his body, it surrounded every inch of me, and I ached to fall into it and lose myself in the expanse of blue-white skin. Soren growled under his breath, a hungry, near-primal growl, as he deepened the kiss, sucking hard on my bottom lip.

Each of us was so wrapped up in the other that we didn't hear the door open and the small "oh" that came from the intruder.

"Um," said an awkward voice. "My mom's looking for you, Soren. Better get on that."

Soren opened one eye and peered over my shoulder at Seppo before growling again and returning to the kiss. It was softer now, sweeter, and our lips lingered together for one more moment before we broke away. "I'm coming, I'm coming."

Seppo's eyebrows raised, but he said nothing as Soren grabbed the sheaths for his swords, threw on his cloak, and headed out the door. When he finally left, a smirk played on the halfling's lips. "That was quite the display of dominance."

I rolled my eyes as we turned down the hallway to the courtyard where I usually trained. "How's your mother?" I asked.

"Pregnant. Again," Seppo said in the same tone of voice someone would announce the weather.

We picked up our pace as we traveled through the maze-like hallways of the palace, by now knowing which places had dead ends or random drops and which places would take us to our destination the fastest.

"Again?" I asked. "Really?" Satu, Seppo's mother, was known to couple with human men instead of other goblins and carry halfling offspring. There were very few halflings in the

Permafrost—Satu most likely was mother to a high percentage of them.

Seppo shrugged. "I'm getting a new little brother. Or sister. One more for our merry home."

"How many siblings do you actually have anyway?"

Seppo paused, frowning. "Um, huh. Hold on, let me think."

"Think and walk," I said, continuing forward.

We arrived at the courtyard far too late, but at least we got there without any hassle. I breathed in the crisp Permafrost air, the cold filling me with energy. The flavors of life danced on my tongue, muted, but there all the same. The changing of leaves, the burrowing of small, hardy creatures that made the tundra of the Permafrost their home, the smell and taste of sweat from people and creatures alike. All of it was covered in canopies of prey lines that glittered like ice crystals across the grounds.

I'd barely been able to take in the beauty of it all before someone grabbed me roughly and pulled me aside.

"Ouch!" I glared at the serious-faced, black-haired she-goblin. Her dark blue eyes sparked with electricity and her touch stung. I yanked my arm away.

Diaval crossed her arms. "You're late."

"I know," I said.

"Incredibly late." Her expression didn't change.

"I had a . . . rough night last night. We overslept," I explained, trying to discreetly glance toward Seppo and then back at her.

Her eyes told me that she understood. "Hey, Seppo. Rose was looking for you. I think he's somewhere in the stables."

At the mention of his boyfriend, Seppo stood a little straighter. He gave Diaval a wary look, like she might possibly bite him. No doubt he would be happy for any excuse to leave the area.

"Oh, well," Seppo said. "I better help him, then. With the horses, I mean. Help him with the horses."

We watched as the halfling attempted to sprint off before we could catch the sight of his ear tips turning crimson.

"Well," Diaval said. "That was easy."

"Any excuse to be alone together." I nodded, looking at Diaval's semi-disgusted face. "Their love is purer than rain," I added, smirking.

Diaval grimaced. "Excuse me while I puke."

"Nice, healthy relationships are that unimaginable to you?"

She waved her hand. "I don't bother with that sort of stuff. Now sit and let's get to work." She brushed back the leather tails of her coat to sit cross-legged on the stone tiles of the courtyard. She rested a hand on each knee, curling her fingertips from where they poked out of her fingerless gloves until blue light crackled from them.

I sat across from her in the same position, though, as usual, nothing ever emitted from my hands. Reaching down into the solid cold of my core, where I could envision my stag powers rested, I tried to pull them up, but it was like fumbling in the dark for something that might not even exist in the first place.

"Stop forcing it," Diaval said. "It won't come if you force it."

I sighed. Not even a minute in and I was already frustrated enough to throw something. I'd been the stag for nearly a year and still had nothing to show for it. Other than the unconscious regulation of Soren's power and the connection we had as the stag and Erlking, I was no closer to unlocking any abilities that the stag might have. Bitterness rose in my throat like bile. The more I tried and the more I failed, the more I couldn't help but feel like I was missing some fundamental part of being . . . well . . . whatever I was supposed to be. That this destiny laid out for me might not truly have been my path at all.

Ah, Janneka. Always conflicted.

"Get out of my head," I muttered under my breath. Diaval raised a fine black eyebrow.

"Still bothering you, is he?" she asked.

"Hence the rough night. Both him and nightmares. I ended up breaking a mirror." I released the tension between my shoulder blades, head coming to rest against my palms.

"Poor Soren," Diaval said dryly, before becoming serious once more. "Have you told him yet? About these things?"

I scoffed. "What am I supposed to tell him? He's got enough to worry about without me seeing the specter of his dead uncle and dreaming of the apocalypse."

"You two are the stag and Erlking. More important, you're partners. I may not partake in relationships, but I think that should mean something regarding these types of situations." Diaval ran a hand through feathery black hair. "What's more is that obviously whatever you're experiencing, it has to do with being the stag. It started with the stag, right?"

I shrugged. "I guess so. At least, there was a month in between all the chaos. But I've never heard voices or seen figures before now, so I guess it must."

"But you're not hearing voices and hallucinating," Diaval said. "It's real, what you're seeing."

Real. It couldn't be real. I didn't think I could possibly stand it if it were real. "It's not real," I said through gritted teeth.

"Denial isn't a very good look on you, you know," she said. "Tell me, do you really think whatever is going on is simple nightmares and hallucinations? Because I know you don't. Also, I *know* the difference between someone who's losing their mind and someone going through psychical magical visions. I do have some experience in this. And you need support for it besides me. Which is why you need to tell Soren."

"Soren was right. The longer you keep a secret, the harder it is to tell," I said.

"Soren kept a secret for over a hundred years. You've kept this for a few months, I believe it'll be easier to break," Diaval said, a hint of snark in her voice.

I groaned and buried my head in my hands. There was a crippling feeling of failure in my chest that blossomed with sharp bursts of anxiety and pain. Shouldn't I know what the Hel I was doing by now? It'd been nearly a year since the events of the Hunt, and I was still nowhere closer to discovering how to use the stag's power actively or figuring out why I was seeing Lydian, why I heard his voice, and why my sleep was plagued with these apocalyptic nightmares. Sure, maybe I was born on the border of the Permafrost and the human world, and maybe it filled me with a type of magic that others couldn't possess. Maybe that magic was why the original stag, the symbol of the Erlking, the great spirit of the

Permafrost, could pass on its mantle to me after its original form had died. It didn't change the fact that I couldn't tell where the stag ended and I began, much less reach the part of my brain that kept the stag powers in check for me to use. It was like an entirely new sphere of my brain had shown itself behind a glass wall, but I couldn't get through the glass to actually reach it.

"You have the ability to do so much, Janneke." She placed a hand on my knee. "The power is in you; you need to understand it."

"Well, it's not my fault being the stag doesn't come with an instruction manual," I snapped, then immediately felt guilty. Diaval was only trying to help. "I'm sorry. I'm frustrated."

Diaval didn't look offended. We were close enough to deal with each other's unique brand of harshness. I never would have believed I'd find others in the Permafrost that gave me the same sense of connection as people in the human realm had. Not to degrade Soren and Seppo, obviously, but I'd lived my human life with six other siblings, all female, and was privy to all the gossip and talk even if I could never be a part of it due to my restrictions. I always had to play rough with the men outside. And maybe Diaval was not particularly traditionally feminine, but she sure as Hel was close to that type of friend I longed for growing up.

Diaval rested back on her heels, looking toward the palace. By now, Soren would be in talks with the svartelves, discussing some type of statecraft or complaint, and if we were lucky they wouldn't fight to the death or deliver some inane prophecy annoying enough for Soren to put a hole in the wall, only to make him angrier when they said they were kidding. It wasn't hard to picture with Soren's annoyance buzzing in my ears like an insect. I prayed to whichever god was listening that he managed to keep his temper. Not that I'd blame him for flipping out on them. I wasn't sure how those creatures got to be so maddening, but by the gods, they made me want to tear my hair out. Even for the Permafrost, they were so . . . unnatural.

"You should ask Donnar," Diaval said, eyebrows furrowing as she continued to look at the palace as if she could see inside it.

"I managed one meeting with Donnar, and I almost lost my wits. I don't think I would survive going on Donnar's idea of self-discovery again. Speaking to svartelves in general tends to make you want to pummel your brain into bits."

"Svartelves know things, creepy little shits that they are. It might help." She shrugged.

Yes, said the voice inside my head. *Speak to him.*

"Like I'm going to do anything *you* say," I muttered under my breath. If Diaval heard me, she made no sign.

Instead, she turned her head around, looking at something over my shoulder. She breathed out heavily through her nose. "Oh, no."

"What?"

She didn't get to answer before the stampeding of hooves and shouting of men filled the courtyard. A dark brown horse galloped past us, her reins flowing free in the wind. Right after her came Seppo and Rosamund, both men shouting at the horse and each other at the top of their lungs.

I rolled my eyes. What kind of idiot doesn't know you don't chase or shout at a horse you're trying to catch.

"Do you think we should help them?" Diaval asked, though she looked reluctant.

"I kinda want to watch this one," I said.

And so we did. For twenty agonizing minutes, we watched as the two males tried everything to get the horse back under control. Everything, of course, besides walking up to it slowly and speaking in a soft voice. Once or twice Seppo dodged a pair of hooves, which was good since, goblin or not, I was pretty sure even the advanced healing ability they had wouldn't fix a caved-in face. Rosamund's red hair had fallen from its ponytail and his face was streaked with what I hoped was mud. He waved his arms, trying to herd the horse toward Seppo, who immediately dove out of the way as the animal continued running at him at full speed.

Diaval and I exchanged glances. "Males," she said, like it explained everything.

Sighing, I got up before the horse could terrorize or be terrorized anymore. Reaching out with the flimsy, almost intangible power I possessed, I brushed softly against the horse's mind. Calming thoughts, peaceful thoughts, fearless thoughts, I sent them all to the creature, breathing in and out as I felt its heart slow to match my pace. I walked toward it slowly, not looking it straight in the face like a predator would. One hand was outstretched as I got closer and closer until I touched the animal's soft, velvety nose and grabbed the bridle there.

"Shh," I hushed, rubbing the great beast's neck. "It's all right, it's all right."

Rose and Seppo approached me, thankfully slowly this time. "Thanks, Janneke." Rose rubbed the back of his neck, trying to hide his embarrassment. "You shouldn't have bothered. We would've caught her eventually."

Diaval gave a delicate snort from where she stood behind him. "Yeah, you definitely had that situation well under control."

With that, I smiled. Oh, how it was nice to be friends with someone who actually managed to use and understand sarcasm daily. Both Seppo and Rosamund stared at her confused for a moment before understanding dawned on their faces.

"Must you do that?" Rose asked.

"Sarcasm is literally the only thing currently keeping me sane, so yes," Diaval replied.

Keeping a hand on the horse's bridle, I turned to give the two men a questioning look. "Do I want to know why you not only managed to let a horse escape the stables but were running after it like two madmen? Or will it cause me to go prematurely gray?" The horse huffed, like it, too, wanted to know what was going on in these guys' heads.

"Oh, okay so," Seppo started, eyes flickering around to make sure the courtyard was still empty. It was. Despite the stones inlaid in the ground and a few of the Permafrost-hardy plants growing, the courtyard lacked most everything that had been in it during the time of the previous Erlking. Instead of plotting goblins lurking in the shadows, it was an open and silent place.

Well, except for when two silly goblins chased a horse into it.

"Well, you know, my mom is pregnant again so we thought—"

"What?" Diaval interrupted, her eyebrows shooting up to nearly her hairline. "Again?"

"That's what I said," I commented.

Seppo glared at us. "*Anyway,* this horse got captured during a raid a little while back, and Rose and I've been trying to train it as a present."

"I wasn't aware newborns could ride horses," Diaval said wryly.

"For when the kid is *older,*" he clarified. "I mean, if the kid ends up staying here. When it comes to halflings, there's always like a quarter chance they end up fully human. In that case, she'll probably drop the kid off on the doorstep of whoever its father is."

Something struck me from our previous conversation. "You never did tell me how many siblings you had."

Rose turned to his boyfriend. "Yeah, how many siblings *do* you have, anyway?"

"The ones currently alive and in the Permafrost that I personally know about?" Seppo said. "Maybe twenty-three. I'm sure there are some fully human ones and some who've died considering my mom's age."

"And here I thought having six older sisters was a lot."

As fascinating as I find the conversation, you should really find Donnar. I gritted my teeth at Lydian's voice in my head. I'd talk to Donnar on my own time. Lydian was probably pissed at hearing about all the kids Satu had with men that weren't him. Ugh, the fact he tried to court her was disgusting.

Rude.

"Fuck off."

The others looked at me for a moment. "Lydian again?" Rose asked.

"He's still bothering you?" Seppo said.

"Does literally everyone *but* Soren know about this?" I groaned, feeling the urge to throw my hands in the air. And also maybe punch something.

"I don't know if you've noticed," Rose said, "considering how close you two are, but Soren is relatively . . . how do I put this . . . obtuse."

"He lacks emotional intelligence," Diaval added.

"You really need to spell things out for him," Seppo piled on.

I pinched the bridge of my nose, already feeling a headache coming on. In that weird shadowy part of my brain, Soren's feelings took over my own, and I watched as the annoyance grew to anger. Whatever was going on with the svartelves, he was not enjoying it. In fact . . . I pushed further into that part of my mind, trying to make out actual images instead of feelings. I closed my eyes, trying to concentrate, before immediately snapping them open again.

"What is it?" Diaval asked, noticing the look of concern on my face.

"I need to go stop Soren from murdering Tibra. Look after the horse for me, will you?" I didn't give her the chance to answer before I broke into a full sprint, hoping to get to the reception hall before Soren did actually murder someone and start a gods damned war.

2

THE MAN IN THE CAVES

A WAR WAS averted, but it was a close call. I got into the throne room in time to see Soren launch himself at Tibra. The female svartelf gave a high-pitched giggle and disappeared from sight, Soren crashing on the marble of the floor.

He pushed himself up, snarling. "Where did she go?"

Donnar was watching the incident with a slightly amused look on his face. "She probably is back in the caverns."

"How?" Soren growled.

The svartelf gave a very dainty shrug for a creature who literally had no skin on his entire back half and shoulders. "Magic, most likely."

Soren still had one of those *I'm about to murder literally everybody* looks on his face. I sighed and decided to step in.

Taking a look around, my eyebrows shot up to my hairline. There were a few cracks in the walls and the giant gash in the floor from where Soren challenged Lydian before the Hunt had grown wider. A few chairs were knocked over, and standing a bit behind Soren, I could see a very exasperated Satu.

"So, is anyone going to tell me what exactly happened here?" I asked.

Soren looked up at me, having the decency to at least act a little sheepish. "There was a fight."

"I can see that."

"Soren attacked my mate," Donnar said.

There was a pregnant pause before I frowned. "I thought Tibra was your sister?"

Donnar shrugged once more. "Mate, sister, same thing."

Soren and I glanced at each other, then to Satu, then back at each other. Even without the connection from the stag, Soren's *see what I mean* was palpable. I resisted the urge to pinch the bridge of my nose to fight off the headache that was sure to come. Being the stag had its ups and downs. On one hand, I was one of the most powerful creatures in existence despite not knowing exactly how to tap into that power; on the other hand, I had to deal with svartelves.

No matter what creature you were in the Permafrost, there was one main consensus when it came to svartelves that could be summarized in a word: nope.

"Why exactly did you attack Tibra, Soren?" I asked. Honestly, even if it was something like an out-of-place comment on his appearance, I didn't really begrudge Soren. I kind of wished I could pummel Tibra too. And Donnar. Really, any of them. Every time I met a svartelf, I left the meeting questioning my own sanity.

"She doesn't understand the concept of inappropriate

touching," Soren explained. Before I had a chance to be out-raged at the idea of Tibra touching Soren somewhere off-limits, he explained. "And by that, I mean she kept *pulling on my braid*. Like a *child*."

"Well," Donnar said, his tail twitching. "She is one."

Mate, sister, and child? "Donnar, you're really not helping," I said. "I can't believe I actually have to mediate this. Are you two children? Donnar, Tibra shouldn't be pulling Soren's hair. Soren, you cannot murder someone for pulling your hair." I wanted to pull *my* hair. Turning away from the sheepish look-ing svartelf and goblin, I nodded a greeting to Satu.

The she-goblin had her arms crossed over her stom-ach, which thanks to Seppo's comments, I now noticed was slightly swollen. Her dark eyes glittered, deep-set in her face. Despite the difference in color, I could see Seppo in them. Satu was broad where Seppo was slim, dark-skinned where Seppo was fair, and well-muscled where Seppo was slender, but the shape of their eyes were the same, the curve of their ears, and the pitch-black color of their hair. Like her son, she had a vine tattoo that spiraled from her neck to around one of her ears. There was something about her that pulled you in, maybe her smile and glittering eyes which managed to offset her otherwise serious features.

"Seppo told me you're expecting," I said.

She nodded. "It's been a while since I've added to my brood," she joked. "Though being on Soren's council is quite like looking after a toddler."

"I heard that," Soren muttered.

"The father is human," she continued. "I've actually had a

child with him before, but the boy was one of the rare ones to come out fully human. I don't expect this one to be, though. I can feel it."

I nodded. "Thanks for keeping everyone from killing each other." I turned back to Soren and Donnar, who were still standing there, silently. "Shouldn't you be leaving, Donnar?" I scanned the room. He was the only svartelf left.

"Alas," he said. "I need to speak with you." He glanced at Soren. "Alone."

Great. Now I got to add half-mad ramblings from *another* madman to my day.

I resent that. I rarely ramble. It'd been maybe twenty minutes since Lydian had deigned to grace me with his presence, so of course, he'd reappear now. Odin's Ravens, I wished there were a way to kill an already-dead person.

But no, Lydian's ghost haunting my brain aside, part of my job as the stag meant speaking with the other residents of the Permafrost. Unlike my predecessor, I didn't immediately *know* what was going on with every living thing, though I had a general feeling of the state of the world.

A rather negative one, that is. This time the voice in my head wasn't Lydian's but my own. Even so, I could feel his wordless agreement.

So, if Donnar needed to speak with me, then it was my duty as the stag to speak with him or any other creature of the Permafrost who desired it. Svartelves may have been . . . well, svartelves, but they were still residents of the Permafrost, and I had a duty to them like any other creature.

"All right," I said. "Let's talk."

Donnar looked at Satu and Soren, who still stood in the room. "I believe I did say *alone*."

"It's *my* throne room, technically," Soren said, but without much malice. "Are you sure you're okay with this, Janneke?" he asked me. "Say the word, and I will gladly kick him across the Permafrost."

I didn't think I'd ever have a better mental picture in my life, but shook my head. "I'm sure."

"All right," Soren said. "You know I trust your judgment. We can catch up later about this morning, I think."

My cheeks felt hot, and I hoped I wasn't blushing as my mind flashed to some of the things that'd gone on before we'd had to officially start the day. "Of course."

I must've been flushed because a wicked smile curled on Soren's lips at the sight of me, and I continued to feel hot as he and Satu left the room.

Disgusting. Now that's going to be in my head all day, Lydian commented.

"Considering *you're* in my head all day, you can deal."

The tapping of claws against marble made me turn. Donnar was still there and had seen me basically speak to myself. Shit. The empty throne room suddenly seemed cavernously big and too open, too vulnerable. I fought the urge to make sure my back was pressed to a wall.

Donnar, for his part, didn't do much to help. One taloned foot clacked on the marble floor as he swished his tail back and forth. The movement reminded me of a cat right before it was about to pounce. He looked over the now-empty hall again before turning back to me, his pitch-black eyes staring a hole through my body.

"How long has he been with you?" Donnar asked.

"Soren and I ha—"

"No, no," Donnar said, shaking his head. "The other one. In your head. How long has he been there?"

"Lydian?" My voice broke as I said the name. Was it so obvious that something was wrong with me? "I'm not mad, then," I said, realization dawning on me. If Donnar somehow knew . . .

"No, you're not," Donnar said. "Soren never completely burned Lydian's body, right? Didn't give it burial rites?"

"No. He kept his heart. It's . . . somewhere around here." I tried to make myself forget about the still-beating heart locked away in one of the various rooms of the palace. Only those with a fully burned body and burial rites could truly pass on to the next life. Otherwise, they became stuck in a hellish afterlife where they were trapped in the void, never seen or heard from again. Or so I thought, until Lydian barged into my head.

Regardless, when it came to the matter of Lydian's still-beating heart, I had enough haunting my brain without that image pushing through.

"He can't truly leave this world until it's burned. His specter has latched on to you," Donnar said. "But I'm sure you know this by now."

"He keeps saying *things* and I don't understand," I said fervently. "I keep seeing these . . . these flashes of the world falling apart. People being undone by the inside out. Sometimes the sound in my head gets so loud that I think it's going to explode. There's death. Death everywhere, and it's all scream-ing to me, and I don't know what's going on!"

Donnar was silent for a moment, and when he spoke, his voice was both soft and sad. "I did tell you your path wouldn't be an easy one."

"Do you know what's wrong with me?" I asked. "Why I'm seeing all these things?"

Because I'm a part of you now, Janneke.

"No!" I shouted, not caring who heard. "Shut up! You aren't part of this conversation!"

"But he is," Donnar said. "He's very much a part of all of this."

It's all about me. What I know. What you can't know. Unless . . .

"Unless you want to end up like him." Donnar somehow finished Lydian's sentence though his voice was only in my head.

"I want an explanation," I said, trying to keep my hands from shaking. Hel, was it too much to ask to have my life for once not be tainted with my tormentor? Was it so hard for the Norns to let me live in some relative peace for once? Was I cursed to this plague for all eternity? He was dead. Dead and gone and cold in the ground somewhere, and yet somehow, he was still here, doing what he always did. What he'd always done. Tormenting me.

"I can't tell you," Donnar said. "But I can show you."

I took a step back, suddenly frightened. "I've seen the things you've shown me. Forgive me if I'd rather not deal with the mental torture." An iron knife with an antler bone handle, shoved deep into my father's flesh, the proclamation that we were all monsters, his body turning into mine as it bled out and then slowly faded from sight. Yes, I'd had enough of what Donnar could show me to last a lifetime.

"You don't have the luxury of refusal, I'm afraid." He held out a hand, sharp talons glistening in the light. "You *must* see. You *must*."

"Or what?"

"The end of the world." Both Lydian's and Donnar's voices spoke at the same time, resonating in my own head and in the space around me, hanging heavily in the air.

"It's never something simple, is it?" I asked sardonically.

In my mind's eye, I could see Lydian. His hair was frazzled and his face was smudged with soot, his clothes ripped like millions of fingers had torn their way into them. But the smile on his face, so much like his nephew's, was the same. *What happens when the serpent stops eating his tail?*

I didn't know, but as I reached for Donnar's hand, I braced myself to find out.

THE WORLD RUSHED around me, through me, inside and out. There was no breeze, but my hair blew in the wind despite that. I was standing still and moving forward. I was rising and I was falling. Bursts of color and blackness danced across my field of vision as the world around me shifted from the throne room to someplace dark and cold. A place where the red bloodwater trickled down from the sky high, high above; where those who entered rarely left with their sanity—if at all.

The motion stopped and Donnar released my hand. Goose bumps rose on the skin of my arms from the cold. Something was different about this cavern—I could tell it was the same one I'd been in long before, the one Donnar and Tibra inhabited, but something was off. There was more moss, rock structures that hadn't been there before were there now, the bones and feathers on the ground were fresher, fewer in number. Around us, the air shimmered as if it were a mirage.

"What is this?" I asked Donnar, but he shushed me and pointed ahead of us.

Standing there was, well, Donnar. Obviously younger, judging by the skin that barely covered his ribs and the talons that had yet to grow into full length. When a svartelf fully matured, the skin on their backs broke and left them open for the world to see. Muscle, bone, veins, nerves, and sinew all on grotesque display for everyone. Or, in theory, anyways. Staring at a svartelf's exposed back was considered one of the highest forms of disrespect and insult one could commit, and you'd be lucky to escape with your eyes intact.

Footsteps echoed in the cavern as someone approached the younger Donnar, and the older Donnar motioned for me to step aside a few paces, widening my field of vision. A shriek rose and died in my throat before it could be released at the sight of the goblin approaching Donnar. My hands balled into fists, nails digging into the flesh, and a cold trickle of terror ran down my back.

Not real, I thought. *He's not real. He can't see me. He can't.*

I've always been able to see you, Janneke. His words rang in my mind, clear as day. *Memory or not. I've always seen you. Always.*

"Stop talking," I growled, forcing myself to ignore Lydian's voice in my head as a younger version of the goblin stepped before the svartelf.

There was no iron poisoning in his leg so he stood tall, his skin was fresher, younger, lacking the multitude of scars from before. His hair was shorter too, only down to his ears. But what really struck me were his eyes. His green eyes weren't clouded, they didn't look as if they were gazing always at something everyone else couldn't see. They were clear and present.

"You seek knowledge," the younger Donnar said to him. "But it's not knowledge you can handle." His tone was not unkind.

The younger Lydian growled and took a step forward. "I *can* handle it! I *can*! For generations my family has had the sight! *Generations* we have been gifted this knowledge. You cannot deny it to me!"

The younger Donnar was unfazed. "You were not born with the sight. You can't handle it. Leave, goblin, there are no answers for you here."

Lydian swiped at the younger Donnar, causing a line of red to form on his cheek. "My father has it! My brother has it! And my grandfather and his! It is my right to also have it! They don't get to be the only ones! It's my blood *right* to be able to see. You cave-dwelling backless bastards should know that!"

A drop of blood ran down the younger Donnar's cheek and

onto his lips. He tasted it with his tongue, before narrowing his eyes. "It's your right to see, is it?"

"*Yes,*" Lydian hissed.

"And what do you want to see? What do you deserve to know?" Though the younger Lydian didn't seem to notice, I couldn't help but feel a sinking in my gut at the look in the younger Donnar's eyes.

"*Everything.*"

The svartelf broke out into a malicious grin. "So you shall."

One second Lydian was standing and growling, and the next he was on the ground, shrieking. He clutched his head with his hands, fingers digging into the skin on his face. His cry echoed off the walls of the cavern, going up and up and up to the mountains above. He contorted, twisting from grotesque shape to grotesque shape, screams of agony never ceasing. Younger Donnar stood over him, smiling.

"They're all dead. They're all dying!" Lydian shrieked. "Little lives snuffed out by feet, and the bird is going to die in the cold. Heartbeats, there are millions of them. Everywhere. Everything. The stone will be unturned, the other skipped across a pond. Even more will stay as they are forever. Ice goes and comes, the world is burning. The serpent is free and he's sitting on his throne, and she's beside him, both of them, the serpent is unwinding. What have you done to me?" he gasped. "Make it stop!"

I could barely tear my eyes away from Lydian to look back at Donnar. "What *did* you do to him?"

Donnar shrugged. "He wanted to know everything. So, I let him."

"Let him, *what*?"

"Know everything. The fate of each insect, each crawling worm and blade of grass, the individual tracks of the particles in the air, the marks in the snow. The deaths and births of all living things and their every single heartbeat, every single breath. Every single second of every single thing from the beginning to the end of the world, I let him know." At those words, Donnar smiled.

Fear formed like a rock in my stomach, and I had to stop myself from taking a step back at the look on Donnar's face. It was so easy to forget, sometimes, surrounded by the ones who I loved and who loved me, that despite everything, in some ways I was always going to be different. It was hard to remember that some of the people I cared for couldn't experience emotions the same way I did and would never know exactly how to empathize no matter how hard they tried. It was even worse knowing that other goblins, svartelves, the creatures of the Permafrost in general didn't care who I was and were perfectly fine with trying to drive me to insanity. Hel, Lydian managed to do it from beyond the dead.

The Permafrost could be beautiful and its creatures did possess some feral form of grace, but above all, it was brutal, unforgiving, a place where the wrong words to the wrong creatures could end my life before it'd even begun and there were no second chances, no take-backs. Brutal, severe, harsh, and cold.

"Knowing all those things?" I said when I managed to get over a bit of my shock. "They could—they'd have to—"

"Drive you mad?" Donnar replied. "Yes. They could. They

did. Granted, he was already unstable before my 'gift' cursed him."

"Why are you showing me this?" I asked. "How is this going to help me with my visions, with Lydian in my head?"

"Perhaps you should ask him, yourself," Donnar said.

"Ask *Lydian*?"

"You're the stag, communicating between worlds should come naturally to you." He frowned at the look on my face. "Don't tell me you don't know how?"

I balled up my fists again in frustration.

"Ask him," Donnar repeated. "I cursed him with the weight of knowledge. That weight would drive the strongest mad. He would never be able to speak about what he saw until his death. He's dead. He'll always be like this. He never was *not*. He'll always be tortured by the endless stimuli of knowing, but at least now, he should be coherent. More reachable. Ask him and you will understand."

With those words, the world rushed around me again until I stood alone in the throne room, dizzy and shaking. For a long moment, all I could do was stare blankly, unable to even think, much less move voluntarily. When I finally regained control of myself, I fell to my knees and wept.

3

THE FLAMING ARROW

I PULLED MYSELF together quicker than I thought I could. Quick enough that should Soren come back, he wouldn't have noticed my tears or distress. Donnar was gazing at me, something akin to pity in his eyes. I glared at him. I didn't need anyone's pity.

"You drove him mad, then," I said, straightening myself.

Donnar shrugged delicately. "If it's any consolation, he was damaged way before I cursed him, and I don't take disrespect well. Your pity should be saved."

"I *do not* pity him. I *do not* feel compassion for him. None of this changes my view of him." The words came out in a near growl. "You made everything worse."

"Yes," Donnar said. "I hope you find the answers you seek." The wind picked up again despite us being inside, and with a blur of color, Donnar was gone.

I scowled. "You could have at least given me more directions!" I shouted at the spot where he had stood. "Damn svartelves!"

I think that's the one topic you, Soren, and I fully agree upon.

Ignoring Lydian, I put my head in my hands, trying to piece together what Donnar had shown me. Part of it was obvious. Lydian had come down to the caverns seeking knowledge, he'd mentioned some type of ability his brother and father had that he didn't, he was hostile to Donnar, who then cursed him with the knowledge of literally every living thing all at once, driving him mad—or, well, mad-*er*.

But even if he was cursed with some type of knowledge, even if he was driven mad, none of that really mattered. Not to me, anyway. It hadn't changed the things he'd done to me. It hadn't changed the pain he caused. I didn't want to talk to him. I didn't want to listen to what he had to say, because even if it was important enough for his specter to hang around me and speak in my mind all day, listening to him felt like giving in. Somehow validating his actions. Maybe it was irrational. But it was how I felt.

At the same time, I wasn't sure I had a choice. Something deep in my gut was tugging at me, a part of my mind that was walled off begged for the blockade to be shattered. There was no voice in my head, yet it was there all the same. My duty did not involve, could not involve, personal feelings. No emotions. No grudges. No pain. Nothing. I was the stag and the stag's job was to keep balance in the world, to find and eliminate threats that would have that balance destroyed. It didn't matter what *I* wanted. It was what the stag had to do. I could hate it all I wanted, I could refuse to do it as Janneke the human, but Janneke the stag would do it whether Janneke the human wanted to or not.

"Janneke?" Soren's voice brought me back to the world, and I tried to discreetly wipe any trace of tears from my face. "Are you okay? Where's Donnar?"

"He left," I said, trying to keep my voice light.

"What did he want with you?"

Soren's concern was written plainly on his face, and it killed me to lie to him. But I couldn't tell him the truth when I wasn't even exactly sure what the truth was. How could I tell him what was going on when I didn't know myself?

I shook my head. "I'm not entirely sure."

Soren stepped forward and rested a hand on my shoulder. "You look exhausted," he said. "Are you sure you're okay?"

No. I feel like I'm going to break into a million pieces. I feel like I'm drowning. But I couldn't tell him that. I didn't know how. Asking for help was still not one of my strong suits.

"I didn't sleep well last night," I said. At least it was partly true.

"Maybe you should rest," Soren said. "The Permafrost won't fall into pieces without you for twenty-four hours."

I snorted. "I was only gone for about an hour when you tried to kill Tibra. Not that I blame you for it."

He brushed a loose lock of my hair behind my ear, finger-tips gently running over my cheek. My skin flushed where his fingers touched and the reaction made him smile with satisfaction. "I promise, I'll be good. Besides, you look like you really need it. Are you sure you're okay?"

I caught his hand in mine and held it to my cheek. "I'll be fine. I promise. It's stress." The understatement of the century.

Gods, I wanted to tell him. The secrets inside of me ached to be let out. Seppo, Rose, and Diaval knew and I was fine with that, so then, what scared me so much about Soren knowing? Even Donnar knew more than him—granted it was probably because he caused the problem in the first place.

Maybe because I didn't exactly tell the three of them out loud. Diaval could sense it and so could Rose, for some strange reason, and whatever Rose knew, Seppo did. They'd approached me about it all three together in what was probably considered the goblin form of a soft intervention.

Or maybe because Seppo, Rose, and Diaval hadn't actually been victims of Lydian. Not like Soren and I had. They hadn't suffered by his hand; they didn't have him haunt their dreams for decades.

Maybe if it'd been me seeing Lydian's ghost, it'd be different. I could confide in Soren about the ghosts of my past, real or imagined. But I was hearing him in my mind. He stood before my eyes. Not only that, but I had visions of the world being thrown into chaos, and if Donnar was right, the one person who could truly tell me what was going on was a person who I'd rather die than see again.

How would I even explain that? I could barely grasp the concept myself. Every cell inside of me ached to ignore Donnar's words, which now bounced around in my brain, and continue surviving.

It should've been, well, not peaceful exactly, but *better* by now. The bad guy was dead. Soren and I were together and safe. My friends were safe. I was finally allowing myself to heal and grieve and let go of all the hate and anger I felt toward myself. Except for that bad guy was speaking to me from beyond the grave. It was so unfair I wanted to stomp my foot on the ground like a child.

It should've been better. *I* should've been better by now. But I wasn't. The very idea of even speaking to Lydian petrified me. Hel, I didn't even want to breathe the same air as him if I could help it. I should've been free of him, but my abuser was hanging on despite every effort to shake him off for good.

But I didn't really have a choice when everything boiled down to it, did I? No matter my human feelings, buried underneath it all was the compulsion to do whatever needed to be done to keep the Permafrost safe. What I wanted didn't matter. If it hurt me, it didn't matter. All that mattered was fulfilling my duty and doing it as quickly and efficiently as possible.

And so despite my feelings, I did what I had to do.

"You're right," I murmured. "I think I may lie down for a bit. I'll see you later?"

He bent down to kiss my forehead. "I love you," he whispered.

"I love you too."

———

I DIDN'T ACTUALLY head back to our rooms. First, I had to have a conversation with a dead goblin, and I wasn't actually entirely sure how to do that. I had a feeling that the limited commentary in my brain was exactly that—limited. Holding a conversation wasn't necessarily something I'd managed to do yet—though it wasn't like I was champing at the bit to do so in the first place. We'd have to create a space where we could see each other physically, and not touch each other. There was only one goblin who could probably get me the results I wanted.

Diaval had a number of haunts around the palace. Normally places that were dangerous, like the chasm I threw Aleksey off of so long ago or hidden passageways that'd been built back thousands of years ago when the palace was made. She'd actually climbed down that chasm to retrieve and burn the remainder of Aleksey's body, saying we didn't want someone who tried to betray Soren's ghost haunting the place. Honestly, I was glad. Aleksey may have been plotting against Soren, but he was also the first goblin I killed. Maybe the first goblin of the total Hunt to be killed. The idea of a proper burial took some weight off my conscience.

Though there was no way I'd climb down a chasm, I still checked most of the known haunts she had, and had nearly given up when I finally found the she-goblin, lying in a small crevice like it was a hammock, reading, of all things.

"Diaval?" I asked.

"Yes?" The she-goblin didn't look up from her book. I tilted my head to try to catch a glimpse of the title, but all I could make out were runes too old for me to know the meaning of.

"That can't be comfortable," I said, frowning.

"Things being comfortable are for the weak," Diaval said.

"Oh?" I raised my eyebrows.

"Besides, I like the pain. Makes me feel good."

Well, I wasn't touching that comment with a six-foot pole, so instead, I counted to five and started over.

"I need your help."

"I'm busy," she said.

I narrowed my eyes. "That was kind of an order, not a request."

She finally looked up, dark eyes twinkling. "There's that backbone. What is it you need help with exactly?"

I spilled it all out to her. Donnar's words and what he showed me, the idea that Lydian might somehow know something about my visions, the plan to try to speak with him on some even ground where both of our spirits could hear each other clearly. Throughout the whole time, Diaval's expression never changed. I wasn't entirely sure if that was a good or bad thing.

"So," she said when I finished. "You need my help to get into a liminal space."

"A . . . what?"

Diaval rolled her eyes. "Liminal space. The space between what is and what's coming. There are liminal spaces when you can contact those not truly dead but also not truly alive— like Lydian. And there are liminal beings that control those spaces and work as catalysts to move from *what is* to *what is to come*. The stag is a liminal being."

I blinked. "I feel like I would've known if I was a liminal being?"

Diaval shrugged. "For you, it's mainly unconscious. You still can't access the stag's full consciousness and scope of abilities while awake and in control. I mean, that's what you and I practice. If you can't do that, then getting yourself into a liminal space would be nearly impossible at your current skill set. If anything, the closest you can get to one is when you're unconscious."

I frowned. Another reminder about how *bad* I was at this entire stag thing. "So, you're saying it's impossible, then?"

"Not at all." Diaval closed her book and heaved herself out of the crevice in the floor she'd been lying in. "You need help. And since I am particularly skilled in this area, I can help. But not now. Later, at midnight, when the others are asleep. I don't really fancy having to explain to everyone what I'm doing. They won't get it."

I nodded in understanding. Magic was not necessarily a thing goblins usually knew how to do. Other than a few of them having extra abilities outside of the scope of normal, they tended to be much more physical and martially focused. They weren't exactly created to do magic, the stag let me know that much. Other creatures in the Permafrost would and could perform it, but like the inability to create without harm to themselves, the inability to use magic was like a check and balance in the system to keep things fair. Finding Diaval had been like finding a needle in a haystack, and her affinity with magic separated her from the rest of her kind. Like me, she understood sarcasm, nonliteral figures of speech, and was deeply attuned to the world around her. While not necessarily physically gifted, she was psychically strong and wasn't afraid to show that off. She also "got me" more than most others did. Soren was my lover, and Seppo and Rose were friends, but Diaval was someone who I could talk to and know she understood the way I was feeling and offer comfort rather than ways to fix it. We were both outsiders in the Permafrost in our own ways, and like me, she was someone often underestimated but not afraid to pack a punch.

She was my best friend. Words I'd never thought I'd utter.

Magic came to her as easy as breathing, which tended to make her more impatient when it came to my own struggles with the craft.

"All right. Midnight," I said. "Where do you want to meet?"

"Courtyard should be empty and horse-free by then," she said. "Best to do it outside where there's a better connection. Until then, try to get some rest or something, okay?"

"Sure," I said. Guess it looked like I was going to take Soren's advice after all. Maybe for once, I could sleep without dreaming. How long had it been since I'd done that? I missed the blackness and utter oblivion that used to come with sleep. Closing my eyes and fearing what I might see once I drifted off did nothing good for my mental state. Not that my mental state was ever in tip-top shape to begin with.

I trudged back to the more livable part of the Erlking's palace. When we'd first moved in, Soren had constantly complained about the décor—something I really should have seen coming considering his original statement about the palace the last time we were there—until Seppo had taken it upon himself to change how things looked. It was starker now, austere, despite the white-and-gold-veined marble, the jutting ice and rock helping complete the image. I still hadn't explored the entire thing, mainly because I was sure there were a number of death traps I didn't need to stumble into, but I was pretty sure both Diaval and Rosamund had the entire place memorized like the back of their hands.

There used to be more thralls too, I noted as I passed through empty halls. Humans that had been taken during raids and enslaved by goblins to do the skills they couldn't, like I'd been.

But Soren had very little need for thralls in the first place, and the dozen he had originally to complete tasks that he himself wasn't physically able to do, like create clothing and plant food, all things to do with creation, had come with him here. It still made my stomach upset, seeing them, even if Soren wasn't going to mistreat them or allow them to be mistreated. Thralldom was still thralldom. It existed even in the human world. When different clans would raid one another, they would often take thralls, and my clan was no different. That changed when I came across humans in thralldom to nonhumans; it made me uncomfortable how much I had accepted thralldom as a way of life.

Still, Soren released all the thralls who originally worked for the Erlking that he didn't have any need for.

Some of them stayed. They were too old or too well adapted or had been in the Permafrost too long to ever truly acclimatize to the world of men again. They continued to work, but now it was on their own time and by their own choice. Some became changelings and I'd witnessed some of the ceremonies I thought originally were going to happen to me when Soren first revealed the reason he took me on the Hunt. Seeing human features gradually change into goblin as the days passed was slightly unnerving.

Those who did leave, which were most, were guided safely back to the human world. Sometimes I thought about them. If they'd found family. Had reunions. Were they tearful? Joyful? Were they accepted once more? I could only hope so. Even with Soren being able to erase those bonds, we were still considered so affected by its magic that barely any people considered us human. Monstrous, animals. I'd grown up listening to my father talk about such things, and in the end, I'd even killed a few of those men.

But this line of thought wasn't going to help me relax.

When I got to our shared quarters and more specifically to our bedroom, I sighed as I took the heavy antler bone torq off my neck and placed it carefully on the table. Doing so gave me a bit of peace. While the torq wasn't in any way a source of my power, it did help amplify my connection to the land. The little whispers in my head and pulls of feeling as creatures completed their natural cycles, loved, lived, died, were louder, and while I could still feel it without the torq, at least I could ignore it a bit easier.

I collapsed on the sleeping platform, suddenly exhausted. Maybe Soren was right. Rest would be good for me.

But it didn't come. Despite my comfort, I tossed and turned in the furs; my mind raced through any attempts to calm it. I was still awake when, hours later, Soren came in. "Can't sleep?" he asked.

"Can't sleep," I confirmed. "Guess I better get used to it."

He unhooked his sword belt and hung it over one of the chairs before coming to sit next to my head. "You need sleep. Even your eye bags have eye bags."

"Gee, thanks. As if I wasn't self-conscious enough with my appearance," I muttered.

Soren rolled his eyes. "You could have three eyes, a horn, and webbed feet, and I'd still think you were the most beautiful person in the world. You are."

I gave him the ghost of a smile. Maybe I wasn't traditionally beautiful as much as I wished, but hey, neither was Satu, and she seemed to be doing fine for herself. I had Soren. Soren loved me no matter what. That mattered.

"You're beautiful too," I said.

"We'd make absolutely stunning children," he replied, smirking. The mischievous twinkle was back in his eye.

"Everyone and babies!" I exclaimed. "Is Satu rubbing off on you?"

"It's an unfortunate trait she shares with her son."

"Can we even have babies? Like, logistically? As Erlking and the stag?" The thought popped into my head before I could chase it away for the ridiculous thing it was.

Soren frowned, thinking. "I'm . . . not sure. I don't believe the original stag ever was in the position to have offspring with the Erlking. Because, I mean, it was a deer. A magical deer. But still a deer."

I smiled. "Yes, it was, in fact, a deer." At least physically. I could attest to how *not* a deer it was in other ways. Deer didn't help regulate the entire universe, for the most part.

Soren had that soft look in his eyes that was always reserved for me. "Do you want to hear a story?"

"A story?" I asked.

"To help you sleep."

"I didn't know you told stories," I said.

He blushed, pink spreading across the gray-blue skin of his cheeks. "I mean, I don't really. Only one. It's true, so I don't know if that even counts. Tanya told me it when I was little."

I raised my eyebrows. I could not for the life of me picture Tanya, red-headed, scowling, snapping Tanya, sitting down and telling a young Soren a story. "Really?"

"Well." Soren rubbed the back of his neck. "My mother and she were very close apparently. I don't know, maybe it was because they were half sisters, so there was less competition between the two. When my mother was attacked by the draugr, Tanya could only save her or me. My mother told her to save me and look after me. So, Tanya delivered me and my mother died."

There was a shine of grief in Soren's eyes, for the mother he never got to know. I felt for him. At least I knew my family before they died. I knew I was loved. Different, yes, but loved.

"I'm sorry," I said, placing a hand on his bicep.

"It's fine, it's why Tanya took so much of an interest in me. She always would tell me stories about how my parents met. I thought it was quite romantic."

"You, a romantic?" I giggled.

He smirked. "Marriages tend to be arranged and betrothals are common. Breaking betrothals, too, which I really should have taken into consideration when I decided to join my ex-betrothed's team on a hunt for a magic deer and take along the girl I'd been pining after for half a century."

"Yeah, you kinda fucked that one up, Soren," I said, but

couldn't help but laugh. Not at the memory of almost being murdered, but the way Soren described the events as if it were another regular evening.

"My mom was notorious for harshly refusing anyone that came at her. But her father was adamant she marry and carry on the bloodline. There were tons of suitors, I was told, but none managed to ever win her heart."

I could picture it. A woman who looked vaguely like Soren, laughing in the face of any goblin brute at her feet, scorning the idea that they would ever be good enough for her.

"She challenged any suitor she had to a competition of her choosing, and she beat them all, one by one. It started to get to be quite the spectacle because goblins from all over the Permafrost were going north to where she lived. That included my father and Lydian and their father."

A montage of the vague woman continuing to succeed and succeed without stopping, hundreds filling a home suited more for dozens, and the crackling of flames filled my senses. The mantle of the stag was letting me taste the past.

"My father was the younger son, so the idea was for Lydian to court her. Despite Lydian still being . . . Lydian, at the time. He continued to compete over and over, trying to find her weakness. Because her challenge didn't limit the amount of times you could go head-to-head with her. But while she was fighting suitors by daylight, by moonlight she was meeting my father. Tanya says they were absolutely infatuated with each other from the first moment they laid eyes on each other."

A couple meeting in secret. Soft kisses in the rain. The giggle of a woman's voice and the throaty laughter of a goblin brute. Clothes soaked from walking through the snow and underbrush at night, explained away with any excuse they could find. Two hearts beating as one.

I ached to share this experience with Soren, what I was feeling now, but I wasn't sure how.

"They got caught eventually, and her father put down his foot. He proclaimed my mother would travel away from her home and that night, any suitor who wished could ride out and try to catch her. A hunt, if you will." A slow smile spread across Soren's face. "So that's what they did. A dozen goblins clambering after another one, trying to get through the thick fog and ice of the tundra of the High North, unable to see even an inch past their faces. All except one."

I was leaning forward now, my heart beating with anticipation at Soren's story. Something about it struck me as familiar, personal, though I'd never experienced anything like that. But her desire, her will, to make her own choices was something I'd always possessed.

"The night before, she'd snuck into my father's rooms and told him that to find her, he only needed to look for the light in the sky. At first, that confused him. He thought she meant stars, but the stars were hard to see through the thick fog. He figured it out, though, when he saw a flaming arrow shoot up in the air. They left a trail for him that he followed while everyone else was still lost in the fog, looking for tracks in the ice."

"She sounds incredible," I said. "I wish you could've met her."

"I do too. Something . . . changed in my father when she died. He wasn't outright hateful toward me. No more than any father-son relationship between goblins. According to Tanya, we looked very similar except for she was less . . ." He struggled for the right word, holding out an arm and glaring at his skin tone. ". . . blue."

"I always wondered where you got your coloring from," I said. I knew at least part of it was some genetic mutation that changed the pigment in his skin, making it not pale but an odd, semitranslucent blue-gray color, coloring his eyes lilac, and leaving his lips a soft powder blue. It was beautiful, to me, even if it was strange.

"Thank you for telling me this, Soren," I said. "Really, it means a lot." While Soren didn't have nearly as many shields up as I did, I knew firsthand about sharing trauma and how painful that could be on its own. There was something comforting knowing Soren was okay sharing this with me.

"A bit much for a story, eh?" he said, the sadness wiped off his face.

"I'll forgive it this time."

Though certain thoughts and a certain voice lingered in the back of my head, asking me why I wasn't doing the same. Soon, though. Soon. As soon as I figured out what was going on, I'd tell him. I'd apologize for keeping it a secret. I'd let him know that I'd been scared. Hopefully, he would forgive me.

Despite the stress and anticipation for the night ahead,

Soren's steady, calm voice did help manage to relax me as I lay there. He pulled up a chair beside me and brushed a runaway curl of my hair back behind my ears. My eyelids became heavier, and I closed them as he sang to me in a deep voice, so low I could barely hear.

He continued even after I closed my eyes.

4

THE KILLING SIGHT

FOR ONCE, MY sleep was blissful and dreamless—that was until the flat of someone's hands nailed me in the ribs in the middle of the night. I woke, a scream on my lips, only for my mouth to be covered.

"It's me," Diaval hissed. "You weren't showing, so I came to get you. Careful, you'll wake Soren."

She nodded over to the chair that Soren was sitting on. His head rested against his shoulders, body relaxed, almost like he was about to slump out of the chair completely. I shook my head fondly, realizing he hadn't wanted to climb over me in order to get to bed, lest it disrupt my sleep.

That was it. I had to tell him about this after tonight. I trusted him with my emotions, my trauma, I swear I did. I knew something had been holding me back from telling him. And I knew that he would be upset, maybe even angry, that I didn't tell him about what was going on while the others knew for months. Keeping this secret needed to end.

Taking a deep breath, I creeped across the room and

toward the door. Diaval made a "hurry up" motion with her hand, eyes rolling so far they were practically in the back of her head. We exited the room and quietly shut the door, and she let out a huff of exasperation.

"Honestly, I offer my time and services, and I'm nearly stood up by you having a nap." She flicked her fingers, taking off the sting of the words. "Poor Soren's gonna have a backache for days."

"Sorry," I said. "He told me a story and I fell asleep."

Diaval raised an eyebrow. "A story? Color me impressed."

This time I rolled my eyes. "Just because you have zero faith in the entire male population doesn't mean everyone does."

"I resent that," Diaval argued. "I have zero faith in everyone equally."

I decided not to continue down that rabbit hole, lest I tear my hair out. I was already possibly going to confront one of the things that'd caused me immense trauma for a hundred years, in a way that didn't involve ripping his guts out, and I couldn't let my emotions go so unchecked already.

Instead, I let Diaval lead me to the courtyard, marveling at how quiet the palace was at night. The once-white marble was now a shiny black with not even the moonlight reflecting from its stone. Soren's household in the palace was relatively small as it was, making it not so loud during the day, but at night, I could hear a pin drop. Everyone was asleep or getting there. I wondered, for those thralls that stayed and converted, did they ever have a night when they could sleep without fear of murder, before we came?

The thought brought me back to my first nights with

Soren. Terrified, bloody, bruised, and hurting in every possible way. I dared not close my eyes during that time, not knowing what would happen to me if I let my guard down even for a minute around the strange goblin and those who followed him. I kept myself so tense, then, waiting for sounds on the other side of the door. A warning that he was coming to hurt me.

But he never did.

I thought it was sure to happen when they moved me from the sickroom I'd been staying in to a room—a number of rooms actually—that could only be accessed or exited through Soren's own rooms. Back then, when they walked in on me, fire filled my body and I thought about killing myself quickly before he had the chance to do anything. Except for the rooms he gave me had nothing I could use to die. No light fixtures hanging high enough, no sharp objects, even the mirror was polished copper and wouldn't break no matter how hard I pounded on it.

But day and night came after day and night, and soon, I eased into the new life. After a year, I understood Soren had put me in those rooms to protect me from anyone who might've wanted to hurt me, and not because he wanted access to me himself. Because what kind of idiot would go through his lord's rooms in order to assault a girl, knowing they'd leave a trail behind, if not run into their lord himself.

Those first nights, those first months, I only slept because the healer Tanya had put me under with herbs while she healed my broken body. Every touch, even hers, burned. I never wanted to be touched again.

I was lucky. I had help from people who cared, even if I

didn't know it then. I was sure, whatever their experience, those who served under the old Erlking had much more to fear.

I prayed they did get a dreamless sleep.

I banged into something hard, and Diaval let out a cuss. "Watch where you're going!" she hissed as I finally noticed the area around me. Outside, the stars shown bright in the sky, the only light to be found. For a moment I stood there, looking up, picking out constellations in my head before Diaval gave my arm a rough jerk.

"Come on, we need to get started," she said, leading down to an area of the courtyard where stone was inlaid on the ground. The dim light of the stars allowed me to barely see the symbols drawn in chalk across the path, and before I could say anything, Diaval pushed me down into the middle of it.

"Okay, sit down, close your eyes, and reach out," Diaval instructed, before adding, "with your mind, not your hand."

"I know what 'reaching out' means in this context, Diaval," I muttered. "Have some sort of faith in me."

She snorted delicately but didn't respond, opting instead to begin chanting in a language I didn't know. Unlike the ancestral language of goblins, which was only used when swearing oaths to the Erlking, this wasn't rough and coarse but smooth, almost lyrical in a sense. It swayed and flowed like branches in a breeze, and as she continued my head grew light. My body was weightless, floating.

My eyes closed and I tried to envision it in my mind. Conjuring up images of the field I'd seen the world created on, the stag born, the creatures who moved north and south, as I was given the stag's mantle of power. I focused on the space between the spaces, as impossible as it both felt and sounded, the idea that the world tree had roots connecting all the realms together, trying to picture the cosmos in my brain.

I tried, I really did. But I still sat there for who knew how long, trying to reach out to a voice calling me, faintly echoing in the back of my mind, but no matter what, I couldn't grasp or reach it. The more I desired to hold it, the more I aimed to catch it, the more frustrated I got for missing it, the further it drifted from my fingertips.

"This isn't working," I finally said, crestfallen.

Diaval sighed. "Time for plan B, then."

"There's a plan B?" I asked, turning to face her as she cracked her knuckles.

"Yep. I'd turn around if I were you, unless you want a nasty bruise." Blue lightning sprang forth from her hands, and my eyes widened as I did what she said.

"What are you do—" The heel of her palm struck the back of my head, and suddenly I was falling forward, landing face-first on the stone of the courtyard. Except, it hadn't scratched me. It hadn't even hurt at all.

Heart racing, I turned to see Diaval examining my slumped-over body. The body I was currently *not in*. The revelation did nothing for my rising heart rate as I brought a hand to my face, realizing it was slightly see-through.

"What did you do?" I asked, but my voice was carried away by some odd, ethereal wind.

"Get back to your body as soon as you can, Janneke," Diaval instructed me. "I don't know how long I can keep you teth-ered to this world."

Now, out of my body, something tugged me deep in my belly. It was like someone had put a hook in my gut and was slowly pulling me forward, giving me no room to argue or refuse. The landscape changed as I walked farther, as my feet began to stand on air and the world turned upside down. The birds swam and the trees had roots for branches, and I was upside down, right-side up, and somewhere neutral all at once.

Focus your energy, I could almost hear the bastard's voice for real this time, and despite every bit of my body aching to refuse his advice to spite him, I did as he said. I focused hard, back on that field where the world began.

Finally, Lydian appeared in front of my eyes.

The first thing I did was punch him.

I wasn't sure who was more shocked—me, expecting him to maybe be incorporeal or untouchable or him, probably expecting . . . well, I didn't think I'd ever be able to guess what Lydian was expecting.

He put a hand to his nose, then stared at the blood on it. "Ouch."

I punched him again, this time in the jaw. "That was for my village and family." Before he had a chance to move, I brought my knee into his stomach and slammed my elbow down on his back. A satisfying groan came from his lips. "That was for Rekke." The memory of the young she-goblin who'd been forced to fight during the Hunt and was brutally disemboweled by Lydian still flashed in my mind from time to time and left me shaking with rage and sadness. I hadn't known her well, but I knew her well enough that she didn't deserve to die. "You know, the innocent child you killed on the Hunt," I explained when he made a confused expression. I brought my knee up again, this time into his crotch. "That's for what you did to me." I released him and watched as he curled up on the ground, huddled in a ball of pain. Then I kicked him in the ribs. "And that's because I wanted to."

Lydian stayed on the ground, his body trembling. Or, at least, that's what I thought until I heard the gasp-like laughter coming from his mouth. He was *laughing*. I beat him to the ground, his face covered in his own blood, and the fucker was *laughing*. Unbidden, Donnar's words came back to me. *If it's any consolation, he was already a psychopath before I cursed him.*

Yeah, I was beginning to see that.

Hot anger pooled into my muscles, but I forced myself to swallow it back. In the back of my head was a foreign feeling, not quite my own but not a stranger's either, that I recognized to be the stag's mantle. It pulsed and vibrated, almost like a voice, though no words were said, telling me that as reprehensible as this all was, I needed to keep my calm. If only it were that easy.

"Well," I said to his still-laughing form. "I'm here. Talk."

He stood, blood still trickling from his nose and down farther to his neck. It made for a gruesome site when he bared his teeth into something a bit too primal to be a smile. "Took you long enough."

My hands curled into fists again. "Tell me what you want to tell me, and then get out of my sight."

"Sight," he mused, eyes getting that faraway look again. "That's all it comes down to. Sight."

Great, now he was going to ramble again. Just my luck. I

wanted this to be over with. Standing this close to the monster, and he *was* a monster, was making my skin crawl.

His eyes cleared up again as he raked his gaze down me in a predatory way. I stared back at him, refusing to flinch. He made another bared-tooth smile at that. "I have to say, I admire your courage being here."

I lifted my chin. "I already told you, Lydian. You hold no power over me anymore."

"Your heart is racing like a frightened rabbit," he countered.

"Your heart is kept locked away somewhere in the Erlking's palace," I said. "Keeping you in this place. Maybe once you cooperate, I'll actually bury it, let you rest." I refused to let him control the situation in any way. I was the one making the threats. I was the one with the power. I was the one in charge. He could try to flip that dynamic all he wanted, but it wasn't about to change.

"I can never rest," he said, beginning to pace in a feverish manner. "Not after all that's happened, not after what I know, not after the world began falling apart."

"What are you talking about?" I nearly shouted. "Enough with the riddles. *Tell* me."

"Are you sure you want to know?" he asked. When I nodded, his eyes hardened. "Very well."

The field around me shimmered in the air and shifted, changing into a different place all together. I could see all of the nine realms; I somehow stood within them and outside of them at the same time. Yggdrasil, the tree of life, held them together but something was gnawing at its roots. A giant serpent with gleaming red eyes, his entire impossibly long body wrapped around the tree. I stared as Lydian's riddle came back to me. *What happens when the serpent stops eating his tail?*

"It eats the world from the inside out," I spoke without thinking, without even putting the words together in my head. Almost like a different force flowed through me at this moment. This was my world, my *worlds,* that I was supposed to protect and balance, that I was supposed to keep steady, and it was being made to shake apart by this giant serpent.

The odd mine-but-not-mine feeling in my head, in my gut, returned, filling me with something akin to a mother's rage at the destruction of their child—or at least being childless myself, what I thought it felt like. The nine realms were my children, and they were going to fall apart.

"I told you," Lydian snarled. "I told you all. It's all your fault. You and my nephew's. You two were always meant to destroy the world."

The vision faded away until I was back on the field, facing Lydian. His pacing had quickened now until he'd worn a groove into the grass, and his hands grasped each other, wringing and scratching his own skin.

"Soren and I have nothing to do with this," I said sharply.

"No?" He looked up from his pacing. "Do you know the laws of winter, girl?"

Girl. He said it with disgust. That is all I ever was to him. A human girl. Easily used. Easily discarded. *I am powerful now. Even if I don't know how to use my full abilities, I won't let him get to me.* Not when I still needed information. When I woke up from whatever state I was in, I could take my anger out in any way I wanted, but for now I was forced to deal. "Of course I do."

The laws of winter. The laws that governed the entire Permafrost. Sixteen in all, though some had been forgotten in time. But as the stag, I knew them all.

The Erlking's word was law.

The Erlking must be the strongest goblin.

Oaths may not be broken if sworn upon land, sea, and sky, unless both the oathgiver and the oathkeeper agree to it.

The stag is the life force of the Permafrost.

Gifts may only be used for the purpose they were given unless that purpose is no longer suitable. This was the law that made it impossible for Soren to change my status as a thrall until I began adapting more to the Permafrost, since I was originally his uncle's "gift."

All favors must be repaid.

Those who consume the nectar of the Permafrost are bound to its lands.

If two or more persons get into a fight, the winner is granted the loser's power and possessions, and gains immunity for any illegal action during the fight under the spirit of winter.

Iron is banned in the Permafrost on the pain of death, unless used by the victor of the fight.

Magic may not be used to alter the events of time.

All of these I knew, along with the ancient forgotten law that had given me the power of the stag in the first place. Yes, I knew the laws, lived by them like any other creature in the Permafrost. I was created in the Permafrost. Changed.

"No, you don't," Lydian said. He continued before I could protest. "Did you ever wonder why the line for the Erlking is not inherited by blood, rather than battle? It's because the blood of the original Erlking mixed with the sacrifice of the stag sealed the realms together and kept the world serpent from waking from his slumber by shoving its tail in its mouth. If their blood was to mix again, then the serpent would awaken and begin gnawing at the roots of Yggdrasil, starting Ragnarök."

Something uneasy was brewing in my gut at what he was saying, though I couldn't truly understand it yet or make any sense of it.

"For that reason, the Erlking's direct bloodline was all but eliminated. But as often occurs, females tend to be overlooked when it comes to bloodlines, and of the few who escaped, none ever participated in the stag hunt, having the knowledge passed down from mother to child." He'd stopped pacing by now, though his hands still wrung together hard enough for his nails to dig into his skin and create welts. "It was a secret, you see. But I know *everything*. All secrets. All thoughts. All breaths and beats and steps, each pulse of blood, each twitch of muscle."

Lydian broke off into laughter. "But of course, I couldn't say anything. Damn svartelf, I had him to blame for that. What's the use of seeing if you can't tell? And when she came, she was the last of them. And I saw her, and I knew she would have a child and that child would find another child, and those two witless children would end the world. So, I killed her, but her spawn still lived. So, I took you because I *knew* who you were even if I didn't know *how* you were going to do it, and you refused to answer any of my questions. Because I *had* to ask. You were my one blind spot, the *one* thing I couldn't see because how do you see someone dead and alive, moving and still, *liminal?* Now that I travel the space, oh, I can see them, but then, no, nothing. But I had to ask, ask or break you, break you or kill you, until you ruined it by shoving a piece of iron into my skin. And well, we all knew what happened after that.

"No one appreciated my attempts to save them all, so I decided to damn them instead, by giving you to him. Knowing maybe his pride would get in the way of you living. I judged poorly, and when I tried to fix my mistakes, save the world from you two children, you fought back and you won, and now the world is dying and it's *all your fault.*"

5

THE MADMAN'S CONFESSION

LYDIAN CONTINUED HIS laughter, breath hitching and catching every so often until it would send him into deep coughing fits. He would recover from them and then continue laughing as his poison-green eyes kept themselves steadily on my face, watching my expression.

I breathed in the air, somehow both cold and warm, in this space in the field between worlds. It wasn't his words that shocked me, not really; it was the scenes behind my eyes that played almost like dreams as he spoke. They flashed so fast, I almost couldn't keep up, but they always ended up at the same place. Soren on the throne, me beside him, dark brown hair speckled with white, and the world tree cracking, breaking and falling, and the cosmos spiraling downward into black nothingness.

No, it wasn't so much this madman's confession that caused the nausea in my stomach. It wasn't that he in some primitive way was, not right, never right, never on the side of good, "right" wasn't the proper word for it, but *correct* in the ramblings about the world being destroyed, and Soren and I being the ones to bring it to its destruction. No, it was the way I could see it play out in my own head over and over again, the wheels of fate turning and turning and never stopping, no matter what got in its way.

The fate that this world would die.

That Soren and I would cause it in our attempt to save it.

That in some sick way, Lydian was doing what his twisted, ravaged mind thought was *right*. Not solely because he was a mad dog that needed to be put down—though that had always been a part of it—but that in some way, he had tried to save the world and that way happened to include terrible, horrible things.

Then the nausea went away when I decided it didn't matter. That I couldn't dwell on it because I knew, *knew,* it would break me if I did. I would not let him break me.

My eyes hardened in resolve and I straightened from the hunched form I'd found myself curling into without thinking. Lydian stopped his laughter, catching his breath, turning his head to the side quizzically, in a move that reminded me uncomfortably of his nephew.

So, he could understand too, the look in my eyes.

"Soren and I end the world, huh?" I said, voice steady.

He gave a quick, sharp nod.

"Well then, I'm assuming you'll tell me you have the solution?" My voice betrayed no emotion, and I tried to focus on keeping my breath and heart rate down and steady.

"I think so," he said.

"You think?" I let the acid dip from my words.

"Before Ragnarök can begin in truth, Fimbulwinter must start." I nodded along. Fimbulwinter. The winter that lasted three years. When I was a child, my father used to scare me with stories of Fimbulwinter. Three years of ice and cold where the sun never shown. All the animals and crops would die, which would make every creature from the smallest mouse to the largest draugr weak with hunger and exhausted and perfect for when Ragnarök and the soldiers of the dead did arrive three years later. Back as a child, I thought they were stories. But I'd lived in the Permafrost, spoken to gods, killed draugrs, and became a liminal being. I was far past believing *anything* was a children's story. "For Fimbulwinter to start, Fjalar must cry three times. His voice will pierce the chains that keep the *Naglafar* from setting sail with the hosts of the dead."

The names were older than legends to me, but somehow so familiar. Fjalar, the giant bird whose cry was loud enough that it broke the chains on the dreaded *Naglafar,* the nail ship, built from the undead's uncut finger and toenails, carrying the unholy, those not put to rest, those who did not earn a good afterlife, to be soldiers in the army of the dead.

He wasn't saying the plan outright, but I managed to follow along fine.

"If we kill Fjalar before he can break the chains on the *Naglafar,* we can thwart Ragnarök," I said, "and with any luck, the serpent will go back to sleep."

A smile danced on the edge of Lydian's lips. Somehow it made him look even more sinister than when he was raving.

"Smart girl, yes." I bristled at the term *girl*, but not enough for him to stop speaking. "The one problem is, Fjalar is a liminal being. You can't hunt and track something that's *there but not there*."

"Not unless you're led by something else *there but not there*," I finished for him.

The hints of a smile on Lydian's face turned into an outright grin. I was the stag and forced a neutral expression.

"You're taking this rather well," he said, curious eyes flitting toward my face.

"Don't mistake me, Lydian," I said, an edge in my voice. "Nothing you did is forgiven, forgotten, excused, whatever adjective you want to think up. You're not some hero who did a bad thing for a good reason. I've met my share of monsters and monster-like heroes to know the difference, and you are, always will be, a monster." The icy tone in my voice made the air around us glimmer with ice crystals, and as I continued, they began to crack and freeze, almost like the water in the air was turning into a thin sheet of ice. "Nothing you did was for the greater good. Nothing you wrought was for the good of the realm, of the people, of anything. The hurt you've caused, the pain, the vile actions I won't even name? *None* of that changes."

I took a step forward, and from beneath my feet, the once-grassy field cracked with ice. Like his nephew, Lydian was taller than me by at least two heads. But somehow in this space, I met his eyes plain as day, face-to-face, heights equal. It was only when the wind tickled my boots did I see the ice had lifted me into the air, holding me on the frozen crystals my power formed. "You're useful now. Your usefulness doesn't absolve your crimes. That's all you are. A *tool*. And once you've finished out your usefulness . . ." I shrugged as my feet returned to the ground. "Well, you know what happens to broken tools."

Something was calling me from the back of my mind, a familiar voice I could barely make out. Suddenly, there was a sharp tug around my navel, like a band about to snap.

"I suspect this is all we have time to speak about," Lydian said. "I'm afraid even I won't be coherent for much longer. Keeping composure for long . . . is hard. But it seems we have some sort of a deal."

"It seems we do," I replied, letting out a bared-tooth smile that would make Soren proud.

"Tell my nephew I said 'hi.'"

Snap. The world around me retracted until I was pulled backward out of the field and into the air, thrown through the cosmos, into the ground, through the rivers and waters, until I burst forth back into my body, drenched and gasping.

Diaval was breathing heavily, her fingers still coated in blue static and her dark eyes glowing unnaturally bright. But other than that, the courtyard was completely silent. I waited semi-patiently as she caught her breath and her eyes returned to their normal dark blue. She gave me an apologetic look. "I kept you in there for maybe around twenty minutes. I'm sorry. I hope that was enough."

"It was enough, Diaval," I said, bending down to take her

hand and help her stand. She stumbled a little, but managed to keep her feet. "Thank you."

"What did you learn?" she asked, a hand on my shoulder as she continued to keep herself steady. I noticed without it, she was swaying slightly as if in an invisible breeze.

I sighed. Out of all the people I could tell this information to first, Diaval would most likely be the least judgmental. Not to mention soon Soren would need to know, because if Lydian *was* right—then, well, we had to do something.

It hadn't hit the *me* side of me. I was still in stag mode, my emotions there but sort of dull, mute, cut off from me as if they were behind a thick fog or glass. Was this how it was for Soren all the time? I wasn't sure. But the information hadn't hit those emotions yet, the mantle of the stag clouded them, focused my mind on one thing only: my duty to the Permafrost.

I told Diaval and watched her expression as it barely changed at all. Once or twice, she nodded to herself, but other than that, nothing. I wasn't sure if that was a good or bad sign. Finally, she spoke. "This . . . complicates things," she said.

I snorted. "You think?"

"Soren's gonna pitch a fit."

I squeezed my eyes shut. That was not going to go well, no matter how I managed it. "Thanks for the encouragement. I was going to tell him everything in the morning."

She *hmm*ed before speaking again. "You seem strangely calm for all of this."

Nodding, I brushed off some nonexistent dust from my pants. "I'm compartmentalizing, I think. It's like the stag half of my brain has taken over, it's not allowing for emotions other than knowing this is fucked up but I have a duty to the world anyway. I'm sure as soon as the human half takes over, I'll be a blubbering mess somewhere lost deep in my trauma."

The words came out sardonically, but they were close to the truth. I wasn't entirely sure when this whole stag-focused mindset would wear off, but when it did, I knew I was going to be a wreck. I knew what I had to do, but that didn't mean the human side of me liked it or could process it.

Maybe the stag-focused side of me would manage to keep me from freaking every time Lydian was near me, but it couldn't stop the disgust his presence pooled in me—toward both him and myself. I still woke up screaming from night-mares about Lydian. Maybe it was dumb, but I thought they'd go away once he was dead. That the flashbacks would fade now that he couldn't hurt me. But that hadn't happened. The mental wounds he created still bled, and the scar tissue was still rough and pulled painfully in my brain. Not to men-tion other dreams where my family gave me their accusing looks or even worse, dreams where none of this ever happened and I was normal. Despite all I had here, I didn't want those dreams to end.

Diaval stood beside me, hand hovering over my shoulder like she wasn't sure whether the physical contact would com-fort or trigger me. I nodded toward her, and she placed her warm, small hand on me. "If it helps, you'll have me there as backup. And Seppo and Rosamund. When you tell him."

I shook my head, unease flittering in my chest like moths. "No, it's already going to upset him that you all knew about

Lydian before he did. I need to tell him alone. It's the only way I can make him understand."

Midnight had long since passed, and I gazed toward the sky. It was still dark, though getting lighter to where the stars were harder to point out unless I really, really looked. Sooner or later, Soren would wake from his uncomfortable sleep in the chair to find me gone, and he would most likely panic because he was taking his role as concerned partner very seriously.

It was funny, some people called him the Ice King, said that his heart was frozen, that he was brutal and without mercy. Of course, all of those things were good by goblin standards and essential for the Erlking. How many people knew that under all that ice was something sweet, like sugar, that under the harsh ruler was a kind and compassionate goblin.

He would understand why I kept it a secret. He had to understand.

THERE WAS A candle lit when I entered the room again, and Soren sat by it, staring in the flames.

"You know if you do that for too long, you'll start to hallucinate," I said.

He stood, chair shooting backward. "I was trying to scry."

"Didn't know you were into magic," I said. "Should I tell Diaval?"

"That's who you were with, right?" he said. I nodded. "Thought so. I could smell her. She's got a peculiar scent."

Scents. One of the many things I did not experience the same way Soren did, though I think I was lucky for that. I wouldn't have wanted to pick everyone apart by a unique smell anyways. Soren smelled nice enough when we were together and he'd not recently been training, and that worked fine for me.

"And no," he continued. "I figured you'd gone off somewhere, and I was trying to see where you were. I know we're technically supposed to be able to do that as the stag and Erlking, but no luck."

"If it helps, I can't do it either. I'm a pretty big failure at this whole stag thing."

"Don't say that," Soren said with some anger to his tone. "You're the first human to have the stag's power, ever. Of course it's going to be hard. Now, are you going to tell me about where you were, or am I going to have to beg?"

I sighed, running a hand through my curls. I guessed sooner was better than later. "Sorry if I worried you."

"Apology accepted," Soren said, sitting next to me on the sleeping platform. "I know you can take care of yourself. But I still worry. Especially lately. You've not . . . been yourself."

I took a deep breath and winced like I was inhaling ice shards. "About that," I started. "Soren, I need to tell you something."

"I'm listening," he said, lilac eyes on mine.

Well, it was now or never. A stone dropped into my stomach as I started my story. "I've been hiding something from you. I know I shouldn't have, but I did. I can't make excuses for it, so I'm not going to try. But you're right that in the beginning, it was nightmares. But a few months after I became the stag, I began . . . having visions. At first, it was fleeting, normal life things. But then they became about the end of the world. Then I started seeing him . . . hearing him, in my head."

Soren frowned, leaning forward. "Who?"

I turned my head away, unable to keep his gaze. "Lydian. His shade spoke to me, appeared by me, taunted me, *warned* me."

Soren tightened one hand into a fist. "I didn't think he'd even be able to, trapped where he was. I'll burn his heart; he'll disappear." He began to stand, but I pulled him back down.

"No!" I said with a bit too much force.

He sat but looked at me oddly. "No?"

"I talked to Donnar today. He told me a few things. Did . . . did your father ever mention that he could see the future?" Gods, this was going terribly.

"Once or twice, just that it skipped my generation, why?"

"Because it's a family trait, but it doesn't show up in everyone. It didn't show up in Lydian. He was jealous of your father and his father and went into the svartelf caverns demanding the gift of the sight. Donnar was there. Lydian insulted him, and Donnar cursed him. He cursed him with knowing everything and never being able to fully tell others. Every breath of every creature, the life of every blade of grass, drop of water, every person who was or ever had been. It drove him mad. Or, well, madder. He wasn't exactly the picture of stability in the first place."

Soren's face darkened and he stood, his hand yanking from mine. I tried not to feel hurt at the action. It was only going to get worse, I knew it. "What are you saying, Janneke?"

"I'm saying he was right. He was a mad son of a bitch who tortured both of us and would've killed us and possibly doomed the entire Permafrost. But *he was right*. We were always going to destroy the world."

And with those words, my own world came crashing down.

6

THE CATALYSTS

SOREN STARED AT me, mouth slightly open before his face morphed into a deep frown. "You can't be serious."

"It's because you're directly related to the first Erl-king on your mother's side," I said. "That, mixed with the blood of the stag, woke up the world serpent, and he began to gnaw at the roots of the world tree instead of his tail." My heart was beating a mile a minute.

"And that causes the end of the world, according to Lydian? Did you ever think he may be lying? Hel, was this what you were doing with Diaval? Does she know?"

I was silent, guilt written plainly on my face as the flashes of Seppo, Rose, and Diaval came through our link. He growled then, a loud sound that made me step backward.

"So, everyone else knew about this but me? That you were seeing Lydian's ghost, what he was saying, and now you're saying he was right?" Soren turned away from me on his heel and punched the wall. I winced as bits of marble crumbled to the ground. "I'm not going to end the world. You're not going to end the world. He was lying."

"He wasn't. I saw it. I saw the world tree and the serpent and the end of the world in my visions. And as the stag, I know it, I feel it in my bones. The world is going to end unless we do something to stop it," I pleaded.

"Are you suggesting we work *with him*?" Soren asked incredulously, then before he could give me time to answer, he shook his head and shoved past me to the door. "I'm not sure what's more painful. The idea you want to work with that monster, you *believe* what he's telling you, or the fact that despite everything we've been through, I was the last person you trusted with this information."

A burst of rage flared in my chest, and I maneuvered myself between Soren and the door. "You think I'm giddy about this?" My breath hitched, and a pain blossomed in my chest that wasn't entirely physical. Finally the emotional dam the stag's powers had made was breaking. It must've been breaking because the cold, calculated thoughts were seeping away from me, leaving me with terror blossoming in my stomach. "You know what he did to me. I'll never forgive or forget that, and this is terrifying. I am the stag. I must do what the powers will."

Soren crossed his arms in front of his chest, glaring. "That's unfair. I have a duty to the Permafrost as much as you. Do you know how many creatures have been changing boundaries because of problems cropping up? I fix one and then there's another. That's why the svartelves came in today too. Their cave is going dry."

I winced, realizing what I had implied. "I know you're doing your job. I'm trying to do mine."

"Isn't part of your job to inform me when this type of thing is going on?" he asked. "Not hiding it and telling all your friends instead?'

"It's more complicated than that!" I shouted. "I was scared. I'm still scared. I didn't want to tell you because I didn't want you to worry about me or know I was scared." There, the truth was out. The burden tumbled from my shoulders and a weight lifted from my chest. The pain purged from me was better, like a catharsis. I didn't want Soren to see me scared or weak. Not when I spent so much time proving I was strong. My hands were now shaking at having anything to do with Lydian since I was fully me again, and my stomach twisted and made me want to vomit.

"I thought I could deal with it on my own."

"Which is why you told our friends, but not me."

"It's different!" I said. "They practically figured it out with Diaval's condition. They weren't affected by him, tortured by him, not like you and I were. There was some kind of emotional buffer. It wasn't as raw. I know I should have told you when I first started hearing and seeing him, but I couldn't. I couldn't."

Soren still had that unrelenting glare. "Step aside, Janneke."

"Soren—"

"Please," he said a little softer. "Step aside."

I moved away from the door and watched hopelessly as Soren stormed out of it.

I collapsed on the sleeping platform, my knees weak and wobbly. I knew he was going to be mad that I hadn't said anything, but I hadn't realized he would be *hurt*. Because underneath the glares and growls, I could feel it inside me, like he could most likely feel my despair, and while anger was there, what really radiated all around him was hurt. Because we promised to be truthful to each other and *I didn't trust him*. Not with this. That was why I was barely able to get a few sentences out about Lydian and Ragnarök before he stormed off—that wasn't what was causing his pain. It was me, keeping a secret from him for so many months.

Which was fair. I'd be angry too if I were him.

For a moment I contemplated following him and continuing to try to fix this mess, but I realized it would only probably make it worse. Soren needed some time to cool down.

I ended up wandering around the palace, making sure to give Soren his distance as I did so. The place was so large and cavernous that I found myself constantly wishing to be back in Soren's manor in the High North, not here. In all likelihood I would never see it again. It wasn't like Soren could retire from being the Erlking and me, the stag.

How ironic to finally accept a place as your home before having to leave it for another. I missed the wood and iron, the simple and not-so-simple designs carved into everything. It was the type of decoration that was subtle but intricate, and I'd spend hours sometimes looking at them, following them with my fingers. And the work. No matter what race or species you were, you worked, and here, the boredom was killing me. Or, well, it would've been if it weren't for a particular voice in my head.

I sighed. But his manor wasn't a place we could go back to anymore.

I ended up in the stables, watching the horses as they slept. They were such magnificent animals, but they still were painful to look at ever since I'd lost my horse, Panic. He'd been bonded to me, we'd been closer than rider and horse, we were something different all together. But still, ever since I became the stag, animals liked me a lot more than they did when I wasn't. Which was saying something because I was the kid who used to get chased by vicious geese daily, and unfortunately, I couldn't put arrows through due to them being our farm animals. I smiled at the memory.

One of the horses nickered and leaned down to push their nose against mine, and I stroked the soft, velvety skin there. "Hello," I said.

"Hi."

I nearly jumped out of my skin at the reply that definitely had not come from a horse. My eyes darted around before latching onto a figure hiding up in the rafters of the stables. He smiled at me, and I scowled back.

"You nearly gave me a heart attack, Rose!"

Rosamund shrugged and with catlike grace, dropped from the rafters to the ground. "You're the stag. I don't think you can have heart attacks."

"You know what I mean," I huffed in frustration. "What the hell were you doing up there anyway?"

"Well," Rose replied, "I saw Soren sulking in the armory,

and I figured that meant you also must be sulking but in a different place, and so Seppo and I battled for who gets to talk to whom, and I was lucky enough not to get the person who can literally rip hearts out of bodies with his bare hands."

Oh gods. Soren was going to kill Seppo if he tried anything. I shook my head. Not my hunting party, not my hunters.

"You two can be so absolutely petty and stubborn when you want to be. Like, as much as I would say goblinkind is not known for our good communication skills, you and Soren kind of make the bar go to an entirely different level."

"We have good communication skills!" I said, glaring.

"Yeah, that's exactly why neither of you can admit when there's a problem, and instead pretend nothing is wrong until you both come to your senses and actually say something," Rose said, voice dripping with acid.

"Okay, we have some snares, but I'm not about to get relationship advice from someone who chased a horse around the Permafrost all day as a present for someone not even born yet."

Rosamund had the gall to look offended. "We had that situation completely under control."

"Under control, my ass," I muttered. "Look, I tried talking to him, and it ended up a disaster. So, now what?" I leaned my head back against the stall door and closed my eyes as a headache began to brew beneath my eyelids.

"So, now you wait until both of you have cooled down and you try again. And then the next time, you know not to hide things like this from each other for months," Rosamund said in a voice serious enough I contemplated punching him. "Seppo and I had a bit of that problem when we first started seeing each other. He was worried about what others would think since he was already judged for being a halfling. For months I didn't know why he pulled away, until it occurred to me to *ask* him." A satisfied smile grew on his face. "And all it took was ensuring I'd rip the spine out of anyone who dared mistreat him, for it all to be better." I had to keep myself from rolling my eyes. Why did all heartwarming goblin stories still revolve around violence?

"I hate it when you're right," I mumbled. "I'll try again once we're both in a better place. I know it must be hard for him. Both what I found out, and learning that I've kept secrets from him."

"Yeah, Diaval filled Seppo and me in," Rose said. "You know we have your back. And Soren's. Things will work out, you'll see." He patted my shoulder before standing. "I better make sure Seppo is still alive. Between you threatening to push him off mountains and shove weapons up his ass, and Soren being . . . Soren, I'm surprised he doesn't resemble a scared rabbit every time he's around you two."

"Seppo is a good goblin," I said, slightly guilty. "I don't mean to scare him. The Hunt was . . . tense."

Rose snorted. "Hence why I stayed out of it. Also, don't feel too bad. Part of Seppo's entire charm is his ability to annoy and instigate fights wherever he goes. It's what makes him so attractive."

I laughed softly. "Whatever you say."

Rosamund put a hand on my knee, and I held back a flinch. All this time, and sometimes it was still hard for me to have casual physical contact, especially with a male. Goblin, human, it didn't matter. Though parts of my trauma had healed, much of it still was left to go, and that didn't include the bits being ripped open again by Lydian's revelations.

The near-emotionlessness of the stag's sense of duty was almost completely worn off, and I had to grip my hands into fists and dig my fingers into the palms of my hands to stop them from shaking. It didn't matter, I told myself. The same message still applied, even when I was more of my human self. I couldn't change the horrors of my past, but I could still fix the problems of the future. I still had the power to fix what was happening now. If it meant arguing with Soren or working with Lydian, so be it. It had to be done. I was only human—well, sort of—and I couldn't fix or change what was done to me. But I could choose whatever I did next. I had the choice.

I had to keep repeating this mantra in my head. Sooner or later, it would stick, and my heart would calm down from its racing in my chest. Because I knew it was safe, even if my hypervigilance told me to dash away and hide from the situation like a frightened rabbit.

Rose noticed my flinch and took his hand away. "Sorry," he apologized.

"It's not your fault. One day I won't flinch, not today," I said, standing and stretching my cramped calf muscles. The horse in the stall I'd been sitting against brought its head down to greet me, and I rubbed its nose. It was the troublemaker that Seppo and Rosamund had been chasing. "Look at you," I cooed at the animal. "Such a good girl."

"A good girl who nearly gave me a black eye," Rose said.

"It's not my fault you don't understand how horses work," I said, continuing to stroke the horse's nose. I sighed. Would that I could be with the animal forever. But there were conversations to be had and people to have them with. "Soren's alone now," I said, feeling through the weak link that we had between us. He wasn't overly angry, and it didn't feel like he'd broken anything, or at least, he hadn't broken Seppo, so that was a good sign. It was time to go and try for round two. "I think Seppo is all right. You know Soren wouldn't actually hurt his friends."

Rose smirked. "I know, I know. But it's fun to make fun of him and his poor impulse control. Plus, maybe *you've* never encountered Soren in a fit of true rage. He's pretty good at not doing that around you, but none of us get the same courtesy, and while I'm sure the brute would never kill me, it's absolutely *terrifying* to behold."

I smiled. "I'll take your word for it."

I left the stables feeling somewhat better about the situation. A little more lighthearted where before I swore my entire body was weighed down with lead. Soren and I had a relationship that was strong as iron, and it would survive this. We would talk, and, considering what Rosamund said, we would talk more often. If two pigheaded people had to be in a relationship and make it work, it was us.

I couldn't hide my surprise at seeing Soren staring at the doorway to our chambers by the time I got there. He caught me in his gaze and managed to look slightly embarrassed. "It's silly," he said, "but opening it's . . . hard. Knowing what we have to speak about."

I nodded. "I understand." Striding forward, I gently pushed the door open.

Both of us situated ourselves on chairs, turning to face each other. For a moment, all we did was stare, neither of us able to think of the correct words or get them to come out.

I managed to start. "I'm sorry," I said. "I should've told you in the beginning. But I was scared. I wanted to prove that I could handle it on my own. That I wasn't still some vulnerable child, y'know? And then Diaval found out because she could see his specter and that led to the others finding out, and soon, Seppo, Rose, and she knew, and you didn't, and I didn't know what to do. It wasn't because I didn't trust you or don't love you. I do. So much. I'd kept the secret and waved off telling you until now, and you were right when you said it's harder to tell someone something the longer you keep it a secret. But I was scared."

Soren nodded, a pensive look on his face. "I can understand that. I know you weren't trying to hurt me. But," he sighed, "I wish . . . if there is one thing I want for us, Janneke, it's for you to feel safe. I know you might never feel completely safe . . . but I want to be there when you don't. I don't want you to feel the need to hide from me when you're vulnerable because you don't want to add on to my burdens or you're scared. If you can't carry it alone, I'll help you carry it. Because I love you."

Warmth trickled inside my chest, and I smiled softly. "I'll try. Next time something happens. Next time I'm scared or feeling vulnerable. I'll try to remember to speak to you and that me speaking to you doesn't make me weak."

One of Soren's rare smiles graced his face. "That's all I ask."

I leaned forward and kissed him on the cheek before he turned his head to meet my lips. It was a soft kiss, a gentle kiss, a tender kiss of forgiveness that didn't need to be spoken. I didn't want to break away, but I knew I had to, because our conversation wasn't over yet.

Both of us sat back in our chairs, and neither of us needed the link to feel the absolute dread at the discussion ahead.

"So," Soren said, leaning forward. "About Lydian."

7

THE WORLDENDERS

BEFORE I SAY anything about what I learned," I said, "I want to say it *doesn't matter*. No matter what he knew or saw, he did terrible things of his own volition to both of us. And what he did was wrong, even if he saw the future, he was still wrong to do what he did."

I'd been repeating this over and over in my head ever since the end of my discussion with him, knowing that if I didn't, it would be so easy to cross over into territory where I would blame myself and go back to the horrible self-loathing I'd been fighting to keep away. No matter what, *he had no right.*

Soren may not have been on the physical end of Lydian's tortured visions, but he was one of the major parts that they circled around. The last known direct bloodline of the original Erlking, who bonded with the first incarnation of the stag, had now become Erlking himself, bonding with the newest incarnation of the stag, setting off the start of the instability that would cause the end of the world. Blood through blood.

That . . . that was a burden he was going to have to bear

and carry on his shoulders, and I didn't need to be the stag to know it wouldn't be easy on him. I wished I could have lessened some of the pain he surely was about to feel.

Soren nodded in agreement. "Continue."

I laced my hands together in my lap. "Lydian was always . . . off. I don't know *how* off he was in the beginning, but literally everyone has been reassuring me that what happened to him wasn't what made him a bad, evil person with a twisted sense of everything. It made that part of him worse.

"You said people in your family can sometimes see visions of the future. Your father and grandfather could, but Lydian couldn't and it enraged him, so he went to the svartlef caves and demanded to have the gift of sight to a much younger Donnar. He crossed the line too far, and Donnar cursed him with the knowledge of *everything* here and now, in the future, of the past, every heartbeat and sway of the wind and future of blades of grass. He broke his mind further by making sure he could never tell anyone what he saw, not flat out."

Soren winced, then frowned. "That actually makes a lot of sense, unfortunately. Why my father said he took a turn for the worse after entering the caverns."

"One of the things he saw was you and me."

"Yes, I remember what you said. I'm related to the first Erlking through my mother, and my bloodline coming back into power along with you becoming the stag started Ragnarök. Together we tried to save the world but doomed it instead, and only Lydian knew the truth." The tone in his voice had lowered and was the only way I could tell he was upset by this. Otherwise, his face remained passive and stoic.

That wasn't good. I knew Soren, and I didn't have to guess about the pain he was feeling right now. Because I'd dealt with it myself many times before. Reaching out, I grabbed his hand in mine and squeezed reassuringly. "Soren, you can't blame yourself. You can't hate yourself for this."

"Why not?" he bit out. "Why did the stag even choose me if I was going to destroy everything? Why shouldn't I hate myself?"

I leaned forward. "Because the stag saw something *worthy* in you. I see something worthy in you. Otherwise, you wouldn't be the Erlking." He turned his face away and I turned it back, my hand resting on his cheek. I stared into his lilac eyes, saw the shimmer of pain in them. "You can't blame yourself. You can't hate yourself. I know that. I've spent a hundred years hating myself for things I couldn't control, and now I realize that's no way to live. Because then, they've won."

For so long self-hatred had held me back, and even now I struggled not to be as hard on myself. I wouldn't let Soren fall down the same rabbit hole if I could help it. Because once you fell down, it was a grueling, never-ending climb back up.

"You really believe that?" he said, uncharacteristically quiet.

"I have to," I said. "I have to believe there's some type of reason that we are where we are right now. That what's happening to the world is something that maybe we caused, through no fault of our own, but years of prophecy instead—but also, something we can change. If we can't hold onto the belief that this fight matters *because* we're fighting it—because even if we can't control what our bloodlines did, we can control what they do *now*—then we fucking have already let everything and everyone against us win by default. And I don't care if it's Lydian or the end of the world, neither of those things are going to win. Okay. Focus on that. Please."

He gave a small sigh, then nodded. "I'll try. I . . . I've never been unsure of myself like this until now."

I couldn't help but giggle. "You're normally pretty full of yourself. But it's endearing, don't worry."

He shot me a cocky grin. "I'm glad you find my arrogance attractive. I'll remember that next time you claim I'm going to turn your hair white with exasperation."

I fingered a curl of my hair, staring with disdain at the white streak. There were only a few, and I hoped they didn't continue to turn. Though it had nothing to do with Soren causing me stress. I was finally beginning to like my appearance. Maybe I'd never fully accept my scars, but I could appreciate them, and looking in the mirror and seeing a reflection so similar to my father's, dark skin and hair amidst the snowy landscape, no longer filled me with misplaced guilt, but pride. I hoped my hair stayed the same color for the most part even if a few white streaks marked the stag's power inside of me.

"You're not the one currently turning my hair white. I seem to be doing that well enough on my own."

Soren leaned forward until our foreheads pressed against each other, and I could feel his soft breath tickling my face. My hand fell away from his cheek as we fell into a kiss, and I bit back a moan as desire flooded through me. One of his hands tangled itself into my hair as we rose together, only to fall back on the sleeping platform. He carefully kept his weight off me as our kiss deepened and his other hand gripped my hip hard, pulling me in toward him. When we embraced this time, I couldn't stifle the sounds coming from deep in my throat. I let myself get lost in his body, in his touch, and let the worries of the past few days melt away.

———

AFTER THAT, WE lay there for a while, breathing hard and covered in sweat. Soren's fingers absently rubbed my shoulders and I leaned into his body, one leg between his, allowing him to shield me from the world. There were many times where being short was annoying and a hindrance, and this was definitely not one of them. I loved the way I could feel so totally protected by him. Even with all the chaos going on, it was one thing I could always rely on. And I was also glad that I even accepted those feelings in the first place, knowing before the Hunt, anything other than coldness would have been unbelievable.

He pressed his pale blue lips to my forehead, and I buried my head in his chest. "We're going to have to get up and make a game plan soon," I mumbled into his body. "Tell the people that we trust. Figure out what we're going to do, how."

Soren sighed. "Well, the cat's out of the bag for Seppo, Rosamund, and Diaval. Satu should know, too, if she doesn't already, and is waiting to approach us about it. As for the rest . . . I have people on my guard and as my advisors, but I wouldn't say I trust them. I trust that I can outmaneuver them should I need to, and I trust that it's more likely for them to get stabbed in the back than me, but not much else."

I groaned. Typical Permafrost relationships. "Maybe you have white hair not because it's a genetic issue; maybe it really is stress. Fuck, hearing that makes me stressed. I'm so tired of having to worry about everyone's intentions."

Soren cradled my face in his palms, lifting my head to look him in the eyes. "You're stronger than you know, Janneke. But know that I would never allow anyone to come even close enough to harm a hair on your head."

"That's what worries me," I said. "I'm the stag. I'm much less easy to get rid of than you are."

"Are you calling me easily replaced?" he asked, mock offense in his voice.

"Promise that if you end up protecting me, you'll let me protect you the same way. We're partners. We protect each other. Not me, you or you, me."

"I wouldn't dream of it being any other way," he said. "No matter what the future holds."

His mouth met mine again, and I became lost in the world that was his lips, his body, once more. It was so nice, so easy, to have this time to take all my worries away, to feel nothing but warmth and love in a way that hadn't existed for years. It physically ached, knowing the danger we were going into, knowing that we both were going to have to face someone who caused us unbearable harm. We could survive it together, I knew that too, but I wished we had time to enjoy one another like we were now. It wasn't even sex that I wished for; his company and my head on his chest and his smell surrounding me, his steady breath and large body that never failed to make me feel shielded and safe. He was all I needed to remain calm in the chaos.

It was a good while later before we finally rose and dressed again. I stared at myself in the mirror. I was different. Healed from trauma but with cracks still running beneath like invisible veins. I turned my body to the side. I didn't recognize myself. Was I human? Goblin? Something else entirely now that I held the power of the stag? I was used to being forgotten, used to sharp edges. I used to be smaller too, back when I ate as little as I could. It was jarring enough to make me wonder if I was even at a proper weight.

I turned to Soren frowning. "Am I still me?" I blushed when asking the question. Was this vanity?

"Of course. The same Janneke I fell for," Soren said as he slid into his clothing. "You were always malnourished before. A bunch of your bones jutted out so that sometimes I thought they'd break the skin. You are stronger now. You eat better. Still not enough, but better. You've never lost your spirit."

"I know it's dumb, but I feel almost . . . bad about my weight," I said softly.

Soren sighed. "I wish you could see what I see, but I know that's impossible. I know telling you you're beautiful won't help much either. But you are. And I'm positive you'll see it one day when your mind is no longer trapped."

Still, I frowned at the swell of my breast and the curves of my hips and stomach. He wasn't wrong about that. I'd filled out a lot more since becoming the stag, but not perhaps in a bad way. Food was still something I struggled with, but as

I got stronger physically and mentally, I didn't need to control how I ate to replace the lack of control in my life. At least, not as much as I had in a long while. Eating still came with a sense of shame though, like I was giving in against the strict discipline I'd forced myself to have for the past hundred years. It was silly, I knew.

But still, staring at my reflection was weird.

"I feel like I have to inform you that if you don't put clothes on soon, I'm about to undo all the progress I've made in actually getting out of bed," Soren said, motioning to his own outfit. Something hot pooled in my stomach as I pulled on my clothes.

"You're very in tune with your vices, you know that?" I said, hopping on one foot to get my boot on.

"I'm merely aware of them and have no objection acting on most of them," Soren said, smirking. "Our codes of honor are different."

"I thought we agreed the whole 'goblins don't feel emotions' thing was biased," I argued.

"Never said anything about that. I feel a lot less sympathy for my dinner." His smile grew wider, and I scowled at him.

"It's *weird* to eat venison while also holding the title of the stag. It feels like I'm cannibalizing in some way."

"See?" Soren said, making his point.

Breathing deeply and pinching my nose with my hand, I turned to him. "Let's get the others. It's time to plan."

8

THE GNAWING SERPENT

EVERYONE SOREN TRUSTED enough for the situation turned out to be fewer people than I thought. We were in the solar that we'd converted to a war room a bit after we came into ownership of the Erkling's palace. We'd replaced the furniture, which had been mostly chairs and loungers, with a large table that mapped the entire Permafrost both geographically and topographically, with a model of the nine worlds placed next to it in scale similar to the map.

I recognized every face currently standing around the table. Of course, there was Seppo, Rose, and Diaval, but also Seppo's mother, Satu. A bright-haired goblin stood by the door, guarding it in case anyone tried to get in. I couldn't remember exactly, but I thought his name may have been Landon. He'd been one of the few people that had stuck around after the Erlking's death, one way or another.

Seppo had joined Soren's circle of advisors right away, which wasn't surprising considering his role during the Hunt. He always had something helpful to say and a new perspective of situations that we got stuck on. He also was the reason none of us fell asleep.

Rose and Diaval had come later, a few months after the Hunt, when we'd finally got all the favor-seekers and bootlickers to leave us alone. Goblins who ignored or despised us before now desperately wanted to be seen as friends and allies. Only after Soren shooed them all away did they come out and ask to pledge allegiance and to possibly become members of his guard if he saw them fit.

It took only a month before the two of them were accepted. Diaval's magic brought us an unexpected boon and me an unexpected best friend, and Rosamund had let it slip early on that he was also dating Seppo and if Seppo trusted him, I couldn't find a reason not to.

Of course, with Seppo, came Satu, his mother. If you didn't know, she could be any adult aging gracefully into her late thirties or early forties, but that didn't fool me. She'd been around for a *long* time. No-nonsense and with years of experience behind her, she obviously found her way on the council. She knew the goblin world better than any of us in terms of society and brought with her others to help with everyday tasks like guarding and running the grounds smoothly and even added a member of the council.

She stood next to Satu, a goblin whose face was wrinkled and leathery, withered by age and the harshness of life in the Permafrost. Even goblins aged, though very slowly, and their skin became old like the rest of the creatures on this world. Whether from the human realm, Asgard, or the Permafrost, none of us would live forever. This goblin preferred to wear the same weathered leathers every day and tied back his graying hair into a short ponytail. His face was decorated with battle scars half-covered in the salt-and-pepper hair of his beard. His name was Ivar.

It'd shocked me at first to see an older goblin who truly looked old. The Permafrost extended lifespans, and goblins in general were slow to age, but Satu had been around forever and she looked nowhere near as ancient. Even the power radiating from him was duller, like it was muted.

Ivar was an advisor brought into the group by Satu, who was genuinely impressed at his ability to strategize for war, famine, and any other disaster one could think of. He was taciturn and never spoke more than a few sentences, but his words were valued heavily just the same. He reminded me a bit of Satu, how he was, except for being older and a male. He tended to pull more weight when it came to the rest of the goblin species and was more likely to be listened to than her. It struck me as unfair because Satu had never steered us wrong yet, but I also couldn't say I was surprised by it.

But if she had a problem with it, it didn't show, because she'd been the one to recommend him, and so he joined Soren's small group of advisors.

The advisor I knew least about was Landon. He made it clear on his first day, not only was he young, but cocky too, and filled with the usual sense of superiority his species had over creatures other than themselves. As far we knew, he was only here because he was one of the few goblins who stayed at the palace during some parts of the old Erlking's life and knew a decent amount of rumors and gossip as well as the secret passageways that lurked in the palace. He may have been an arrogant ass, but he knew the relationships between younger goblins the same way Satu did with older goblins and that was information we needed.

And of course there was Tanya. She wouldn't separate from her nephew even if you threatened to cut her in half with an axe. The perpetually curt she-goblin stood slightly off from everyone else, most likely by her own choice. She sent scathing glares at anyone who dared approach her, and so we all stood away, hoping not to get on her bad side. Other than Soren, who was liked solely because he was a blood relative, the only other person whose presence she tolerated was Diaval.

Out of the many, many creatures in the Permafrost, Tanya terrified me.

And that was it. Three elder goblins, three younger goblins, and myself. Out of the entire Permafrost, these were who Soren trusted with the information at hand.

He was tense. I could feel it in my own shoulders, like a second sense, and he closed his eyes and breathed in and out a few times before opening them again and leaning forward to rest his hands on the table map. A few cracks appeared in the table as he dug his fingers in, and I touched his arm in sympathy.

Soren began to tell them what I'd told him, about Lydian, about the end of the world and how it was caused, about the plan not to let it happen no matter what. Those who originally knew something was up didn't look surprised as Soren revealed detail after secret detail, and those who didn't know anything had jaws that became slightly more slacked, eyes that widened a little more, and faces that changed color for the briefest of moments. Satu, as I predicted, was not fazed by the news, instead only narrowing her eyes in thought.

Self-hatred wafted from Soren, and I tasted it on my tongue, in the back of my throat. It vibrated in me like I was the one feeling it. Despite our talk, he was still angry at himself for the cosmic fate he'd been given, as if any of it was his fault in the first place. It was only natural and definitely not something I could judge since I wallowed in it for the better part of a century, but it was something I ached to feel in him. Especially since I knew how dangerous it was.

But he had me, and I'd be damned if I'd let him get anywhere near the level of self-loathing I'd gone through.

Even after Soren spoke, the others still silently processed his words. He looked at me, almost helplessly, and I stroked his hand reassuringly. This would be okay. It would all be okay.

As usual, Seppo was the first one to break the silence. "You're not . . . you're not considering bringing Lydian *back*, are you?" His response reminded me of someone being informed a murderer had been asked to a casual dinner.

I folded my hands in front of me. "Not exactly. See, we need him in the current state he is. Not dead and crossed over completely, but also not living. That way, he inhabits a liminal space."

"And we need him in a liminal space because . . . ?" Seppo pressed.

"We've deduced one of the few ways—perhaps the only way—to stop Ragnarök before it begins is to stop Fimbulwinter from starting. Fimbulwinter lasts three years and won't spare us any more than it will humans. Thousands will die from famine, plague, and at the hands of others. Those left over will be what's left to fight in Ragnarök. To stop Fimbulwinter, we have to kill Fjalar. His cries start Fimbulwinter in the first place. But he's a liminal being. We need another liminal being to guide us through the realms to find him."

"Janneke still can't access the liminal realm by herself," Diaval said, "much less bring us all there. And while I managed to push her in there for twenty minutes to speak to Lydian's specter, I won't be able to do the same for everyone here for even a quarter of that length."

I looked away from the rest of the group as they began to murmur, and shame tightened my chest. Another reminder that despite the stag choosing me for the job, I was absolute shit at it. Unable to even reach the liminal realm by myself despite the stag being a liminal. Despite trying to keep my failures under wraps, now multiple people knew. I didn't blame Diaval for disclosing the information. It was needed in this context. But the sick feeling inside of me, the one of bitter disappointment, was hard to ignore.

So what, a voice told me, and it thankfully wasn't Lydian's. *You'll get better at this. You can master this.*

This time, Soren grasped my forearm with his hand and squeezed gently to comfort me.

Right. Self-loathing gets you nowhere.

"The problem is that Lydian's shade is still being held by Hel," I continued. "He's not dead and can't properly pass on due to not having the burial rites done, but he's also not alive either and that means that he's the property of Hel. We need to get him back, one way or another."

Once again, the others stared at me blankly. "You want to haggle for Lydian's spirit with *Hel*?" Rosamund asked incredulously. "Even Frigga couldn't do that for Baldur. Like, she managed to rally up every creature *ever* to bring back her son, and she was the *queen* of Asgard, and even she couldn't get him out."

"Technically, Baldur was already dead, and Frigga wanted him to come back to life fully. Lydian's still kind of existing. So, the situations are different," Seppo said, earning a glare from his partner. "What? It's true!"

Rosamund pinched the bridge of his nose. "You get my point. She's not about to hand over someone's spirit even to the Erlking and the stag. She's *Hel*."

"While Rosamund could have said it more tactfully." Satu spoke up for the first time, her voice low and calm. "He is right. Hel is fickle and will do anything to keep what she has in her grasp. She's cunning, possessive, and dangerous. She's also much less forgiving of slights than, say, a giantess goddess like Skadi." Satu's dark eyes flickered over to Soren at the last bit of her sentence.

"Am I ever going to find out what you did to piss her off?" I asked Soren.

Blood pooled in Soren's cheeks as he blushed, turning the white-blue skin a darkish purple. "Not if I live to be a million years."

"Jeez," Seppo said. "You look really weird when you blush, Soren."

Soren narrowed his eyes. "I was not blushing."

"Liar," Rosamund muttered from his place at the table.

"I think it looks wonderful," I cut in, hoping to stop an argument.

"As much as I'd *love* to spend this time talking about Soren's vanity," Diaval said, earning a glare from Soren. "What?" She shrugged. "It's true. Don't worry, Soren. If you were my type, I'd absolutely ravish you."

Seppo raised an eyebrow. "You have a type?"

Diaval didn't blink. "I'm fond of the nonexistent variety of partners."

Ivar sighed in a purposefully overdramatic way. "*Anyway,* Satu is right. Dealing with Hel and dealing with Skadi are two different things. Janneke, especially, will be in danger as she'll have to be the one to make the deal, being the most powerful of the group. We don't know what Hel will demand, or if she'll attack outright. And Janneke being the stag and you being the Erlking"—he gave Soren a pointed look—"will not save you if she decides she wants you gone."

I wanted to rub my temples because pressure was beginning to build underneath my eyes. We definitely weren't dealing with Hel until I got rid of this oncoming headache. "I can do whatever task she asks of me, and I know she'll make me do something terrible, but I've survived worse than Hel. We can win Lydian's shade back."

"Then there's traveling to the liminal realm with Lydian's shade," Ivar continued. "Is Diaval able to open a portal for you all to get there, even if she can't fully lead you into it?"

"Diaval can definitely open a portal anywhere she wants

even if she's going in blind," Diaval said. "She can also understand the common tongue, and dislikes when old men talk
about her like she's not sitting literally right next to them." The
she-goblin crossed her arms and glared at the elder goblin sitting directly to her right.

I tried my hardest to hold back a snicker, but obviously
the others weren't even trying as small chuckles erupted from
everyone at the table. Even steely-eyed Satu was hiding her
smile.

"So, Diaval can get us where we need to go and then
what . . . we trust Lydian to lead us?" Soren brought up. "I
know we don't have a lot of options, but does anyone here
really trust Lydian to not, you know, try to kill us?"

"We don't have 'not a lot of options,'" I said. "We have one
option, and that's Lydian. And I have to believe that stopping the destruction of what he showed me means more to
him than killing us because he's feeling a tad murderous. The
original reason for wanting to kill us doesn't exist anymore,
and while I won't ever trust him, I think the five of us can take
him if he tries anything."

It was a little more complicated than that. I wouldn't trust
Lydian to lead his own horse to water if it came down to it.
The stag, however, had a different opinion regarding being
able to trust the goblin enough to be led through a realm only
he could inhabit fully.

I pressed my fingers to my temples and rubbed away the
ache before continuing, forehead still in my hands. "And what
I saw, what the stag tells me—it trumps everything, anyway.
It doesn't matter that the entire thing personally makes me feel

like a million spiders are crawling all over my body. I don't necessarily get a choice in this."

"How do you know the stag is right, anyhow?" Landon spoke from his position at the door, lip curled in a sneer. "You can barely access its power after a year of training, but you still think you know enough to make the decision to work with an absolute madman? How do we know this isn't your incompetence?"

My eyes blurred, but before I was able to do anything, Soren rose from his chair. There was already a dagger impaled in the wooden door right next to Landon's head. The goblin took a hand to his ear and marveled at the blood coming from this small cut.

"Landon, right?" Soren growled. The other goblin nodded as Soren continued. "You were put on this group of advisors due to the many years you survived the previous Erlking's court. It would be a mighty shame if your tenure ended so quickly under mine. I won't tolerate that language to the stag."

Eyes flickered to everyone else in the room as we tried to identify the thrower. All of them quickly latched onto Tanya, who had another thin blade in her hand and was using it to clean her nails.

She gave a half shrug. "I would suggest you not talk to your superiors like that, Landon, as my nephew calmly pointed out. The situation with the stag isn't one we've ever seen before. Of course she doesn't know immediately how to use it or train with it. Were you able to defeat strong enemies with a sword when you first picked it up? Are you some kind of god among goblinkind? No? With what we know—which is nothing, I might add—about the stag's mantle of power transferring to Janneke, she's done remarkably well trying to figure it out. I doubt you could do better. So, do us all a favor and keep your mouth shut."

She said all of this without looking up from her handiwork. Her voice was calm and even—she would've been *less* scary somehow if she yelled.

I felt a flash of gratitude toward the she-goblin. We'd never been close, frankly sometimes she scared me more than Lydian, but I never doubted how much she cared for Soren. Never in a hundred years did I think she'd willingly stick up for me. Honestly, I was pretty certain she didn't like me very much.

She finally looked up from her nail care and around the room. When her eyes met mine, she gave a small, almost undetectable nod before continuing her journey. "Does anyone else have anything to say or are we done with that?"

When nobody else spoke, she nodded. "Good. So, the plan is for Janneke, Soren, and Diaval to go into Hel, bargain *with* Hel, and free Lydian's spirit, track down the liminal being most likely to signify Ragnarök's arrival, then kill it."

"Well, when you put it that way . . ." Soren's words lingered in the air like smoke. But he was right. When you put it that way, it did sound fucking ridiculous, didn't it? But then we had some crazy plans during the Hunt, and that worked out for the better, mostly, until now.

Besides, it didn't matter how outlandish the plan sounded. We needed a plan. Because I could see it now, every time I closed my eyes. The serpent gnawing on the roots of the world tree. I could feel it as if it were sinking its fangs into my very flesh and tearing me apart bit by bit. Every time a little chunk disappeared from the trunk of the tree, the branches, the worlds, they all shook and rattled like they were loose rocks about to topple over. If no one stopped it, they *would* topple over. Then we wouldn't have to worry about silly things like the stag or the Erlking, Lydian, or Satu's new kid, because we'd all be very much dead.

"Rose and I are going too," Seppo announced, undaunted by the tone of Soren's voice. Rose grasped a hand over his partner's and nodded in agreement.

Tanya rolled her eyes. I had a feeling she probably considered hand-holding a gross and inappropriate display of public affection. Personally, I thought it was adorable.

"It'll be dangerous," I warned. "I don't want you to needlessly risk your lives."

Seppo smiled. "Needlessly risking my life is my favorite hobby, right, Mom?"

Satu pinched the bridge of her nose. "I blame your father. You definitely didn't get that trait from me."

"If we fail, we die either way," Rosamund said. "Whether that's in Hel, in the liminal world, or down here on the ground, so to speak. No matter what happens, we die if we fail. So I don't really consider it risking my life. More like not twiddling my thumbs as the apocalypse comes knocking. Besides . . ." He smirked. "Seppo has told me *all* about your adventures together during the Hunt. I'm kind of happy the world's ending if that means I get to also go on a similar type of adventure."

I raised my eyebrows. "Literally?"

"Literally."

"Okay, I was making sure." Whether I was making sure Rose was up to the task, or whether I was making sure Rose had a bizarre definition of "adventure" could be left up to interpretation.

"I'll have the best chance of successfully opening a portal in two days," Diaval said. "During the new moon. So, we have two days to gather what we need and prepare."

"Two days, then," Soren agreed. "Any objections?"

Landon's face contorted like he'd eaten a rotting fish, and Ivar didn't necessarily look *happy* with the idea, but neither of them said anything about it.

"All right," Soren said, placing his hands on the tabletop and standing. "Meeting adjourned. Get ready."

As people began to file out of the room, my stomach began to do twists and flips inside of me. Two days. Two days until I had to face him in something more than my dreams or a flash in the mirror, more than the occasional voice in my head. I wanted to say I was strong, that after the Hunt, he no longer held any sway over my emotions, that I no longer feared him. But that wasn't the case. My stomach still turned. I still had phantom scars in my mind.

But I wouldn't let my scars control me. I couldn't.

Soren and Tanya lingered behind after everyone had left. He clasped his hands together in the front, one thumb rubbed the top of the other hand. "Tanya," he said. "Did you . . . did you know? About me? About my mother?"

Tanya smiled softly at her nephew. "If it was something your mother knew about herself, she never disclosed it to me.

I met her later on in life when our mothers happened to be in the same place at the same time." She put a hand on his shoulder. "No one could've known, Soren. Even then, I still say you were the right choice for the Permafrost. You were chosen for a reason. This isn't your fault. No one could have known."

Soren nodded, though his eyes grew dark. The link between our minds buzzed as his thoughts spilled over into mine. *No one except Lydian.*

PART TWO

THE WOMAN

9

THE VOW

WE SPENT THE next two days together, Soren and I. Never leaving each other's sides unless we needed to eat or relieve ourselves. Whenever we slept, we would stare at each other as minutes and hours blended together like spilled paint. My gaze would be half-lidded as he brushed his finger and thumb over the sore spots on my neck and shoulders, and I pressed my head against his chest and listened as his heartbeat—so much slower than a human's—thumped a lazy rhythm between his ribs. No matter what we did or how close we got, we never could get our fill of each other, I thought, as he pressed his pale blue lips against mine for what was likely the hundredth time. Not that I was complaining. If I had my choice, I'd stay curled in the furs and into his warm body forever. In a world where so often we were unsure of ourselves, the clarity of us together, in peace, shone a bright light into the darkness, and I could feel every inch of me saying that everything would turn out fine.

During this time, there was blessed silence in my head.

Lydian had stopped speaking with his snark and taunts and nagging commentary, and I relished my head belonging to me again. Even if it meant that I would have to soon meet him in the flesh. It wasn't a problem—he couldn't hurt me and he couldn't scare me.

Besides, having my mind as my sanctuary once more was sorely missed. It was worth it for that alone.

Despite the peace we found in each other, I could sense through the bond, through his tighter-than-normal muscles, and the frown he was struggling to keep from his face even during bliss, that Soren was grappling with the knowledge we'd all been given, and I could feel him take it and hold it to his heart like glass shards. I kissed him right over the heart and hoped that my feelings of calm and healing could be absorbed by his skin. He grumbled a little—a type of growl he some-times made when he was content that resonated in his chest.

When he fell asleep before me, I lay there gazing at him, rubbing the lines of his frown on his forehead with my finger until his face relaxed and he sank into deeper, undisrupted sleep. He changed when he was asleep; the worry and stress of being the Erlking melted off him like two large chunks of ice he was forced to carry. As if the weight of the Permafrost weren't on his shoulders, as if he didn't need to worry about anything, much less bringing psychotic uncles back from the dead, as if we were back in the Higher North in his own manor and he was sleeping soundly in the room he slept in all his life.

It struck me as odd, how many goblins fought to become the next Erlking without thinking about the responsibility behind the job. Only the power and prestige at being the best hunter, the most powerful predator, out of the group. How many other goblins were unprepared for what actually lay ahead of them once they started their rule?

And what of me? I took the stag's mantle, knowing it was the correct choice, the one needed to save what I loved—or at least I thought so at the time—but in the end, I was still a human in the Permafrost trying to control magic that was beyond the scope of my very reasoning. It was like trying to move a limb that you couldn't see or feel, but you knew it was there.

Had it been different, had Lydian and Soren's confrontation not caused the Erlking to die and thus not trigger the Hunt, where would we be now? Not together, that was for sure.

I wished I could take the burdens off Soren and carry them myself, to take the pain from his shoulders and merge it with my own. Let him understand that there was no reason for him to feel guilt, to blame himself. I'd been through a crisis of identity before and I could do it again. But Soren was always so sure of everything. Until now, when his very existence was revealed to cause calamity.

I stroked his hair, brushing the feathery white strands out of his face, and kissed his forehead softly. He moved a little but remained asleep as I pressed myself against him once more, hoping to get lost in the warmth his body created.

WHEN NIGHT CAME on the second day, both of us somberly got ready for our mission. I put on my hunting leathers—worn and broken in until they molded to my body—and pulled on boots with the similar comfortable feeling of being made solely for me. Underneath the dyed-black leather were warm cotton underlayers that acted as a shield against any bit of cold that might slip through. On my forearms were leather bracers: my shooting arm had two thin rods of metal attached across the bracer by straps and it covered the top of my hand until it met my archery glove; while on the other arm, the bracer was more traditionally covered with steel boning so it was flexible, but could also be used to stop an attack from a sword.

Two axes hung from my hip—courtesy of Rosamund—and my quiver was attached to my belt, my bow slung across my back.

From beside me, I caught glimpses of flashing metal as Soren tucked away knives and daggers in hidden spots in his own leathers. Two in each bracer, one on a sheath on his leg, another hung subtly from his hip, before he reached for the scabbards that held the two swords he carried on his back. From his hip hung his own quiver and his longbow rested on one shoulder.

"A bow too?" I asked, surprised.

Soren snorted. "Just in case. You and I both know that you're way better than me with a bow. I use one to keep up pretenses, but it's not like my eyesight has gotten any better." He waved two fingers across his eyes. "It'll be more cumbersome to carry something I can't use as accurately as I need to be. But we don't know what we're up against, so I'd rather not take the extra risk of someone finding out their Erlking is a bad shot."

"If it helps, I think your eyes are pretty."

His lips twitched into the hint of a smile. "Pretty, not practical. That's what I miss most about home. The sun wasn't nearly out as much for most of the year except for that one week in the midsummer." His eyes had a faraway look to them.

"During that one week, you couldn't even go outside because it was so bright out, and you couldn't see and would burn so badly," I remembered. "You were so grumpy."

"Then the dark would come again and the days would be muted, and I wouldn't have to worry about wearing a cloak that covered every inch of skin," he continued with the memory. "I really miss it. Here is fine. It's not completely in the south, so it's not as extreme as, say, where Seppo grew up, but it's still a bit too bright for me."

I nodded, looking around at the stone and marble walls of the palace, the artwork etched into the very stones themselves, the archways and high ceilings. I thought about the millions of secret passageways and how random hallways could lead off into a sharp fall into a pit and the multitude of traps set up that kept travelers and visitors on their toes. So elegant in its own lethal way, yet I also found myself longing for the solitude of the small manor up in the High North where Soren originally lived. It was far less grand, colder, made of quarried stone and wood, and so austere compared to the Erlking's palace, but it was also a place I called home for a hundred years.

"I miss it too," I said softly.

He raised his eyebrows in surprise as he fit another small dagger into a hidden sheath in his boot. "Really? I would've thought the memories . . ." He trailed off.

"The worst memories I have aren't from your home," I

said. "And even afterward, after all I'd been through, nothing overtly traumatic happened to me under your protection."

"Yeah," Soren said, a glint in his eye. "You were a thrall for a hundred years before I finally had the stones to tell you the truth of everything."

It took me a moment before I realized he was actually being sarcastic. Soren's sarcasm came in fits and starts; he had a rather shaky grasp of the matter, but then there were times like this when he really hit the nail on the head.

"Well, yeah," I acknowledged, "you did kind of mess up there. But we're both past it now. Everything about us, our relationship, it's different."

He nodded before slipping one more small knife into his other boot. Adding the axe that hung from his hip, he had nine blades in total on him. Normally, I'd say that was overkill, even for a goblin, but he was right. We didn't exactly know what to expect, and it was better to be prepared.

"Still, sometimes I look at my past and get so embarrassed, I want to stay in a hot spring until my skin melts to cleanse myself of the shame." His voice was dead serious.

"I'm no perfect princess either. Even with my life outside the Permafrost combined, I'd want to join you," I said.

"Our only saving grace is there's no hot springs here, not like farther north." A wistful look passed over his face.

"I wouldn't worry about it," I said. "Once I expressed a similar sentiment to Diaval, and she politely informed me that she can mimic the pain you feel during certain deaths without it actually killing you. I think she was trying to be helpful."

"Diaval terrifies me," Soren said, no hint of a joke in his voice.

"Diaval terrifies everyone who isn't Diaval," I responded.

"You look tense. Need some help with that before we go?" he offered. I sighed. I didn't really want to get up. Soren had the same reluctant look on his face.

"What?" I said. "I'm not—"

Soren's fingers curled into my neck and upward toward my head with the force of his thumbs. Pain blazed down from my neck to my spine. Ready to yell at him for whatever he did, instead, I found the blood flow increasing in my head and releasing the headache I had had for days.

He did the same thing with my shoulders. Pressing on knots of muscle, not too gently, causing me to cuss a few times when he did so, but the knot disappeared, with only smooth muscles left behind.

There was a type of painful pleasure to it. Painful because of his fingers digging into the ultra-tight parts of my body, but also pleasure when he released his grip, endorphins rushing in as the oxygen-starved muscle finally was let loose.

I let myself relax muscles I hadn't even known I'd been clenching. The smooth rhythm of his fingers across my scalp sent a shiver through me. Intimate. My eyes became half-lidded as I tried not to fall asleep while Soren worked on me.

He only stopped when his hands started to burn.

Erlking and the stag we might've been, but the ancient rules of power still applied. Goblins risked burning themselves if they did deeds that were in no way related to hunting or battle; which was a shame because whatever Soren did to my neck and shoulders made them feel like melted butter.

He must've picked up on that. "Don't worry about the burns, Janneke. It's worth it to see you relax. You carry so much tension. And I promise I'll stop if I hit first-degree wounds."

I gave him a withering look as he rubbed his hands, already red from what he'd done so far. "I'm not going to lie. I *really* liked that. But don't injure yourself for my sake."

"It hurts you more than it hurts me." Soren shrugged as his hands turned back to a normal—or normal-for-him—color.

Moonlight covered our room in a blanket of silver, and both Soren and I sighed, wishing for the moment to never end. Despite his calm demeanor, his heart thumped fast in his chest. My loosened muscles already were tightening again.

The closer and closer we came to getting ready, the closer we came to midnight, the closer we came to the portal, meant the closer we'd come to Hel and Lydian. Nerves fluttered in my stomach like moths.

THE MOON WAS high in the sky as we entered the courtyard. I clenched Soren's hand, careful to not put too much pressure on the areas where there might be burns. But I needed his reassuring touch right now. With what we had to do, I didn't think I'd be able to go on without it. It was amazing my spine hadn't turned to butter and melted. Without the nature of the stag taking over part of my brain, I was still left with my human emotions.

Other than us, only Diaval was out. She sat in the center of an elaborate circle drawn from chalk. While I could recognize some of the runes—Hagalaz, Raidho, Jera—there were multiple markings that I couldn't recognize. The she-goblin had her eyes closed and was muttering quietly to herself, but stopped as Soren stepped forward.

She held her hand out in a stopping motion, and Soren took a step back. "Don't get anywhere near the circle," she said, eyes still closed. "You'll ruin it, and then we'll have to wait another month."

With that, she continued her chanting. From beside her, I noticed a small flask that she took sips of every so often. It stained her lips a violent reddish-black color, almost like viscera, and looking at it made my stomach twist.

It didn't take long until Seppo and Rosamund came too, leading the young filly that they'd been chasing a few days before. Satu stood with them as well as Tanya, here to see us off, apparently. Part of me wondered about the rest of the council, before I came to the conclusion that even if they were plotting something, leaving the Permafrost in the hands of Satu and Tanya was more than enough protection.

"What's with the horse?" Soren asked.

Seppo sighed. "Well, my baby sibling isn't getting this horse any time soon."

Satu rolled her eyes. "It would take a few years for it to even be able to ride anyway. I'm sure we'll find a new horse."

"If we don't die from the coming apocalypse," Rosamund muttered under his breath.

Diaval breathed out heavily through her nose. "Not

helping, Rose." She stood and came forward, though carefully remained in the circle as Seppo led the filly toward Diaval. She cooed and spoke softly to the young creature, ruffling its mane and rubbing its nose.

A sour feeling spread throughout my body. My grip tightened on Soren's hand, causing him to wince.

"You don't have to watch," he said.

"Yes, I do." This animal was sacrificing its life for us. The least we could do was watch as it died.

Diaval sat back down in the middle of the circle, holding the rope of the filly tight enough that it couldn't escape. She continued her muttering as the young animal blinked at her with large, brown, trusting eyes. Another ignorant lamb—technically horse—to the slaughter.

She shivered as she took another, longer sip of the dark red liquid in her flask, and I found myself asking, "What is she even drinking?" Some of the liquid escaped her mouth and ran crimson down her chin as she choked on it.

A hand on my arm caused me to jump almost a foot in the air before I realized it was Tanya. She beckoned me over to where she stood, and with a lingering glance at Soren, I went with her. "It's venom," Tanya said, "from the snake that hangs over the bound Loki."

"She's actually ingesting that?" I said, shocked. "Won't it kill her?"

"Diaval's been at this a long time," Tanya said softly. "She's immune to most venoms and poisons. It won't kill her. It won't be a pleasant experience throughout the ritual either, but that's what you get with magic. It's never pleasant. When a goblin creates on the scale of magic, it always changes them, always." She smiled humorlessly. "I originally wanted to follow that path, but it wasn't for me. Which ended up being good for all of us, eh?"

Her gaze shifted to Soren, who watched Diaval's work with an intensity to his lilac eyes that he normally reserved for intimidating or fighting his foes. "Take care of him, Janneke," she said. "I know we aren't close. I know I've never been what you may consider kind. That's how I am," she explained. "But Soren is the one thing I have left in the world. I can see that he loves you dearly. Don't take that for granted."

"I won't. I promise," I said.

She took my hands in hers and squeezed. "He's doing a good job of hiding it, but I've taken care of him since he was a babe. He's in pain, turmoil. All of this, it's making him second-guess everything and shaking him to the core. Please, keep him safe, even from himself."

"I promise," I repeated.

A fevered look passed in Tanya's gaze. "Swear it. An oath. Please."

We locked eyes and I nodded. "I swear by the gods by whom my people swear. I will keep him safe. If I break my oath, may the land open to swallow me, the sea rise to drown me, and the sky fall upon me."

A cold feeling passed through me as we gripped each other's forearms; it grew hotter and hotter until both of us winced with the pain, but neither of us let go. When it finally died down and we let go, the spot where our forearms met was branded with a small Eihwaz rune. It was done, then. For that second, the magic of the oath rooted us both to the ground, and the tremor of the very earth itself rocked beneath our feet as if recognizing my words.

The others still hadn't noticed anything, and we were quick to rejoin them. I pulled down my sleeve to cover the new brand on my arm.

From where she sat, Diaval was now chanting louder in another unknown language, her hands running across a black blade that shined slick as oil. I might've not been able to understand her words by themselves, but I could *feel* their meaning deep in my bones. It was a blessing.

She stood then, knife hidden behind her back with one hand, and pressed her forehead to the filly's. "Forgive me," she whispered, and with a flash of the blade, blood came pouring down into the circle.

10

DWELLINGS

I WINCED AT the horse's shriek and watched with muted horror as the poor animal fell to its knees, blood gushing from the slash on its throat. The thick blood covered the circle and Diaval, but if it bothered her, she didn't show it. Instead, she carefully dabbed the blood on different spots—her forehead, elbows, collarbones, and the back of her hands—then spread her hands out on the blood-coated ground and smeared the blood all over the circle with the horse now lying dead next to her.

My stomach roiled, and I was forced to swallow vomit. It wasn't the worst thing I'd ever seen in the Permafrost, but there was something different about it. When goblins fought one another and other creatures, there was a sense of . . . normalcy involved. Even if there were deaths and murders, that was pretty much on par for the creatures of the Permafrost. With death came energy, and with energy came power. A type of power I didn't normally come across. There was no crushing sensation to it, but it was one of the strongest, and it vibrated in my chest like a swarm of wasps. My skin itched at the unnatural way Diaval contorted her body as she changed, at the glassy eyes of the horse, and I could swear for a brief second that Diaval's own eyes turned completely black.

Her head snapped back with a force so strong, I was sure her neck would crack, and blackish red lines spread from the venom-covered corners of her mouth throughout the rest of her body, making it look like she'd dined on blood.

"Hall of thieves, dogs of men, three stars that break apart at dawn." Her voice shook with a timbre deeper than her own, as if something had crawled inside of her throat and was now speaking for her. *"The black sun falls, the blood thins. Twenty acres of suffering and demon light pulled into the bosom of spring."* Blood trickled from her nose, and my eyes widened when I caught sight of it coming from her ears as well. The black color had completely taken over her eyes again, and they dripped with blackened liquid that I couldn't be sure was venom or blood or some unholy mix of the two. *"Where order and chaos go to die and strength of icy currents pull. Darkness, bitch goddess, the turning worm. Cast upon our ready forms. Avaa ovi ja anna meidän porteista!"*

Lightning struck and hit the ground, right in the center of the circle. As it did, all of us stumbled backward except Diaval, whose head was back to a slightly more normal position but who was now bending forward with her palms on the blood-soaked stone of the courtyard. Blue light flickered from her hands. I'd seen her light before, but it was only in sparks. These flickers grew and grew until they threatened to spill outside the circle, but all they did was create a fiery boundary around it instead.

There was a collective sigh of relief as Diaval's eye color changed back to its normal hue, and she observed her handiwork, blinking in confusion for a second before standing. She stumbled a bit as if she were slightly drunk, but managed to grab her pack and sling it over her shoulder as well as shove the flask back into a holster attached to her pants.

I only noticed then that out of all of us journeying to the lowest realm, only she had no physical weapon. Sure, she had whatever was in her pack, and I noticed some hidden pockets that must've been full of *something*, but she wasn't carrying any blades as far as I could tell. Compared to my axes and bow and arrows, Soren's many, many different types of blades, Seppo's featherstaff, and Rosamund's double-bladed axes, she was going in completely naked.

No, no, she isn't, a voice told me. *No one with this type of power is ever naked, ever powerless.* Diaval's power did not come in the traditional goblin form. The small she-goblin had given up the right to wield traditional weaponry when she turned to magic and walked down the solitary path of a mage who happened to be a goblin as well. Two things that weren't supposed to ever mix, but somehow . . . they had. The part of me more in tune with the Permafrost recoiled at the blatant disregard for the proper laws, but the rest of me had always recognized she was something different, since the day she appeared seemingly out of nowhere to offer her services to Soren and me.

"All right," Diaval breathed. "I need everyone who is coming to step into the circle. No pushing, no shoving, and for the love of all the gods, *don't speak*." She narrowed her eyes at us, and I winced at the blood still dripping down from them and her nose.

We all nodded with a tinge of terror radiating into the night air, at the blood dripping on her face and her black-red stained lips, the black veins that spread up one side of her face, and the way one of her irises glowed in the darkness. This was the toll on goblins who did magic in the Permafrost. No wonder Tanya hadn't gone down that path when she came across it.

Silently we came into the circle, with Seppo looking down uneasily at the flames before also crossing through. They didn't burn when they touched my flesh, but they still were . . . off somehow. Not cold, not hot . . . *wrong*. This entire thing wriggled in my gut like worms crawling to the surface of the earth.

Diaval looked around at us, pulling Rose's sleeve so he stood closer to the center. She handed off one of the bags she was carrying to him. When she finally approved of us, she gave a sharp nod and clasped her hands together. Dark blue light flared from her fingertips as she muttered one final word: "*Laskeutua.*"

The world turned, my stomach dropped, and for a single terrifying moment, I was weightless. Right-side up, upside down, left, right, and every which way in between. My body fell like a rag doll, down and down but also up and up, as I crashed through the primordial darkness that swallowed my entire body. One second I was falling, and then the next I was floating in the blackness only to fall once more. At first my heart rate spiked at the sheer terror that flooded through me, but the terror was chased away by the pure darkness that surrounded me. It cradled me for a moment like a mother might her child, and I hung in what might've been midair or underground or beneath the water. It could've been seconds or minutes or hours, and I'd have no way to tell until my body finally crashed down onto the muddy embankment of two large rivers.

I lay on my side for a moment, panting to recover my breath after the fall—*was it even a fall?*—that had brought me into this realm. Around me the others, save Diaval, were also catching their breath. When I finally rose, my eyes caught sight of how massive the two rivers were.

They were connected together in the middle as if to form one giant, impossible river. Ice floes littered the incredibly large body of water like plains, and they crashed and churned in the rapidly moving, dark water. Something clenched deep in my gut; this wasn't a place designed for any fast movement, any escape for the people who crossed it if they survived the crossing at all. Again the *wrongness* of the entire thing lay heavily inside of me, but try as I might, I couldn't shake it off. Even if we got through the river, how in the world would we be able to go back? I smelled the protections on the river, the source that it came from, and the stories of my childhood many, many years ago echoed; a voice spoke in my head—not Lydian's, not mine, but a voice all the same—and whispered the name of the massive river. *Gjall.*

Nights around a burning fire, huddled up between my sisters and their families, as my father animatedly told stories by firelight came rushing back to me. So, so many stories. How Skadi's giant father was killed, how the Valkyries picked the dead from the battlefield, and how those who'd died by sickness and old age were forced to cross a mighty river of ice where not even gods could return from, in order to get to their afterlife.

A final test, he'd said.

Hel is a place as well as the name of its ruler. This voice I recognized as Lydian's, and if I had enough energy after having fallen for who knew how long, I would've groaned. After two blissful days of silence, he was back. At least soon he wouldn't be speaking in my head and driving only me to want to rip my hair out. *It's not for punishment, not all of it.* Lydian continued without acknowledging my frustration. *Sure, there are some parts that are less desirable than others, especially if you were not properly buried.* He let his words linger for a second, and I swore I could see him in my mind's eye, glaring at Soren. *But in reality, Hel means the grave. The dwelling of the dead. Nothing more, nothing less. You cross into its borders and you become its citizen.*

"And now we're going to have to cross back," I muttered out loud. The others turned to me in concert but shrugged it off when I tapped my temple. By now, I was pretty sure they were used to me speaking to what seemed like myself. Thank the gods they all knew the truth now, so I didn't look completely out of my head.

"Is he bothering you?" Soren asked.

"Always and forever," I replied. "But in this case, it's more of an annoyance. As if I don't know my own theology."

"Theology?" Soren raised an eyebrow.

"I'm getting lectured about the river, Gjall, like I'm a kid at a teacher's knee. It's almost worse than when he's taunting me," I said, acid dripping from my voice.

Rose shot a wary glance at the rushing water. "We're going to have to cross that, aren't we?" His face had turned a pale shade of green at the sight. Other than Diaval, the other goblins also were swallowing back roils of nausea at the proximity to rushing water. Because of course, fast-moving water was one of the ways to ward off creatures of the Permafrost. Surprisingly, my stomach wasn't turning itself into knots and loops.

"I'd say it's not as daunting as it looks," Diaval said, "but I'd be lying. Besides, I'm sure you've done much more dangerous things."

Well, she wasn't wrong about that. But still, rushing water didn't even have a negative effect on me, and I was terrified to get in there. Not only could I not see the bottom through the rapids and the ice floes, but I was sure the temperature had to be absolutely freezing.

A memory over a hundred years old came back to me. Some cocky kid trying to prove their manhood to the rest of the others by jumping into the half-frozen river and going into shock and drowning right after. Would being the stag keep me from dying? Or would it keep my body alive as a vessel and kill the part of me that was human inside of it? I had a feeling I didn't want to know.

"Either way," Diaval continued, "I have safety measures at hand. Rose, toss me the pack I handed you."

Rosamund tossed the packed bag he had slung across his back, and Diaval caught it effortlessly. "What was in that anyway, rocks?" he said.

Diaval let out a small, mischievous smile. "Something like that." She dug into the pack and pulled out a casing of thick leather rolled up as many times as it could go. She carefully placed the parcel on the ground and began to unroll the leather bindings until the roll was opened, and two wickedly sharp stakes peered out from view.

Immediately Soren, Seppo, and Rosamund took a step back. "You had me carry that?" Rosamund exclaimed.

Diaval examined the iron stakes with her bare hands, not even hissing in pain at the touch of the forbidden metal, and shrugged. "You didn't die, now did you?"

"Pretty sure one of the unbreakable rules of the Permafrost is not carrying iron into the Permafrost on pain of death," Soren muttered. "I mean, it's not like I'm the *king* of the Permafrost or anything, so how would *I* know, but I have this hunch."

"Impressive use of sarcasm," I said, while simultaneously trying to hide my laughter at the childish tone of his voice.

"Thank you," he said, the compliment thankfully distracting him from executing the king's justice on Rose and Diaval. "I've been practicing."

Diaval rolled her eyes and continued with her work. Sooner or later, she was going to get her eyes permanently stuck there.

If it were any other goblin, the iron would've burned right through her skin by this point, but Diaval wasn't a normal goblin. Like Tanya said, she could do some amazing things but they all came with a price. In the time I had known her, I'd seen her handle iron, cross rushing water, take down wards, break oaths, and create in ways other goblins couldn't. So much power that went against goblin nature itself. Whatever the cost, to her it must have been worth it.

"Janneke," she said. "Can I borrow your axe?"

I eyed the iron warily—it may not have hurt me anymore, not like back when I held it in my hand to light up a flame to kill the draugr during the Hunt—but I still had an almost superstitious bad feeling in my gut when I was around it.

I lifted my axe out of its holster and handed it to her. She wasted no time hammering the back of the stake into the earth with the blunt, back side of the axe until it was grounded into the bank of the raging river. The land screamed out noiselessly at the painful intrusion, and a sharp bolt of pain went through my side as if someone had hammered the stake into me instead of the ground. Despite it staying the same on the surface, I could *see* behind my eyelids, almost like a second scene, the ground writhing and thrashing beneath us, trying to expel the foreign object inside of it. Blood leaked out of the land as it cried out in pain. I offered a silent apology, though I doubted the land cared as we forced poisoned iron into the ground.

When she was done, she tied a rope to the end of the iron stake—something else that came out of her pack—and tied it tightly around the stake, making sure it wouldn't slip off.

"All right, I'll be right back." She rolled up the leathers again, this time with my axe and the rope inside it as well as the stake, and tucked it under one arm. I frowned. Was she going to do what I thought she would? Surely even *she* wasn't that bold.

"Wait, Diaval—" Rosamund said in horror as the she-goblin plunged into the icy water. For a moment, she was thrashed by the current, bobbing up and down, being thrown left and right by the torrents of water and ice. She went under as an ice floe hit her, and despite the pain of the running water, all three male goblins and I stepped forward, peering into the churning darkness.

It was quiet for a long, painful moment, and I gripped Soren's hand, squeezing it as my heart raced for my friend. But as I was starting to truly fear she'd drowned, Diaval burst out of the water on the other side, breathing deep in the cold air. She pulled herself out of the river by her arms, crawling low with her belly until she was all the way onto the opposite bank. I let out a breath I hadn't known I'd been holding and relaxed my grip on Soren's hand. He gazed at the redness, the mark of strength from my grip, in surprise.

She immediately went back to work, pulling out the leather bindings again and hammering the iron stake into the opposite side of the bank. Then she pulled the rope taut, so it was visibly hanging over the torrents of water and ice before she tied it to the other stake in the same way she had the first.

"I know I'm not one to talk," Seppo said, "but that's unnatural. She's not even bothered at all."

"Magic," Rose replied, "really messes with people."

"Remind me never to piss off Diaval in the future, will you?" Soren asked.

"I'll try my best but . . . you do have a very special skill when it comes to pissing people off," Rose said.

Soren turned to look at the two men, then back at me. "If I ever piss her off, are you going to protect me, Janneke?"

He had that stupid smirk on his face as if he already knew the answer. Which, he might've. "Whatever she does to you, you'll probably deserve."

"Oi!" Diaval yelled from across the river. "We can play 'house' later! Get in the bloody water!" The three goblins cringed.

"I'm going to put this out there," Soren said, "but I really hate this idea."

"It's either this or having to fight the giant wolf that guards the other gate of Hel!" Diaval shouted from across the river. "You don't want to fight the wolf, believe me!"

"I'm with Soren," Rosamund said. "I kinda prefer taking my chances with the giant wolf."

"Where's your sense of adventure?" Seppo grinned, eyeing the river like any other challenge.

"Honey," Rose said, "I think what you call a sense of adventure is what most people would call 'poking a dragon with a stick to see what it does when it wakes up' or 'jumping down a random chasm to see where it leads after hearing a strange noise from it.' So, believe me when I say that I love you, but your idea of an adventure is pretty much suicide." He crossed his arms. "That being said, where you go, I go."

I looked over at Soren, who was staring transfixed at the water. "Do you see the faces?"

"Faces?" I asked. "What faces?"

Soren shook his head. "It's the ice floes playing with my head. Don't worry about it. Let's get this over with. Single file, everyone. Can everyone here at least swim?"

"Well, obviously you know the answer for me and Seppo," I said.

Soren rolled his eyes.

"I can swim," Rosamund said. "I'm not going to be winning any competitions any time soon, but I can swim."

Soren nodded and approached the head of the line, where the stake was firmly planted into the ground. He glanced uneasily at the metal before taking a step from the solid riverbank to the muddy mix of the two and then right into the water. He gasped as the water quickly rose up to meet his chest, and for a terrifying moment, his lack of breath suffocated me in my own lungs, gasping for air that wouldn't come. But as quick as it hit, he shook it off and continued, holding tightly onto the rope Diaval planted for us and using it to maneuver his way through the cold water and icy floes.

He gasped, spluttering in the icy water as he pulled himself forward one strong tug at a time. When he was halfway across, Diaval signaled for Rosamund to go in, then Seppo. Both had similar reactions to the cold and the veins stood against their skin as if they were going to pop. Every one of them, even Seppo, was having a hard time not morphing into their true forms, which would include claws and sharp teeth that would undoubtedly shred the rope to bits.

My heart rose into my throat as Soren lost his footing and was thrusted underneath a sheet of ice. I could barely make out his shadow under the water, twisting and turning as he tried to find a way to break through to the surface again. His body was wrapped around the rope like it was his lifeline, which, to be fair, it was. I stood anchored in my spot, knowing I had to wait for Diaval's say, but all that changed when I got a good look at the thing in the water. Made from the river foam and broken chunks of ice was a face, a hand, a body. Person or creature, I didn't know, but their fingers were like claws pulling on Soren to keep him down and underneath the ice. He struggled to get a breath and fight off the creatures, and both Rose and Seppo were too far away and too busy fighting the icy current themselves to be of any help.

So that left me. Diaval shouted something at me—a warning or a word of concern—I wasn't entirely sure what was said because her words were wind in my ears. There was only one thing important here, one thing that mattered, and it was Soren. Soren. Soren. Soren.

All that mattered was Soren.

Pale hands grabbed him and pulled him under, and he was yanked free of his grip on the rope.

I plunged into the icy water.

11

SISTER SPIRITS

WHEN I FIRST was dragged into the southern part of the Permafrost, I thought I'd never feel a cold like it again. When I traveled with Soren to the High North where he lived, though I was still unconscious half the time, I once again thought I would never experience a cold worse than that. But plunging into the icy river proved how wrong I was.

The cold stole the breath straight from my lungs, and I broke the surface, gasping for air as my chest tightened and my instincts told me to thrash and panic. But now was not the time to panic. Rose's and Seppo's struggle in the water I could feel if I reached out with my power, but it was Soren's that was the most severe. Whatever creature or monster or thing that had its claws in him was desperate not to let him go until he drowned and stayed underneath the water forever.

All the blades in the world couldn't help him in the rapid, icy current, and my own weapons were useless as well. Still, I couldn't, *wouldn't*, let that *thing* have Soren, and so with another gasp of icy air, I thanked my lucky stars that I'd been taught how to swim so well all those years ago and plunged my head back under, forcing my eyes to remain open despite the sting.

I'd had my share of salt water in my eyes before, growing up so close to the coast, but I'd never had it like this. It burned like salt water but also gave the distinct feel of river water, the taste of lake water. Was this the river where all bodies of water came from? I didn't have time to ponder that thought because despite the current pushing me farther and farther away—or trying to, at least—I dug my hands into the stony muck of the ground to pull myself forward. Unable to shriek as rocks and sharp edges ripped at my fingers and dug into my fingernails, I pulled myself forward to the thing attacking Soren, not entirely sure what I was going to do, but knowing I was going to cause it a world of pain.

Somewhat surprised that I could easily touch the creature, I yanked it away from Soren and watched as Soren broke to the surface, hopefully getting in breaths of blessed air. I was ready to unleash the fury of the nine worlds onto the thing until I got sight of its face, and time stilled, despite the swirling, chaotic water and ice around us.

She was young, and the wounds in her body wept blue blood as she shrieked in pain. Her anguish radiated through me like it was my own, and flashes of memory that didn't belong to me forced themselves into my head as she spoke to me without words.

The men who'd come to her home, normal men, human men, who'd ended up burning it all down, taking the women and children to a fate worse than death. Walking dead-eyed with the others, a bundle of cloth heavy in her arms. She cradled it close to her chest and her eyes softened when she looked down upon it. Then they hardened as she stopped in her tracks and another woman bumped into her. She dug at the swaddling with her hands and exposed the babe fully to the cold air, hoping to rouse it, but it was already dead and cold. No, not "it." He. I knew, rather than saw. He. Her son. Too innocent and fragile to endure the grueling conditions of this walk of captives. Too young to even have a chance at life the moment the village burned down.

She wailed and flung herself to the ground with the body of her child, pulling out her hair in grief. There was no charcoal to blacken her face, nor were there any knives to mar her skin so the world would know her pain, but she still had her hair.

It was a death ritual, to make yourself ugly or harm yourself because a loved one had passed on. It was meant to show how strongly one grieved for their dead loved one, slashing cheeks and nonlethal parts of one's arms and body, smearing mud and thick red paint that took weeks to wash off.

It assured the dead they'd be mourned, and this young woman couldn't even do that. Another man from the raiding village yanked her up and shoved her forward, tossing the small corpse of the baby behind. The woman cried out, and she was met with a slap in the face and forced to keep moving as her precious child dwindled farther and farther away.

I reached out and gripped the woman in the water. Because underneath her silvery appearance, burning white hair, and wraithlike eyes, her true face appeared—a young woman with pale skin and a small nose with a soft bridge, rich brown eyes, yellow hair that fell like feathers around her face. Her claws passed through me like wind through leaves as I took hold of her forearm and reentered the memory with her.

The men camped at the top of a cliff and harsh winds blew. The captive women and children huddled closely together to share their warmth despite the lack of adequate clothing and blankets. Every so often, a child would stir and cry before being shushed by its mother or someone would hide a cough knowing any sign of weakness could get them killed. The survivors all came together as one.

Except for the woman with the brown eyes who sat to the very edge of the group and toward the craggy rocks. She stood in one fluid motion then and stepped forward, again and again, one more step, just one more, until the other women were calling for her, and some of the men were screaming in a language she didn't know nor would ever learn. But none of them ran after her, none of them stopped as she stood at the top of the wind-battered cliff and calmly unlaced her boots. They were pretty, made of doeskin, and the beadwork was impeccable. Nothing I could recognize, but then again, who knew how far back in history this was?

She stood straight with the self-assurance of a lady who knew exactly what she was doing and had already steeled herself for it a long time ago. Clarity swept over her pained features as she stared over the water below, watching it crash against the rocks, and the white foam swirled into faces that called her down.

She stepped out of her boots, wincing at the pain in her sore, aching feet, and stood on the cliff face a moment longer, head raised to take in one last breath of salty, ocean-borne wind before she calmly stepped off the cliff and to her death.

We locked eyes again, the spirit and I, and suddenly I *knew*. Not sure how, not sure why, but I *knew* that she was no monster or creature or thing attacking Soren for the sake of it. Not for the revel of the kill or the glory of the hunt or even for hunger. She was a mother reaching for a boy whose skin had turned blue-gray in death, whose lips became the color of frost, whose blond hair was so fine that if he'd actually been a goblin, it could've been white as snow.

She was reaching for what she thought was her son.

Underwater, I could shed no tears, but I didn't let go of my grip on her even as she fought and called out under the water to what she thought was hers. Instead, I reached out with my mind to that one shimmering place that always evaded me, and I called to it, and for the first time, a call came back.

Go through to your dwelling, sister spirit. A voice that was mine but also not mine spoke beneath the water. *Do not linger in the river. There is peace on the other side.* I took the spirit's clawed hand and pressed it against my chest, against the wounds I'd received a hundred years ago, and I watched in amazement as those clawed hands transformed back into the hands of a human woman's. *You will be with him on the other side of the river, sister spirit. I know this, for I have crossed this river many times over.* The voice that was me but was not me continued. *Do not let your sorrow drown you anymore. Do not let the cold water freeze your heart from feeling. Cross the river, sister spirit, and emerge from the other side into the glory of your dwelling.*

The wraith breathed out a sigh in the water as she transformed back into a woman and then shrank until she was a silvery wisp floating high and away from the torrents of the icy water.

I had a moment of pure peace fill me when I closed my eyes and smiled before realizing I was still in the frigid rapids and needed to cross to the other side myself. I came up to the top again and took a gulp of air, grabbing at the rope. Soren rushed forward from where he was pacing and grabbed the hook of my tunic and pulled me until I was on the muddy bank of the river, then the brown, dry grass of the other side.

Coughing and spluttering, he thumped on my back hard with one fist as water exited my lungs and was expelled onto the grass below me. I continued to gulp at the air like a beached fish in between choked vomits of water, until I could take a deep breath again, and with trembling muscles, I collapsed into his arms.

We lay there, a desperately breathing mess, as the world beneath us slowly began to warm us again. Steam rose from the ground where our bodies lay, and I had no energy to think anything of it other than *huh, neat.* Soren and I buried ourselves in each other until our heaving chests slowed, and we began to come back to the world. Weakly raising my head, I saw Rose and Seppo in a similar embrace while Diaval sat off to the side, rolling her eyes at all of us. But for someone who scoffed at personal relationships, she had sounded particularly worried when I jumped in after Soren.

"That thing tried to kill me," Soren breathed. "It almost did. I couldn't—the water—the ice—it was like nothing I'd ever imagined. What did you do to it, Janneke?"

"I'm interested too." Rosamund sat up. "I swore I heard something shrieking, but I couldn't get anywhere near whatever it was. I failed as a guard member."

Seppo rubbed his boyfriend's back. "There, there, now, you'll have to be a disappointment like the rest of us."

Only Diaval didn't inquire about my "fight" with the thing in the water. Instead, she had a sly smile slowly spreading on her elfin face. "You finally did it, Janneke."

"I did," I agreed. "What did I do, exactly?" I did definitely get the feeling I'd accomplished something major as the stag but wasn't entirely sure what that thing was in the first place.

"You reached into a liminal space and pulled something back from it. The memories of the spirit in the water. You let them play out and then let the spirit pass on to the afterlife."

"Did you *know* that would happen, Diaval?" Soren asked, a slight growl coloring his tone.

"Don't be ridiculous, Soren," Diaval said. "I knew that crossing was dangerous, and I made that very clear. I also knew, as should you *all* know, that Gjall does harbor spirits of water-based death if they cannot fully pass on but aren't wicked enough for the *Naglafar*. I wouldn't have made you cross this way if there were an easier or safer way to do it."

Soren made a noise in the back of his throat but didn't comment further, laying his head back down against the warm ground. It was nice after the freezing water and part of me wished it would swallow me up and wrap me tightly in its embrace. My gaze flickered to the others. Usually things in the Permafrost were not pleasantly warm unless you were in immediate danger, and I had no reason to believe that Helheim didn't work the same way. But even Diaval was relaxing slowly from her swim.

"We'll need to continue on," I spoke, though my voice sounded tired and I held back a yawn. My muscles ached from the swim, and I was beginning to feel a sharp pain in my temple that was no doubt the beginning of a headache. "We can't stay and relax. We have no time."

A couple of groans came from the pile of sleepy goblins. "I get that," Rose said. "Truly I do, but give us a moment. The water takes a lot out of us. You and Diaval are lucky. Even Seppo's got the muscle strength of a particularly limp noodle right now."

"You're a limp noodle," Seppo muttered.

"He's not lying," Soren said. "Running water is awful."

"She's right," Diaval said, standing. "We don't have time for this."

"You weren't affected the same way; you don't get a vote."

Diaval raised a finely shaped eyebrow. "I wasn't aware we were voting."

"Technically, Soren's the king, so even if we were going to pull that card, Soren would come out on top," Seppo said helpfully.

Diaval sent the poor goblin a withering glare for his effort.

"No," Soren said, heaving himself up. "She's right. We'll feel better the farther away we are from the water, and we can't relax on the banks of Helheim, anyway."

Well, he was right about that. I scanned this side of the riverbank, trying to figure out where we possibly needed to go next and hoping that all it involved was walking and not fighting some infernal creature or passing another test of strength. Stag or not, I was pretty wiped out from my experience in the water, and my muscles felt like heavy lead.

Rosamund stood, shaking. "Can't you feel it?" he asked. When we met eyes, I was shocked to see his pupils blown so large that they almost engulfed his entire iris. "We've got nowhere we need to go. No need to travel to any place. We're already there. Anywhere we want to be. We've passed; we're at the dwelling. If you look, you can see the roots."

Anyone who remained on the ground stood with a new, burning fire as we looked at Rosamund with confusion in our faces. Even Seppo, who knew him better than anyone else, was confused at the blown-out pupils and rambling words that had come out of his boyfriend's mouth.

Rosamund lurched forward, taking a step and then another before reaching his hand out.

There was a shimmer and the world surrounding us shook and turned. My feet nearly fell from under me when the glamour in front of us was physically forced open by Rosamund's hands as he yanked and pulled it apart like a piece of tough meat from a bone.

"Rose—" Seppo said but that was all he had time to say as with a loud grunt a ripping sound sent shivers down my spine and the glamour faded away.

There was no river around us now, nothing but the fields of brown grass, and the massive roots of a tree where a skeletal goddess sat watching us with amusement on her half-rotten face. She was terrible and she was beautiful; somehow managing to be seductive with the side of her face that hadn't gone to rot, the beautiful alabaster skin and a shining blue eye, the golden-white hair flowing down one side, tucked behind one ear with her milk-white hand and shimmering nails. And then the other side of her body, a hollowed-out corpse, shot through with rot, like a carcass that'd been picked nearly clean by dogs. Dead flesh hung from her face and her eye socket was dark and empty, other than the maggots crawling out of it.

The goddess lounged on the roots of the world tree, delight in her single shining eye. "Oh, I was wondering when it would hit you, dear brute," she said with a laugh that managed to sound both like a hyena and tinkling bells.

Rose's eyes slowly turned back their normal green, and I breathed a sigh of relief, knowing whatever had happened, it'd passed. "No." He shook his head. "I'm past the age where it would've first developed. It's impossible to have it now."

Have what? I mouthed to Seppo, but all the halfling did was shrug and shake his head to indicate he too had no idea what his boyfriend was talking about.

"Did you not tell them?" Hel said, amusement in her tone. "Did you not tell them the truth of why you wanted to come?"

"I came to help my friends," Rose growled. "And that's what I'll do."

"But that's not all you came for, right?" Her voice was an impossible dichotomy of soothing and taunting, soft and harsh, dark and light, like her own body.

"We all came for the same person," Rose said, his growl a little deeper. "If I had personal reasons, those are my own."

"Wait." Seppo took a half step toward his boyfriend. "What do you mean? Rose?"

"Yeah," Soren said, in a much less friendly tone than Seppo. "What *do* you mean?"

Diaval's head tilted to the side like an interested cat, yet she said nothing.

Deep inside my gut, something churned. The feeling of not-right and darkness, anticipation of betrayal, the idea that one of my friends could have some ulterior motive . . . Had I grown too complacent? Had being the stag lulled me into some false sense of security? Out of the group, Rose was always the one with the littlest to share. He, like Diaval, didn't participate on the Hunt, but like Diaval, he'd pledged his services after. He had an uncanny ability to nearly predict my moves before I made them in a fight, but swore it was years of talent, and had no family to speak of.

But there was something more, and my stomach lurched painfully as a shimmering spirit emerged, trapped in the roots of the world tree.

His face was haggard, his once-luscious blond hair limp and tangled, and his bones jutted out from his skin like a skeleton's. His once-nice clothes had been torn and ripped almost to shreds, and there were bruises littering his skin. Some were dark blue, new and growing darker, while some were yellowing and fading. A large cut marred one of his cheeks and ruined the perfect skin he'd once possessed.

He gripped at the roots holding him in place as if they

were iron bars, and they might've well been as they held him securely to his prison, some even running through him in painful penetrated areas where blood oozed and mixed with green sap.

This was the fate we'd elected to give him when we didn't give his body funeral rights. This was the fate that Hel elected to give him for his deeds in his life. Slowly being consumed by the world tree, demolished until there was nothing left.

I wanted to throw up but was stopped in my tracks as Lydian's catlike green eyes met mine and then slid right over to the staring figure of Rosamund.

"Hello, son."

12

SINS OF THE FATHER

BLOOD SHOT LIKE frozen water through my veins. *Son?* Rosamund was Lydian's *son?* My gaze bounced between the two of them. They resembled little of each other, Lydian being lean where Rosamund was stocky, and of course Rose had his telltale red hair. But the eyes . . . both men had the exact same color eyes in the exact same shape in their faces. That alone could be proof enough. It wasn't like Rose was denying it.

From beside me, a low growl built up in Soren's throat, and I grabbed his wrist, running my thumb over the finger-nails that were slowly lengthening to claws in hopes that they reversed the transformation. Luckily, the soothing gesture worked, but who knew for how long. The upset wouldn't get any better with claws out.

I glared at Lydian, who while still in his painful prison managed to look very amused with himself. The damn brute was impaled by thorns and still managed to rile up everyone in the group with his words without even being a threat to us physically. I took a deep breath, wincing at the pain in my head that was becoming an ever-constant headache.

"You have no right to call me that," Rosamund said, voice in a deep growl. He turned to Soren and me, green eyes pleading. "Believe me when I say there is no sort of relationship between the two of us, not in the way you think. Not in *any* way." I wasn't sure who was more upset in the moment, him or Soren.

Soren's bloodlust was palpable, but even he could hear the truth in Rosamund's words. The truth and the pain behind them. Blood or not, Lydian's revelation held no type of positive emotion for Rose. No goblin could lie without the other one knowing, and both of them could tell he was speaking the truth. He couldn't hide his true feelings.

"The only way that monster is my father is that one night he and my mother both had too much to drink. I'd barely ever laid eyes on the brute my entire life," he said, voice rough. "My mother hates him. I've seen him maybe thrice in my entire existence, and it was never good. I've spoken to him personally once. The fact that he calls me *son* so casually makes me feel sick. I came here as a member of your guard. I joined your guard to protect you two, not for him."

"That's not fully true, though, is it?" Diaval asked quietly, for once all the emotion and teasing gone from her voice.

Rosamund shut his eyes tight.

"What does she mean, Rose?" Seppo asked, looking slightly like a hurt puppy.

Rosamund shot a glare at the goblin being slowly impaled by the roots of the world tree and the goddess sitting on the throne they made. "I bet you're loving this."

Lydian shrugged, wincing in pain as the movement ripped his skin. "I've been without amusement for far too long. And well, here it is for me right now. How can I not indulge?"

If we hadn't needed the brute for our mission, I would've killed him a second time right then and there.

"I needed to see if it would happen," Rosamund said after a moment. "They always say if latent abilities don't wake after seeing the world tree, they never will . . . I needed to make sure . . ."

"And you are, now, aren't you?" Lydian's own voice was poisonous. "Congratulations, son. You have the ability that I drove myself mad to get."

"You were always mad," Soren spat as Rose said, "Don't call me son!"

Soren turned to Rosamund once again. "What ability? Are you claiming you've got the sight?"

"It was in bits and pieces before now," Rosamund said. "Just little things. Knowing reactions to things that hadn't happened yet. Knowing someone's moves before they happened. I could see Lydian's shade hanging around Janneke sometimes. But nothing full on . . . like *that*." He indicated between himself and the now-visible world tree, to the veil he pulled off. "Until now. But you have to know that while that was a *benefit* of this, it was not my goal. My goal is to serve and protect both of you to the best of my abilities. You know that. I need the sight like I need a hole in the head. It should be obvious how I feel."

And it was, because we could hear it resonating in his voice. But still. How much I'd shared with the son of the monster who tormented me, about what his own blood had done. I felt strangely violated, though I couldn't figure out in what sense. Rose hadn't done anything to hurt me or Seppo or Soren; he'd kept a fact from us. And did it matter if Lydian was his father if he'd had such a little role to play in Rose's life as he'd said? It didn't matter who Seppo's father was. Seppo had been raised by his mother, same as Rosamund had.

While he hadn't told us of his heritage, I could hardly blame Rose for the sins of Lydian, especially if they barely knew each other. From what I knew, Soren was raised by his father, who was not a good person and someone who did not care about the pain and suffering of others and who treated those weaker than him cruelly; someone who treated his own son cruelly enough for Soren to murder him for his seat as lord without so much as a single doubt. But I couldn't blame Soren for his father being cruel. And what about my own father? Who while good-hearted and well-intentioned instilled in me a self-hatred I fought every day because of his hatred of the Permafrost? Was I really one who could judge Rose?

No, as much as it made my stomach flip and sink, and as much as I wanted to be outraged, I couldn't. It wasn't like any of us had a choice who bore us, and in truth, I could see why Rose hadn't shared the knowledge. I don't think any of us would've let him near us had we known, and then I wouldn't have a friend, and Seppo wouldn't have his boyfriend.

"I understand," I said.

Soren turned to me, frowning. "Just like that?"

"He's not Lydian. Why punish him for what Lydian did?" I replied. "You're not responsible for your parents' crimes.

We have more important things to worry about than Rose's parents. We can discuss his withholding of information after we've done what we came here to do, but I doubt it's necessary."

Soren nodded but still had a sour look on his face. Seppo looked visibly relieved if still a bit hurt. Diaval looked bored. She'd known about this too—how? Was it part of her magic?

Hel smiled, and the way the rotten half of her face moved made me shutter. "Yes, what did you come here for?"

"I think you know," I said, nodding toward the trapped Lydian. "Considering you're dangling him in front of us like a lure."

The monstrous goddess of death cocked her head to the side in a coy gesture. "I have no idea what you mean."

The frustration and anger coming off my companions was nearly palpable. "We want Lydian's shade. We need it released out of Helheim. He doesn't have to come back to life, necessarily, him and his shade will do," I demanded, and hoped I sounded a lot more sure of myself than I truly felt.

Hel threw back her head and laughed. The sound was like nails against a chalkboard, like shattering glass, and I fought not to cover my ears. "*YOU*," she said, laughing. "You and your ragtag bunch of heroes think you can demand from *me* the shade of a member of my realm? What right do you all have to do such a thing? Even the mighty Frigga couldn't bring Balder back from death and away from my realm. And yet you think you can offer me something the goddess queen could not, in return?"

I focused on breathing steady, keeping my body from tensing up. I shot furtive looks at the members of my party and they did the same as well as they possibly could. No one said this was going to be easy and being mocked by Hel was probably something we all should've expected. There was no use in getting angry or offended or even irritated by her. We had to keep pressing our point.

But it was impossible to stand in front of Hel and not feel incredibly intimidated by her size and features and the strength of her voice. Her straightened and squared shoulders as well as the way she almost lounged on her throne only proved how confident in her power she was.

"Frigga may be the goddess queen, yes," I said, "but I am the *stag*, and as such, my jurisdiction is much different than her majesty's."

Hel let out another ear-splitting laugh. "Yes, you are the little stag who can barely control or use even an eighth of the power the real stag possessed. You may bear the mantle and you may have the name, but you are nothing—*nothing*—compared to the great beast the original stag was. Why should I concern myself with the opinions of a weak fawn?"

The goddess of death knew to hit me right where it hurt. Yeah, sure, I'd managed to do something in the water that I hadn't before. I saw that trapped soul, her pain, her past, her grief, and set her free so she could pass across the water, but that was literally the only thing I'd yet to do with the stag's powers that came directly from my own ability. She was right. I was less a stag and more a little white fawn. Weak and trembling in a world too strong for her.

No. I couldn't let myself think like that. That's what she wanted me to think. To feel weak, to give up, to lie down in her hall somewhere and let the water and mud take over me and turn me into stone. I needed to stop pitying myself about my powers not working right. It didn't matter. I'd find a way, and Hel wasn't going to stop me.

"If you don't concern yourself with her," Soren spoke up, his voice in a low growl, "perhaps you'll concern yourself with the Erlking. Like it or not, we have power and a place in this cosmic game you gods like to play." He stood with his arms folded across his chest, glaring so sharply, it could probably break glass.

"You at least offered Frigga a trial," Diaval said, "a way to prove whether or not she was worthy of taking Balder and bringing him back to life—to have every being ask for his existence back, and it would've worked if not for the trickster god, Loki. We're not even asking for you to bring Lydian back to life. We want his shade. We're not asking for a god either. Just a lowly goblin!"

"Hey!" Lydian objected from his cage of roots.

The goddess sat back on her throne with a smug smile. "Oh, yes, and I'm sure you'll do nothing that could ruin my own plans with him now, will you?"

I held out a hand to keep the others from speaking, knowing that we'd almost fallen into her trap. Hel couldn't know why we wanted Lydian's shade. In the prophecies surrounding Ragnarök, she was always one of the ones who brought it forth, fought against the gods. There was no way she'd give us Lydian back if she knew what we planned to do with him.

I stepped forward, hands on my hips. "And what do you care what we do with a simple shade?" I asked tauntingly.

"You have so many others to deal with, after all, and so many things to attend to. We have his heart beating in the Erlking's palace in the Permafrost. Perhaps we want to taunt him, hurt him. You must've known what he's done to me. Maybe I've decided I haven't had enough revenge."

The lies slipped through my teeth like millions of tiny snakes, but better they came from me than from the others who couldn't carry such a hoax. Their curious stares lingered on my back, but I was happy enough to know they trusted me for whatever I was planning on doing.

"Diaval is right," I said. "Are you so scared of a little fawn you won't even give her a trial?"

Hel narrowed her eye, and I held back a flinch at the way the rotting side of her face moved. "Hmm. We could do a trade. Direct blood for direct blood." She pointed a finger at Rose who stood frozen to the spot when he realized what she meant.

Thank the gods no one here considered it. "No," I said. "Rose is our friend and we won't exchange a fully living being for the shade of another. That's an unfair trade and I'm not willing to kill him so you can technically have his shade. No, you'll give us a trial like you did Frigga."

The goddess snorted in amusement. "You couldn't handle any trial I gave you."

"I don't know," I said. "I've handled quite a lot of things others expected to break me."

She narrowed her eyes at me once more. "If you want to free a shade from its fate, then you yourself will have to give your fate up, blindly. I will let you have a trial, but only in time shall you know what I want you to do, only in time will you be able to complete your mission, and until then, your fate should hang in the balance like a fraying thread."

"What do you want us to do?" Soren asked, but the goddess shook her head.

"Not 'us,'" she said. "Her." She pointed one crooked finger at me before beckoning me forward. Unease crawled through me like insects down my spine the closer I got to the roots of the world tree and the goddess of death herself. Looking down, I noticed the ground right below the roots crumbling away and leaving spots of dark nothingness in its pathway.

"Ginnugagap," I whispered in awe below my breath at the darkness.

"So, you know what this is, then," Hel said.

"Of course. I was raised on these tales," I said. "As every human child was."

"Then you know what it means when I tell you to jump into it," Hel said, smiling a wicked smile. "Jump into the yawning grave and meet your fate inside of it."

My eyes widened, and I hastily took a step back as the soil beneath my feet began to crumble and fall into the primordial void. They said while the stag created the creatures and worlds that lived in Midgard, the Ginnugagap, or *yawning grave,* was what lingered before there were gods and other worlds and would be there long after. That on one side of the void sat Niflheim, the land of ice, intense cold, and mist, and on the other sat Muspellheim, the land of fire, heat, lava, and smoke. And in between the two sat a nothing that was something—a space between spaces that took you wherever it desired. To jump into the gap between two worlds would be to give up all control and knowledge of what surrounded you, what held you to the world, what made you even you. Yet this was my task. Not to jump into the gap, but to complete whatever Hel desired of me while I could be in an entirely different world as an entirely different being seeing through entirely different eyes.

Looking down at the gaping void, I couldn't suppress a shudder. In tales, the gap was supposed to be filled with roots from Yggdrasil, the world tree, but there was nothing peering back at me through the yawning, obsidian nothingness. Only a feeling of terror deep in my stomach that got larger and larger the more I peered into it.

It radiated darkness and despair—the darkness of the unknown and the despair of not being able to ever know. The vast void led to somewhere at the same time as leading to nowhere at all.

"That's suicide," Diaval hissed. "How is she supposed to know what you want her to do in the gap? How is she supposed to know what her tasks are?"

Hel's ghoulish gaze raked over Diaval, but the she-goblin didn't waver. "Your friend is the stag. If anyone can survive a jump into the gap and wherever it leads, where it follows, and understands my own messages that come after for her, then it is her and only her." Hel let out a surprisingly ladylike laugh.

"Do you accept this?" Hel asked.

"So, the gap isn't the task by itself, is it? It's what awaits me on the other side?" I questioned, brows furrowed. "It's the choices I make inside?"

"Janneke," Soren said, "don't do it. We can find another way."

"Janneke, I'll gladly sacrifice myself for the good of the Permafrost," Rose said.

I turned back to my friends. "No words of protest, Seppo? Diaval?"

Seppo shrugged. "If anyone can do it, it would be you. You never cease to amaze me with how powerful you are. I don't doubt you."

"It's not that I don't believe in her—" Soren said, but I held a hand up.

"I know. It's your instinct, your fear, and it's perfectly understandable."

"I won't lie and say you'll be okay," Diaval said. "I don't know what will happen. But if this is our only option, then I trust your strength."

I took a deep breath in and let it out sharply, then nodded. "I accept your tasks, Hel."

Carefully I picked my way around the roots of the world tree to find part of the gap that would be the easiest to jump through. As I did, the hair stood on the back of my neck from Lydian watching me. For once, he didn't look like he was about to taunt me. Instead, an intrigued expression crossed his face, as if he couldn't quite understand what I was doing. A flicker of respect passed his expression and was gone in almost an instant.

I found a spot between the roots big enough for my body to fall through without banging anything on the way down and turned back once more to look at the people I loved. I wasn't sure what type of world I would enter into once the gap had me in its grasp, but in case they didn't exist there . . . I made sure to memorize their faces down to the shadows below their eyes. Soren gave me a small, reassuring nod. My mate believed in me.

Turning back to the gap in the world tree, I took one more deep breath and jumped into the darkness.

13

THE YAWNING GRAVE

I wasn't sure, but I was expecting to feel like I was falling when I jumped into the void. Instead, it was almost like I was rising, floating, my body caught in the air and held there in some space and time that existed solely for that moment. My eyes were closed, and when I opened them, I still didn't see myself fall even though the roots of the world tree should've been rushing past me. They went down and down and down forever, and yet still, no matter how far I traveled down, I didn't feel like I was falling.

Reaching out, I grabbed one of the roots and my vision went blurry, transporting me to another place in time.

Specifically another place in another time, as I stood in front of my parents and watched as they tanned hides and sewed them together, dyed white wool and white pelts of animals; even the shoes themselves were made of white leather. A me who was not really me shivered in the body I stood in.

Something wriggled in my brain and screamed at me to leave, that my thoughts weren't welcome here—where was here? Why was I here? Why was I thinking I'd be anywhere else but here? Hadn't I been observing my parents doing this for weeks? Hadn't I been listening to my mother sobbing when she thought that we were all asleep? And the other members of the village—the men *and* the women—hadn't they treated me somewhat nicer or at least with more respect? And why had my sisters repeated my name to their children so often when they would hear it for their entire lives anyways?

I fidgeted in the open hall of my home, unable to stop my fingers from shaking. Why would I be anywhere else? Why was I even thinking such a thing? This was my home. This was my body. There was nothing wrong with it. Nothing wrong at all. I must've caught a fever or something because I was led back to a space by the fire by my sister, blocking off the actions of my parents, and giving me a place to rest.

"Janneke," my mother said softly, coming forward. She gracefully knelt beside my bed and bent my head forward as she kissed my brow. We'd never really got on as well as me and my father had. Too different of people, too different of personalities. But I loved her. She loved me, and I could feel it in her kiss. But her eyes were watering. "My sweet girl."

Blinking in surprise—it wasn't often I was referred to as my birth gender—I frowned at her. "What's wrong? Father, Mother, what's the matter?"

Both of them were close to tears. Worry gnawed in my stomach as they looked at each other before my father sighed heavily and spoke. I stood shocked and numb as he explained the circumstances of my birth, the goblin that nearly stole me as a child, and the deal he made with said goblin to stop the village from getting slaughtered and to keep me with my family until I at least turned eighteen.

Now my eighteenth birthday was approaching and the goblin was coming to fetch me, take me "home" to the Permafrost to do . . . what? I wasn't sure, but it couldn't have been anything good.

It had to be a joke. A really bad joke. There was no way the *ground* of any area, whether or not it was magical, could bring a dead baby back to life. And a real goblin wouldn't have given my father eighteen years, he would've stolen me right away, probably massacring the village as he did. Not to mention why would a goblin want me to think the Permafrost was my home, anyway? One of my sisters had gone into sudden labor and delivered her child at the creek, and no one was saying the creek was their home.

The same feeling of something wiggling in my mind again hit me. Like a memory just trying to reach the surface. But I couldn't have because the sick shock to my system had me staggering outside of my home and retching onto the ground until there was nothing left inside of me. Funeral clothes. They were making funeral clothing for me, tailored for the harsh cold of the Permafrost, because that was where they figured I was going. To my death.

"I'm so sorry, my girl," my father said, his hand on my shoulder. He rubbed my back as I continued vomiting until I was dry heaving on the cold, frozen ground. Hel, if I thought this was cold, then how bad would the Permafrost be?

"When?" I asked, my voice cracking with pain.

"On the next claw moon," my father said. Both he and my mother embraced me.

Then I was falling again, and my eyes were open into the black void as my body slammed against the roots of the world tree. The roots reached far into the gap and high up into whatever stood above it, and lying on one caused an uneasy feeling—like I was staring into a mirror image. I was both right-side up and upside down, lying on blackness. From somewhere both above and below me, Hel's voice echoed. "Each root represents a different path your life could have gone. Prove that the current path you're on—the one which brings you so much insecurity, which brings you to free the shade of your worst enemy—is the one which your heart truly desires. Escape these worlds by root, by fang, and by iron, or stay in them forever."

With that, my back hit another root and I was standing by the border of the Permafrost, dressed in the funeral clothes my parents had painstakingly made. White leathers, white furs, and an iron knife tucked deep inside the folds of my sleeve so that hopefully I could protect myself in the one way I knew how—protect myself from the goblin studying me with such intensity in his lilac-colored eyes that I wanted to take a step backward.

I knew there was something I was supposed to be remembering, something that was supposed to be familiar about him, safe, but those were fleeting thoughts and feelings that left as soon as they came and slipped between my fingertips like water in a sieve.

The goblin held out a hand to me as if he were trying to

coax a frightened animal closer to him, and I raised my chin to meet and keep his gaze as I took an unsure step forward, then another, and then another after that until I crossed the invisible line between the worlds.

"Not very hard now, was it?" he said, voice soft, still in the tone of trying to calm a frightened creature.

A blast of coldness hit me the minute I stepped over the border. *How is it the temperature is so much colder a few steps away?* I wondered as my body began to shake violently, and I clenched my jaw in order to keep my teeth from chattering. I was wrapped in furs from my family and yet they did as much to the bone-deep, chilling cold as if I were naked and exposed.

The goblin eyed me calmly, still. "Noble effort," he murmured. "And very symbolic, the clothes. But only clothes specifically made in the Permafrost will keep you from freezing to death. Here." He reached to unclasp the cloak around his shoulders. It was dark and heavy, bearskin maybe, or shadow cat, and I stood still, frozen to the ground by fear, as he brushed aside my hair and placed the cloak over my shoulders and gently closed the clasp in front of me. The cloak did seem to block out most of the chilling blast I was receiving where it covered my body, though I was still unbelievably cold.

He was still looking at me, somewhat expectantly. Did he want me to thank him? I wasn't about to thank him when he was ripping me away from my family and home and everything I'd ever known.

This man, this *goblin*, was taking me to what was most

likely my death. Thanking him for a stupid cloak was out of the picture.

"You'll be happy there," he said, as if he could read my mind. Maybe he could. "You were born to be in the Permafrost. I know it. You'll know it too. Now come on, we won't be walking far. I have horses up ahead."

The utterly preposterous promise brought a bubble of laughter I was barely able to hold back. Who was *he* to say I'd be happy, that I was meant to be born there? I knew myself and my own mind much better than he ever could, and both of those things filled me with the desire to run straight back across the border into my own world. Hel, I would now if I didn't fear for the safety of my family.

He didn't look back as he started north, and with a twisting in my stomach, I realized all I could do was follow him. If I went back home, I'd risk my family and village getting slaughtered, risk my father dying from breaking the oath that he made, risk this goblin's wrath. So, I forced myself farther north into the cold region as the trees and shrubs began to become thinner and thinner, sparser, until there were no more green leaves coating them but merely skeletons waving somberly in the wind.

He didn't lie. We didn't walk for long before we came upon the horses, somehow perfectly obedient despite not being tied down. His—I figured it was his since it was a giant destrier—was solid black with a black mane to match and shaggy fur around his hooves. The gray mare beside him was slighter and smaller though still bore the distinctive shaggy fur that fell over one of its eyes. I ran a hand through her hair and she pressed her nose into my hand.

"Do you need help getting on?" he asked.

"I can get on a horse," I bit out, not wanting to talk to this goblin more than I had to, despite the annoyance bubbling on my lips. Of course I could get on a horse! It wasn't like children in my world weren't taught to ride from a young age either! It was one of the few things encouraged for both boys and girls. If this was a sign of things to come, I would end up in the grave from sheer exasperation alone.

Something tickled in the back of my mind as the anger faded. A word repeated over and over and over again. Root. Something about a root. A feeling like I didn't belong and a root. But I could barely make sense of the current situation I was in, much less the hypothetical one that kept brushing my consciousness.

We rode hard that first night and camped out when it got dark. He started a fire that glowed an unnatural blue color—normal fires didn't light in the Permafrost, he explained, though I hadn't asked—and was roasting a rabbit carcass on it. He'd nearly dug into it raw before realizing that we had different eating habits, and cooked it instead. He needn't have bothered. I wasn't in the mood to eat anything he had to give me even if my stomach cramped from the lack of food.

Instead, I wrapped myself in some of the furs he'd thought to bring and leaned on a bedroll with a saddlebag as a cushion. I had the iron knife. All I had to do was wait until he was asleep and then shove it in some soft place. His gut maybe or in an eye, his throat even. It wouldn't be hard. The blade was sharp enough. I needed the courage to do it and not worry about the consequences if I failed.

"You must hate me so very much," he said, noticing my deep frown.

I would've laughed in any other circumstance. "As if anyone likes the person who takes them against their will to do what—what will I be? A thrall for you? Shall I call you master?"

"You're not going to be a thrall," he said. "And my name is Soren."

"What then? A concubine?" Gods, the mere thought of that had me shiver in distaste. The white hair, the blue lips, the blue-gray tinge to his skin was weird enough to be around, but to be forced to *lie* with that . . .

"I'm quite capable of getting sex from willing participants," he said dryly, "so, no."

"Then what?" I spat out. "What's the point of you taking me? What will I do when I'm there?"

He shrugged. "I hadn't actually planned that out entirely. I know you need to be there, with me. The rest will come."

"You're very cavalier about the future of someone whom you've ripped from their home."

"The Permafrost will be your new home. My home will be your home."

"And how do you know that?" I asked sharply. "Can you tell the future?"

He wasn't making it easy not to stab him. Did he really think it was that simple—that easy? That I'd forget my home, my people, my *species*, and grow to love the Permafrost and his freezing pile of stones like it was my own? I knew what went on with humans in the Permafrost, and it was not something I'd call pleasant. I'd even seen two humans who managed to escape from the place where they'd been held, telling stories of monsters who eat uncooked flesh of any creature they desired, including themselves, of the brutality, the fights for food, the jobs they were forced to do because goblins themselves couldn't do them. If he thought I would be happy there, his brain was a crock of shit.

"You don't have to believe me now," Soren said, obviously reading my facial expression, "but you will sooner or later. I know that."

I shook my head and turned my face away from him, pressing it on the saddlebag that rested against the roots of a large, lightning-struck tree. Again, with the knowing. He had the stones to go into this situation and declare that he knew how I would feel, if not now, then in the future. He didn't know a thing about me or my life or what I wanted. Unwillingly, warm tears slipped from my closed eyelids and down my cheeks, dripping down onto the dead roots.

Roots. There was something about roots. Even with the emotional pain trying to break my chest into two, I still remembered that. Something about roots was important, and I didn't know why it kept buzzing in my head.

That's how it stayed as we went farther and farther north. To where the dead skeleton trees were the only foliage to be seen, to where any grass was stained white and gray with death and snow, where the rocks were sharp and covered in ice. It could almost be beautiful, almost, had I been here willingly. But I wasn't and every single bone in my body ached with that knowledge.

Soren continued to try to engage me, and despite the harshness of the environment, the starkness that made it hard to bear alone, I did my best to ignore him or shut him out. But he managed to whittle out answers from me sometimes when I was doing something rote and mindless like dressing the rare rabbit or squirrel that we came across. Stupid things like my favorite color or if I preferred dawn to dusk. Most of the time, I answered sarcastically which left him confused—I was finding out the whole spiel about goblins not able to understand sarcasm was actually true and very annoying—but sometimes when he caught me off guard, I answered honestly and in return, he gave his own answer. So, I learned that his favorite color was dark green, that he preferred the dawn right as the sky went from gray to pink, and that he abhorred the taste of herring. I learned that he preferred vines to flowers, grass, and even trees, that he let them grow almost wild around his home, that he had no siblings and sometimes he wished for that to change despite knowing it was easier to be an only sibling as a goblin.

I didn't like how human he was after these sessions and how they slowly got my tense muscles to relax as he talked, almost to himself considering the little I had to say to him, and shared and became a tangible person versus a *thing* taking me from my home.

The night I fell asleep in front of a roaring blue fire before he did, closer to him due to the warmth that radiated from his body, lulled and comforted by it all instead of repulsed, I knew I'd lost the battle and I would continue to drift farther and farther into this world as we traveled. Drift farther and farther into him.

A voice in my head whispered *no*, whispered *roots*, but another voice asked me if it would really be that bad to fall into this place, fall into him, and I woke up in blind terror one night, gasping from the voices and feelings in my head.

There was something I needed to do. Somewhere I needed to go, and I couldn't keep falling into this world. If I fell asleep, I would never wake up again, not to the world I needed to, somehow I knew. I palmed the knife that I was given so very long ago, the iron smelling unpleasant in the Permafrost, so strong that it woke him up from beside me. He gave me a resigned look, like he'd expected this to happen, and moved to disarm me, but I turned away before he could and began hacking at the exposed roots at the base of the tree I slept near, eyes widening as the roots began to bleed a thick, dark sap. I hacked and hacked, cut and jabbed, and then as the thick sap flowed, I took it in my mouth and drank like some type of creature was possessing me.

All of a sudden the fire fell away, the Permafrost fell away, the trees fell away, the horses fell away, and the goblin man beside me fell away, and all that was left were the roots. So impossibly long and thick.

And I was falling once more.

———

MY BACK HIT the roots as they spiraled down and once again the voice of Hel spoke. "You're a clever girl." The condescension in her voice was so thick, you could cut it with a knife. "Aren't you? Or is it luck that keeps you from losing yourself completely in your other selves?" The void called out to me, shimmering like skipping a pebble over water, and I glared at the vast darkness.

"Did you truly have so little faith in me?" I snarled to Hel's voice, but all I could hear was her laughter—grating and painful to the ears.

Her voice faded away as the other, more ancient voice spoke, *By root, by fang, by iron, come back to us. By root, by fang, by iron, seal your fate.* Though there was no speaker, the words brushed against my skin as if someone whispered softly against me. The words ran down my body like a gentle caress. Unlike the mocking of Hel, this voice called out encouragement as I closed my eyes once more.

The world exploded back into color. This time grim, the sky right before dawn looming over me with a heavy, almost oppressive feeling to it. Something was familiar about the sky, about the day, but nothing I could really put my finger on as I hefted the axe upon my shoulder and carried a few blocks of firewood beneath my free arm. The cold months were coming soon and my sister's newborn needed to stay warm if he was going to survive. As my father's heir, it was my duty to help take care of all of my six sisters and their children, working side by side with my father and some of their husbands, until we had enough to live off during the months of severe cold when the ocean water froze and nothing grew in the hard, dark ground. When the daylight disappeared completely and all we could do was huddle by the fire and each other, pressing our freezing skin against one another to share heat, until the warm months came again.

There was an odd tinge in the air, almost like ash, a metallic type of taste in the wind that brought me discomfort and unease that traveled down my spine. I crouched and pressed a hand to the ground, trying to listen, to feel, the way the earth was speaking to me. The minute the ground spoke my eyes shot open and wide. Hoofbeats, the sound of dozens of horses against the frozen ground, the cries of hunters who had no human blood, their faces flashed in my mind from the connection in the ground, and I dropped the firewood and raced back to where I knew I'd be safe—in the lake under the rushing water of the falls the river made.

I stopped dead in my tracks when I realized what I was doing. I was no coward. I couldn't run, not when I had a family to defend. So, I turned on my heel and raced back to my small village and into the midst of a slaughter.

Never before had I seen such creatures with so much speed, ferocity, the animalistic way in which they hunted and killed, and the way their faces contorted into monstrous features as they reveled in their kill.

A sword came for me and I blocked it with my axe, twisting until the weapon was locked in the space between the blade and the handle and yanking it out of my attacker's hands. The effort left my own hands red and smarting, but I followed through until my blade was embedded into my attacker's side. Wrenching it out, blood splattered onto my body as I took a deep gasp of air and attacked another foe. It didn't matter if they were human, goblin, some unholy mix. I fought my way step by step to where my family was.

Most of the blows coming at me, I dodged, and most of the blows I threw, I missed. But I was doing better than the other humans surrounding me who were getting mowed down like flies. If I had a moment, I might've stopped and wondered why there was almost some supernatural type of quality to how I fought. It wasn't like I didn't train hard, but this was different, it was like every single step was made with invisible strings pulling me around. One step to the front, dodged a blow, a step and swing to the side, wounded an enemy, like a dance that my body innately knew, even if my mind didn't.

Something hard smacked me in my face, and I went down to the ground, gasping for air. The dirt was soaked with blood, and I gripped a handful of it, screaming and throwing it in the face of the goblin who came down upon me. He spat as he swiped away the bloodied dirt that muddied his pale face and got into his emerald eyes. His hair was long and blond and unbound, and even with my distraction, he quickly fell upon me.

I aimed a kick toward his chest only to be kicked roughly in the stomach in turn, and I curled up into a ball as the pain exploded, sharper than knives, bringing blood up to my throat and lips. Eyes shut tight, my stomach curdled as I realized there were no more sounds of battle around me. Only whooping of victorious monsters and the dying, ragged breaths of my fellow man.

The goblin pulled me up by my hair, and I hissed in pain but opened my eyes, resolved to look at them until the very end.

"You smell like the Permafrost," he muttered before throwing me down once more. "Why do you smell like the Permafrost?"

I got to my hands and knees only for another gut-wrenching kick to force me back into a ball on the bloody earth. Around me, bodies were cut open, bashed in, bruised and torn apart, bloodied until I no longer knew who they were in life. Bile rose in my throat at the smell of the corpses, but I'd had nothing to eat and so I had nothing to throw up other than the blood dripping from my lips.

"Run," the goblin who kicked me said.

I stared at him with wide eyes. His brethren were coming behind him into a half-circle, jeering with devious looks on their faces.

"I said run!" he yelled, and I scrambled backward until I was on my feet and sprinting toward the woods.

Raucous laughter came from behind me, and deep inside, I knew it was only a matter of time before they caught up to me and finished the job. This wasn't mercy, letting me run, this was releasing a hare for the hunt. Despite the pain where he kicked me and the other blows I received, despite the blood dribbling from my lips from some internal wound, I raced through the forest like an injured doe trying to escape her hunters. I'd never thought about how the animal must've felt when I hunted it down and killed it, and the irony of the situation tasted bitter on my tongue.

My chest tightened as I panted in deep gasps of air, but

nothing worked to quench the fire in my throat. Pushing on, I jumped over a pile of dead wood and rotting plants and landed with a cry as my ankle gave out.

Stumbling through the underbrush, I finally crashed and fell down a ravine. My leg hit hard stone, and I nearly shrieked as blinding pain filled my vision. When I tried to move the leg, the blinding pain came again, white and hot. One leg most likely broken; one ankle at least sprained. There was nothing I could do anymore.

My vision fuzzy, I waited until they caught up to me. They would torture me, assault me, then if they were feeling merciful, they would kill me fast. But more likely than not, they would play with me like a cat did with its prey.

Something slithered beside me, the cold, clammy scales making me freeze up as a little albino snake in the dirt slithered past me. It had puncture marks on its tail from another snake, most likely, unless it had bitten its own tail. Even with its muted coloring, my father's lessons came back to me—it was most certainly venomous.

There was crashing in the trees up above me, and a voice whispering in my head *by fang, by fang, by fang*. Whatever they had in store for me, whatever they could do, it would be much worse than what I could do for myself now, in this moment.

And so I grabbed the snake, enraging it, until it bit into the soft flesh of my arm and the world turned black.

14

WHAT IS AND WHAT NEVER WILL BE

I BOLTED UPRIGHT in my bed, my breath heaving in my chest. It was so real . . . so, so real. His voice, his touch, his men. I took a few deep breaths before I realized that I wasn't where I thought I should be. Not on the muddy banks of Hel but in a house—more specifically, the wooden house I grew up in. The loft with the low ceiling. It'd always been a little cramped in here with six other sisters, but I couldn't tell where anyone was.

I thought I wasn't supposed to know I was in a trial? I thought, hoping the voice of Hel would hear me.

Trust me, darling girl, the voice replied, and what it said sent shivers down my side. *This is the one trial you will remember and wish to forget.*

My eyes darted around wildly as I tried to pull myself up, only to fall back down onto the bed in a fit of dizziness. The bed stands grinded against the wood as I fell over and lay there with hazy vision, trying to figure out what the fuck was happening.

It was there, lying on my side, that I realized something. I was . . . whole. My injuries from Lydian were gone. There was no aching scar tissue, and I gazed in wonder at the smooth skin of my arms and the lack of calluses on my hands. If anything, both of my breasts were a bit swollen, and when I touched my cheek, there were no markings from goblin nails. What? How?

"Ebba!" A voice that sounded so familiar raced up the ladder to the loft. Whoever it was was keeping low as to avoid bumping their head.

Ebba? Ebba was my middle name. My mother had insisted that if I was to have a boy's name for a first name, she would give me a female middle name and so she had. But no one ever called me it, no one ever referenced it. What was the point? I wasn't supposed to be a girl anyway.

I stared open-mouthed at the figure coming to lean by my bedside. It was . . . Soren, but not Soren. Innately, somewhere in my heart, I could *feel* that he was the same like Lydian had been the same, like my parents had been the same, except for this time . . . he was the same, but different.

His skin was the color of alabaster, and despite the summer heat, he wore a light, hooded cloak to cover it. His eyes weren't the color of lilacs, but instead, a pinkish color almost bordering on red. His hair remained white but without the blue undertones that his goblin-self had. But other than that, he was unmistakably human.

What had he said once? The reason he looked like he had as a goblin was due to a genetic mutation. So, if this was a human form of Soren, if this was the *same Soren* but in a different life—a life where we were both human—it made sense he had the same mutation.

Like all the other versions of my life the roots had shown me, this world was as real as any other, despite it feeling like a dream. This perfect path with no blood or violence and no goblins or other creatures, but still with Soren, human, deeply in love with me.

He leaned forward and kissed my sweaty brow while I was still too shocked to do anything.

"Ebba," he whispered as if he were tasting the name, like it was fresh water after not drinking for an entire day. "Ebba, you're awake."

There was more ruckus downstairs as multiple other people began climbing into the loft. My mother's voice, loud, demanding, and totally in charge, ordered everyone to give me room as a group of people huddled around my bedside. My father, my mother, the town healer, Soren, and a man that I didn't know but had the strange feeling I should. He also, like me, took after our father with his dark skin and curly hair, and he might've been a few years older. Did I have a brother?

The healer bent down, feeling my forehead with the back of her hand. "You gave us quite the scare, child."

"I— What— What's going on?" This was too much. Too much information trying to cram itself into my head and my head wouldn't let it. It was too different, wrong, yet also so, so familiar and so, so right.

"Do you not remember?" My mother fussed over me. My mother never fussed over me. We had a cordial relationship, but there'd always been distance. Whether it was because I was meant to be a boy or because I was meant to be given to the Permafrost when I reached my majority, I'd never know. Not in this world, at least. I didn't blame her. Living with the knowledge your child was going to be ripped from your grasp for years probably meant some unintentional emotional boundaries. "You fainted, caught a fever. You've been asleep for two weeks."

Two weeks? Asleep? I blinked again, trying to clear the gunk from my gummy eyes. "I—what?"

The healer held up her hand. "It's possible her brain needs a chance to recover. The fever was strong and likely affected her memory and thinking capabilities. She'll be back to normal soon."

"Magda," the human Soren said, "what about . . . ?" He trailed off, anxiety written plainly on his face in a way it never would have in the Permafrost.

Magda pressed her hand on my lower belly; there was a small but noticeable bump between my hips. "If the child survived the fever without miscarriage, then it should be fine."

Child? I was with child? My hand went down to press against the small bump. It was more solid than the rest of me, definitely not distended gas or from eating too much. The moment my hand brushed against it, a fierceness flooded through me, stronger than I'd ever known before. A child. With Soren?

It was something I'd thought about before, but doubted was possible for either of us. I wasn't in the position to spend nine months pregnant, and who knew how the stag's power would affect the child. Not to mention the child of the Erlking would be in incredible danger from those that wished us harm or wanted a bargaining chip. And Soren? He might've been less physically vulnerable, but he'd never put me in harm's way. A child was out of the question.

Until now, that was.

"Thank the gods," Soren said and rested one of his large hands on top of mine. His hand was warm and callused against my softer ones, and I could only stare in shock, knowing that I was pregnant in this world.

Pregnant. Whereas before, in my other life, I took herbs that stopped my menses from coming, terrifying me that I may never carry a child. Though perhaps I was grateful I'd had my monthly dose soon before Lydian decided to tear apart my village. Pregnancy and childbirth were things I'd thrown out long ago as something I would never experience.

And here I was, pregnant, carrying this human Soren's child within me, seeing it grow inside of me. Something inside me was warm but broken all the same. *By iron, you must leave this life,* the voice whispered to me. I'd done it all so far. Left lives by root, by fang, and now I must by iron because others were counting on me. But a sweet dazzling smile from the human Soren made all those thoughts melt away.

"You scared us all, sweetling." My mother brushed a lock of my hair back from my sweaty face. "It came on so sudden."

"I fear I don't remember much," I said, glancing around at the people in the room. Many of them were strangers to me. Soren was Soren yet he was a stranger, the man who was most likely my brother, a stranger, Magda, a stranger. Was my mother a stranger too? Was I a stranger to even myself? The thought wiggled like a worm in my brain, unsettling me.

Magda nodded with sage wisdom. "A fever will do that to you. You'll probably regain more of your memory as the days pass on. But for now, rest. Be loved and taken care of. It's best for you and the babe."

I found myself nodding when I should've been searching for my way out. But oh, to be loved and taken care of without the worry of assassins and monstrous creatures, without the weight of the Permafrost on my shoulders, in a simple life with simple comforts and simple love. Was it so wrong that I wanted to experience that for a few more hours?

Even then, I didn't think I could get up and search for my escape anyway. My body was heavy and tired, and my eyes already were slipping closed again. Soren brushed my forehead with his lips. "Sleep, Ebba. You need it. We'll be here when you wake up."

The man who must've been my brother grasped my hand tightly with his own. "Sleep, little wild thing. You'll feel better soon. I'll catch your favorite, and we can have rabbit stew for dinner."

So, some things in this life were the same across all prospective futures. Perhaps the scenarios were different but deep inside . . . I was still me and I was surrounded by love and warmth and normalcy and the lack of the burden of the entire world, because here, if the world were ending, then no one paid any notice to it or even knew of its changing.

I would need to rip myself away from this warm, comfortable place, and I feared I may not be able to do it. *Just give me a day,* I prayed. *Just give me a day to enjoy this and live in this soft, wonderful world.* It wasn't like I could get up to search the source of my escape anyway. I was still incredibly woozy when I even tried to sit up. I doubted I could move anywhere. I had all the reason to linger in this beautiful world a while longer.

"Jannek." Both I and the man who was my brother turned. Of course, he'd be the one named Jannek, wouldn't he, since I was considered a girl and my name was Ebba. "Stop crowding everyone and go and actually do those chores I asked." My mom's exasperated voice was the same in both worlds.

Jannek shot me an apologetic look before getting up and climbing back down from the loft. I watched him go, wondering what else was different about this world where I wasn't needed to fulfill a male role, where Soren was already human, and where life lacked the magic of the Permafrost.

"Sleep, love," Soren repeated, and my eyelids grew heavier and heavier until I complied and drifted off to sleep.

For a few days, I was still too weak to even get up. Soren had to help me with the simplest of tasks that always had me blushing with embarrassment. My sisters and brother visited me on the regular, telling me of their day, and I lay there marveling at the normalcy of it all.

When I slept, the voice would come, reminding me of my trial by iron, but it sounded fainter and fainter as I began to move around. My body was different now, not because I was pregnant and uninjured; it wasn't as muscled as it had been in my previous life. While I was still athletic, I was softer and I doubted my arms could ever pull back the bowstring on a regular bow, much less a goblin-forged bow.

Once I was cleared to do light chores, I was put in charge of sewing and mending the clothes of others, which was something I'd never done before, not in my other life at least. I did manage to get the hang of the patterns pretty quickly and blamed my clumsy stitching on my recent illness and pregnancy. Sitting inside all day—or sometimes outside if the weather was nice—bent over my work while the men played their hunting games, had me bouncing my knee and tapping my foot, looking around at every place I could, trying to count the number of rushes on the floor. My body itched for the sport and the contact, the thrill of the hunt, even if it was in this weak body where I doubted I could pull back a bowstring.

"I didn't think it was possible, but somehow your stitching got worse," Avette joked from where she sat beside me.

"And she's so antsy!" replied Sigfrid, one of my middle sisters who I'd never gotten along with, even in my other life.

I glared at her but didn't have any answer. While I didn't have my previous skills from my other life, I lacked the skills most women my age would've developed by this point. So, throwing an axe at her head was out of the question.

"Don't tease her," Ika scolded. "She's getting over being sick. Besides, it's her first child. You were an anxious mess during your entire pregnancy. You couldn't stitch a straight line even if Freya above led your hand."

Sigfrid rolled her eyes, but my other sisters giggled and I found myself laughing too.

"Besides, I bet her baby will come out more handsome

than yours did," Jerry teased, bringing back the memory of
Sigfrid's squalling newborn with his pinched red face and
hungry mouth.

She sniffed. "It'll come out a freak, like its father."

I narrowed my eyes. "Soren's not a freak."

"Even if he were," Ika said, "he's a very attractive freak."

"Ika!" Avette scolded. "Stop being mean to Ebba, Sigfrid.
No one likes a bully."

The banter, the comments, the insults thrown easily back
and forth like a . . . like a family, gods, how I missed that.
Squabbling with my sisters, the time I got to spend with them,
even if it was doing a chore I didn't particularly like and wasn't
very good at. I would take this part life. I would take it forever.

Just give me another day, I thought. *Just one more day of this.
Please. I've never known this peace.*

But that night, I found something hard under my pillow—
an iron knife. *Escape this world by iron.* I gripped it in my
hands, forcing back the tears in my eyes that threatened to
spill over.

Soren came over to me, already in his bedclothes—which
consisted of a light pair of pants—and any other time, I'd
stare at him, but this time something inside me felt like it was
breaking. I didn't want to leave this light and happy world. I
couldn't. It wasn't a trick more than any other universe the
roots held within them were a trick, and maybe if I stayed
here, then Ragnarök would never come. Inwardly I knew that
wasn't how it was going to happen, but gods did I want it to,
practically needed it to.

There was some comfort. A version of me would remain here after I was gone. This was one of the many simultaneous paths happening all at once, after all. Jealousy struck me like a brand at the luckier version of me, so soft and calm and safe.

But this version of me wasn't made to be soft and calm and safe. It was meant to be a bloody fighter who stood even with both legs broken, who fought even with no more breath, and who brought balance to the chaos that controlled the nine realms.

As much as I wanted to, this version of me couldn't stay here.

"What's wrong, little heart?" Soren asked, his head against my shoulder as his body cradled mine.

"I don't want to go," I whispered, voice cracking. "I don't want to go and yet I have to go."

He turned me to face him, pushing some of my hair behind my ears. "You don't need to go anywhere, little heart. Why would you think you have to go somewhere?"

"You don't understand!" I sobbed, gripping the knife in my left hand with a pained expression. *I just want this moment. Just this moment, please. Just this love.*

"Shhh." He quieted me down, his forehead pressing against mine, his nose rubbing against mine. "You're here, you're safe, you don't have to go anywhere. Breathe and lie here with me, okay? Breathe and lie here with me."

Escape by iron. Prove you are worthy of Hel's favor. Kill him and escape by iron.

No. No, I couldn't possibly kill him. I could do anything else, anything else, even kill myself, but him? Soren? No. No matter what form he took, no matter what life we lived, I couldn't bring myself to hurt him.

Then fail the trial and let the world burn.

I blinked back tears and clenched my hand around the knife. It would be one stab. One quick stab right in the eye, deep inside to his brain, and he would be dead. One quick movement and I would be back among the roots. One more painful task and I would be free, home, ready to save the world.

Soren still had his forehead pressed against mine, and I took my chance at surprise, slashing with the iron knife at his face and hearing him scream. It broke my heart, shattered it to a million pieces, as he clutched his injured eye in pain and looked at me incredulously.

Finish it. Finish it! Gouge out his eyes and win.

But I couldn't. I couldn't look at the betrayed expression on his face. I couldn't watch as people came into the loft, alerted by the screams. I couldn't kill Soren. I gritted my teeth and turned the iron knife on myself, slashing deep lines in my wrists. Blood gushed out of the gashes in my skin faster than I thought possible, and the screaming and shocked voices quickly became a background to the pain and dim feeling that I was floating away.

I closed my eyes and let myself float. I was done.

I woke up back in the gap, staring at the opening hundreds of feet above me. Would I need to climb to get there? Did I even have the energy to climb anymore? My bones felt brittle, like an old woman's, and something inside me ached and ached and ached, though I could not pinpoint where.

I wanted to go back. To the nice, safe world. To the world

where Lydian never came for me and I still slowly fell for Soren. I wanted to go back to those bright, happy spots that led to certain doom one way or another once Ragnarök hit. It would be worth it to feel the comfort again.

Deep inside, the voices from the roots called to me in sympathy before sighing and apologizing that my destiny was so painful.

Wearily, I grabbed onto one of the tree roots and let visions flash before my eyes. I didn't see any of them. I pulled myself up root by grueling root, until there was some form of light, some form of voices, and I emerged from the gap to the world I belonged in, covered in a wet, dark fluid as if I'd been birthed into the world again.

Gasping, I lay on my back as my chest heaved, and the others stood with shocked silence when they saw me, confusion, hopefulness, terror on their faces. Soren rushed to my side, and I almost winced before realizing this wasn't the Soren from my other life. This Soren's hair was tinged with blue and his skin had a grayish hue, his eyes were lilac, and both of them were intact in his face.

"Janneke," he breathed a breath of relief. "Are you okay?"

Unable to speak, I nodded and closed my eyes. I couldn't get the images out of my head. The other futures that were as real as my own.

From her throne on the roots, Hel tsked at me. "So close," she said. "You were so close to gaining your shade. Your blood may be of the Permafrost, but your heart is foolish and human, child. All you had to do was kill him, that was all."

I growled at the beastly goddess. "I could never kill Soren, in this life, in the next life, in another life! You know that! You set me up to fail because you want Ragnarök to happen!"

From his cage in the roots, Lydian laughed like a hyena. "Oh. She has you there, goddess mine."

"I don't understand," Soren said. "What is she talking about?"

He aimed the question at Diaval, but it was Rosamund who answered, his eyes looking strangely vacant. "She forced Janneke into a bunch of alternate universes in which she had to escape to come back to us, to prove that she was willing to do whatever it took. But each of those universes were as real as this one, and her final task to prove herself—kill you—she couldn't do. She tried but merely gouged out your eye."

Soren absentmindedly rubbed a hand over his eye, and I shuddered when I realized it was the one I stabbed in my ordeal. "How do you know—? Right," Soren corrected himself. "Seer now, I forgot. Say, if you're a seer, can't you guide us? We don't need Lydian, then."

Lydian laughed. "Is Rosamund a liminal creature? He's another hunk of meat on your plane of existence to be consumed by those who destroy the failures." He shook his head. "I had better faith in you all, I did, I did. But turns out, it was for nothing. Not when you pick the heart over the head."

"I'm disappointed," Hel said, "but not surprised. Frigga could not bring back even a beloved god to the world above, the likes of you could not do so for a lowly shade. And you have crossed the deathly waters into my domain, making your fates linked to mine. If you try to leave—not that you even could—I would know in a second. But," she said delicately, "I won't leave it up to chance anyways."

The goddess merged back into the tree roots, and Lydian screamed in pain as the roots entered his skin and dragged him back with her. I sat, head in my hands, muttering curses.

"Don't be mad at yourself, Janneke," Diaval said. "You're not the first person who couldn't complete Hel's challenges. You won't be the last."

"We'll find a way," Seppo said, patting me awkwardly on the back.

Soren crouched down to my height. "I, for one, am really glad you couldn't kill me, even in an alternate universe. I love you, Janneke."

He reached around me and held me tight, warming my body up from the blackish goo I was covered in. For a moment, there was the singular feeling of peace, like we were the only ones in the entire world.

Something rustled around us, but I paid no mind as I buried my head in Soren's shoulder and let out a sob. "I'm sorry."

"Don't be," Soren said. "You have no reason to be."

The rustling came again and along with it some odd, foreign sound. It could've been a growl despite the way it echoed, almost like a human's screech mixed with barking.

"Diaval," Rosamund said, "remember back before we crossed the river when you mentioned the giant wolf?"

"What of it?" Diaval asked. "Also I was technically wrong before. Garm's a giant hound, not a wolf."

"That doesn't make it better, Diaval," Seppo said, staying close to Rosamund.

The humanlike animalistic growl got louder as *something* invisible stepped through the shadows, only showing itself through the paw prints in the muddy earth.

"Well, I think we may have a problem with it," Rosamund said. "Unless I'm the only one who can actually *see* it . . . because a giant dog appeared and it doesn't look . . . nice."

"Fuck," Diaval said.

Fuck, indeed.

15

THE WORTHY DEAD

THE GROWLING-SHRIEKING SOUND intensified as the invisible creature took slow, stalking steps toward us. The only way we could tell was the paw prints appearing in the sinking mud. Immediately, we formed a circle, each of us guarding the others' backs so there was no way we would be taken from behind.

"Hold the circle," Soren said, swords out. "Whatever happens, hold the fucking circle."

"So, Diaval," Seppo said in a tone of voice more suited for a friendly conversation than a battle. "When were you going to tell us that the giant dog-wolf thing we might have to fight would be invisible to the living eye?" He unhooked his featherstaff from where it hung on his back, the long, wickedly sharp blades locking into place.

"I figured we'd cross that road if we came to it," Diaval said, her hands crackling with the blue lightning that signified her magic.

"You didn't once think, 'huh, maybe it would be good for everyone to know we may be fighting an invisible monster'?"

"Now is not the time for arguments," Soren hissed at the two of them. "Bicker about Diaval's lack of transparency later. Right now, we have a giant invisible hound to deal with, so draw your weapons and get ready."

I drew my twin axes. While I still wasn't nearly as good with them as I was with the bow, it would've been foolish to attack an enemy I couldn't see with arrows. That was how you wasted all your ammunition. I was skilled enough to stay alive with my axes though, and that was all that mattered.

From beside me, Rosamund's eyes had the glazed look over them again. His weapons were in his hands, but he wasn't paying attention to the growling or looking wildly around. Instead, his eyes were tracking something that none of us could see, and I had a feeling I knew what it was.

"What's it look like?" I asked Rose out of curiosity.

"Big, mean, and scary," Rose supplied. So much for that then, I guessed.

"Okay," I shouted. "Here's the plan. Rose can see the thing. He's going to tell us where it is, what it's doing, when to attack or dodge. Got it?"

There was a general murmur all around as the others agreed. The paw prints now were circling us, a hound circling its cornered, captured prey.

Despite the many monsters I'd fought in my life, fear leapt in my throat as I watched the paw prints in the mud, knowing that without Rose, we were absolutely helpless. The eerie growling turned into a shrieking cry one more time before the monster became completely silent.

"On your left! Swiping paw!" Rose cried out, and Seppo parried the blow as best he could with his featherstaff. The weight of the hound's paw had him staggering backward, but he still held his featherstaff strong in front of him, keeping the hound from doing any damage.

Diaval, quick as a snake, slunk under where the massive beast supposedly was and chanted a spell too quiet for me to hear. But whatever it was, it did the trick as the hound yelped and backed off, leaving Seppo room to breathe. His arms shook with the effort of holding back the giant creature's blow.

"Janneke, Soren!" Rose called out, and immediately Soren and I pivoted until our backs faced each other. My blood was pumping so intensely that the sound vibrated in my ears. I once again pushed down the terror that came with the invisible creature growling and snapping its jaws somewhere we couldn't see but already so close.

"It's lunging!" Rose said. "It's going to reach over to Soren, I think!"

Which gave me an opening as I stood before Soren. Like Rose said, I swung upward with my axe and a yelp came from above me as the giant creature began to ooze blood from a wound in its belly. But the yelp left as quickly as it came and was replaced by an infuriated snarl. Slathering jaws and wickedly sharp teeth quickly filled my imagination as hot breath blew on my face.

It was an eerie sight. Blood dripped from seemingly

nowhere as the hound stalked, painting the muddy ground red. Up close, blood and saliva dripped from its jaws, and I froze in terror. Only to be pushed away as Diaval made another chant, and a burst of blue kinetic energy hit the creature. The energy continued to spark around the creature almost like it had been wrapped in glowing lights.

"That should make it easier," Diaval panted, her pupils blown from the magic use.

But as she said that, the monstrous hound struck again, and this time Rose barely had a chance to yell out a warning before its massive paw nearly shredded Soren, and before he could say anything, something hit me hard and I flew backward, rolling over a few times in the muck.

I gasped, trying to catch the breath that had been knocked out of my lungs by the blow, but thankfully there was no stinging to suggest I'd been cut. Only a sensation similar to that of being whipped by a dog's wagging tail. Except in this case, instead of a light sting, I swore that deep bruises were already forming where the tail knocked into me.

"Janneke!" Soren cried out, but mentally I willed him to stay where he was.

"I'm okay!" I said, rolling back to my feet.

The hound was after Rosamund now, but out of all of us, Rose was ready and he stepped backward as the creature came at him. Dodged left, then right, at swiping paws, jumping over a lashing tail, and rolling underneath what I assumed the belly of the beast was. He continued this dance, not even lifting his weapons, but slowly drawing the creature away from the rest of us and toward—toward the Gjall.

"Brilliant," I said. "Everyone, keep the hound directed to following Rose! I think I know what he's doing." Or, at least, I hoped I did.

We created a semi-circle, all of us baring our weapons whether they be blades or magic, and slowly stepped forward, crowding the monster so it had nowhere to go. When it did try to lash out at one of us, the blow was quickly parried and Rose shouted for its attention.

"Good doggie," Rose muttered. "Keep your eyes on me."

As far as I could tell, it did. Rose was now standing at the bank of the rushing icy river and breathing hard from all his dodging and dancing around the large hound like a piece of prey might do. The hound's prey drive was too strong to ignore Rose's dashing figure, and it too stepped onto the muddy banks.

Rose didn't dare look behind him at the flowing ice chutes as he tempted the hound to lunge at him one last time, and like any animal obsessed with the kill, the hound fell for the bait. Rose dove to the side as the creature fell into the water which began to run red with blood.

Panting with exhaustion, Rose watched the river for a moment before nodding. "That thing isn't coming back for a long time."

All of us regrouped far away from the river, near where Hel's throne of roots had been.

"Well," said Seppo. "That was fun."

"Are you being sarcastic or did you actually think that was fun?" Soren asked. "It's really hard to tell with you."

"A little of both," Seppo replied, shrugging.

"Are you okay, Rose?" Diaval asked.

He nodded. "I . . . It's weird. It's like I have double vision. Sometimes it's normal and sometimes I'm seeing two very different things all at once." He ran a hand through his hair. "I shouldn't have come."

"If you hadn't come, we'd have been eaten by that thing," Soren said. "I couldn't care less about your lineage. It's not like my father was a stellar person either. I'm glad you came."

There was a stunning silence as everyone stared at Soren who began to blush a pretty lavender color. "I do have the emotional and mental maturity not to hold things people can't control against them, you know," Soren said. "I have a reputation to uphold."

"Of being an emotionally constipated jackass?" Seppo asked.

Soren gave Seppo a withering look but didn't press the issue.

"We need to keep moving," Diaval said from where she was crouched on the ground, filling a small bag she had in her hand with the dirt and muck from near the river. "Hel will figure out we escaped Garm in no time. We need to get to wherever she's keeping Lydian and then get out as fast as we can."

"How do we know where she's keeping him?" I asked. "I can't even see anything but mud for miles."

"There's only one place a soul like his would go," Soren said. "The shore of corpses."

"You know," Seppo said. "I wish we were going somewhere pleasant for once. It's always draugr lair, lindworm nest, shore of corpses, can't we go anywhere *nice*?"

"Next time we need to save the world, I'll make sure to ask the Norns for it to happen in a nicer place, okay?" I said, though I doubted the ancient crones of fate had any care for our small mortal lives.

"So rude," Seppo said. "Why is everyone so rude to me, Rosamund?"

"You can be uniquely annoying," he answered. "As your partner, I find it endearing. Many don't."

"Will you all shut up?" Diaval was close to shouting. "I'm trying to figure something out here, so we can actually get to the shore of corpses!"

There was something in her tone that had us drop all conversation, and we stood in silence as Diaval fiddled with the bag of dirt from the bank of Gjall.

"*Olla silmäni.*" The ancient words and the magic they created swirled around us like a breeze as Diaval made a small cut on her hand and let the blood drip into the bag. Coming over to all of us, she held out the bag of mud and passed over her ritual knife, hilt-first. One by one, we all took the knife and made a small cut, letting the blood drip into the bag of muck while Diaval kept chanting the same words over and over again. Her pupils blew up, almost covering her irises entirely, before slowly returning to normal. A flicker of electric blue light danced inside the bag before sinking into its contents.

"Take some of it and smear it under your eyes. Even you, Rose," Diaval ordered. "It'll help us get to the shore and hopefully avoid any dangers on the way."

"Seer's mud?" Soren inquired.

"Would you prefer to go in blind?" Diaval asked.

"No, ma'am," Soren replied, a hint of humor in his voice as he, like the rest of us, smeared the muck under his eyes.

The underworld burst to life. No longer was it muck and mud for miles to see but a wild plain where my inner stag could sense the powerful creatures it contained. There were paths in the ground, colored and stained all different shades, twisting and spiraling each way to a distant destination. A field was to our left, the grass grown so high that even Soren wouldn't be able to see over it, and to the right, there was a thick forest full of undergrowth that held millions of little yellow eyes, staring back at us.

Diaval waited until we were accustomed to the sights before she spoke again. "We go down the red path," she said, toe tapping the red-stained earth under our feet. "It will bring us through to the shore and the unworthy dead."

Nervously, we all filed down the red-stained path, only to hear Diaval in the front say, "Oh, and try not to pay attention to anything you see."

Well, that made the sinking feeling in my gut *so* much better. I grasped Soren's hand, and he squeezed it tightly in response.

"You look ashen," he said. "What happened to you during your trials? I mean, I know they tried to make you kill a version of me, but I'm assuming details were left out."

I shivered despite the fact I wasn't cold. With my eyes focused to the ground, I said, "I kept hitting different roots of Yggdrasil, and they all showed different lives I could have lived. Or, well, not *showed* me them, but I lived them. I didn't remember anything about this life or what was going on above ground." I motioned around us. "And each life I was shown, I was told there was a way to escape it. I had to escape it to prove I was worthy, but I still didn't know what I was escaping to or proving I was worthy about. I knew I had to do it."

"What did you see, if you don't mind me asking?" Soren said.

My foot kicked a red rock out of the pathway; it'd now turned from muck and dirt to gravely rocks sharp enough to pierce the skin of one's foot if they weren't wearing sturdy boots. "They were all designed to challenge my life and desires. All of them were actual lives a different me was living right now.

"The first one was a life where Lydian never had raided my village. Instead, I'd turned eighteen and you took me to the Permafrost." I paused, trying to collect myself. "My family dressed me in funeral clothing as if they were sending me to my death, and I was so scared of what you would do."

Concern flickered on Soren's face. "Did I do anything to you? Anything bad, I mean?"

I shook my head. "I would scream and rage at you, and you would take the anger and continue on until I was too tired to scream and rage anymore. You told me little things about your life, like your least favorite food and your favorite color."

"Herring and dark green," Soren answered, despite the fact I already knew.

"I think I would've stayed. I was lulled into the rhythm we created as we traveled. But then a voice told me I had to escape. By root, by fang, and by iron, it said." I shivered at the last one, the look on Soren's face when I slashed his eye out and the deep cuts bubbling with blood on my wrists coming back so clear, I could be experiencing them again.

Soren put a hand on my shoulder, holding me close. "It's okay; you're back now. That's all that matters."

"I ended up using an iron knife my parents hid in my clothes to attack a tree and drink the black sap from it; that was the way out apparently. The second trial was . . . different."

If I strained my ears, I could still hear the screams and cries of my family and the people in my village. I could still hear Lydian yelling at me to run and hunting me down like prey.

"I came back to my village as the slaughter was taking place," I said quietly. "And survived. Lydian made me run so he could chase after me, but I was injured and fell into a ravine. I knew they were close and they'd do horrible things to me . . . but then I remembered *by fang* and noticed the albino snake near me, one of the venomous kinds, and I grabbed it and let it bite me so I would die before Lydian ever got his hands on me."

"Gods," Soren said. "That must have been terrifying. I'm so sorry."

"The last one was the worst."

"What happened?" Soren asked. "Only if you want to speak about it. I understand if you can't bring it up again."

I shook my head. "That's the thing . . . it wasn't horrible. It wasn't horrible, so it was the worst because I had to leave." My eyes were stinging and I quickly rubbed them before any falling tears could betray me. "I was a normal person in a normal life, but you were there too, also human. My body wasn't scarred, we were going to have a baby, there was my family all around, and I don't think the Permafrost even existed." My voice shook a little. "It was like someone dangling everything I wanted in front of me. And the worst part is that it wasn't some illusion. The roots weren't making me see things. I was actually living an alternate life."

"I'm so sorry, Janneke," Soren said softly, his hand squeezing mine gently. "I'm so sorry you had to choose."

"They said that I had to kill you in order to get back. Kill that version of you in a perfect life, and I couldn't do it." My voice broke. "It's my fault we had to face Garm and that we couldn't reach Lydian. I couldn't find it in myself to kill you—any version of you. I tried," I said. "I ended up slashing one of your eyes, but I couldn't go any further, and so I slit my own wrists in the hopes that I'd wake up back in this world."

Soren was quiet for a long while, but he still pulled my shivering body close and I leaned into his warmth. His heartbeat, slower than a human's, began to relax me as the fear and despair from what had happened left my body.

"You're so strong, Janneke," Soren said. "I hope you know that."

"I was so close to giving up, to living in that world forever."

"And yet you still came home at the end of the day. Like I said, you're strong. Don't doubt it." He kissed my forehead. "I'm still so sorry you had to go through that, and none of us were able to help."

We were so wrapped up in our conversation that both of us nearly banged into Rose, Seppo, and Diaval where they stood staring into the distance. The path now had a sandy texture to it, and somewhere far away the crashing of waves echoed off rocks.

"Well," Diaval said. "Here it is, the shore of corpses. Don't do anything stupid. Walk quietly, stay behind me, and don't interact with anything."

I was about to say I didn't even see anything I could interact with, until right before my eyes, they shimmered into vision. People of all ages tied to the rocks, their bones broken, and ravens picking their faces apart as they lay there helpless. The water crashed into them and deprived them of breath, creeping higher and higher as the tide came in. They screamed, some of them, who had newly bloodied wounds and mostly intact clothing, whose chains weren't rusted, but most of them moaned in agony with their eyes closed.

We passed by men hung up on crucifixes, trying their best to hold themselves up with their nailed feet so they could breathe, only making the wounds deeper and more painful. Some of their gazes followed us while others stared blankly into space with dead eyes.

The sand below our feet shifted, and Diaval held up a finger to her lips as a giant serpent rose out of the sand. Its scales were dark and shiny, a mixture of black and purple with little veins of green shooting down its long body from the throat to the tail. The creature shook the sand off of its body before turning its giant head to us.

A million cuss words formed in my head, but my mouth was too dry to say anything and fear had closed my throat shut like a trapdoor as the serpent rose high above us. It observed us with unblinking red eyes before turning away and lunging at one of the men on a crucifix. It tore the body off the wooden structure and swallowed it whole, so we could almost see the outline of the condemned man inside of him. But no sooner had the serpent consumed the man than the man was back on the cross, and the serpent slipped away down into the earth.

Diaval lowered her hand, indicating we could speak.

"What," Soren said, "in the entirety of the nine worlds was *that*?" He sounded like he'd run a mile, breathless from the fear the creature put in him. I couldn't blame him. Now that it was gone my heart sped up faster than a storm, and I began to feel faint as I gasped for the breath I'd been holding.

Seppo leaned against Rosamund, who was softly petting his hair and whispering soothing words to the shaking half-ling. His eyes widened to the size of dinner plates and he shook his head. "Nidhogg," he muttered. "Nidhogg."

"*What?*" Soren and I asked at the same time.

Diaval rolled her eyes. "You two really need to brush up on your cosmology if you're going to be the Erlking and the stag successfully. Nidhogg is the serpent that helps chew at the roots of Yggdrasil, and it eats the bodies of the unworthy dead on the shore of corpses." She scanned the corpse-dotted beach. "It'll be back. We're not dead, so it's not going to attack or eat us, unless we take away one of its treasures."

I had a sinking feeling in my gut.

"Why do I feel like we're about to fight the giant, people-eating snake?" Seppo said.

"Because," Soren huffed, "if we want to free my uncle from this—arguably suitable for him—afterlife, we're going to need to fight the giant, people-eating snake."

16

THE CORPSE EATER

THERE WAS A collective groan from everyone in the group. Muscles were still sore and aching, and a few of us favored certain parts of our bodies over others since the fight with Garm. Nobody wanted to get into another battle so soon.

"Maybe if he doesn't notice us freeing Lydian, he won't attack us," I offered, trying to sound optimistic.

"When has our luck *ever* been that good, though?" Soren asked.

"Just trying to be positive," I said.

"Well," Diaval said, "we need to find the ass first. That could take a while." She motioned to the hundreds of writhing bodies that were chained upon the rocks and pinned down with stakes in the sand.

Rose squinted at the open sands. "We'll never get it all done in one group. We need to split up."

"I can't believe I'm saying this, but Rose is right," Diaval said. "But just in case, Rose, go with Seppo, and Janneke, go with Soren. Pairs are safer than being on your own."

Seppo raised an eyebrow at Diaval. "And who will you be going with?"

The she-goblin quirked a crooked smile. "Me, myself, and I. Don't worry, I can take care of myself."

I nodded. Out of all of us, Diaval did seem the most capable. "So, Soren and I will head toward the shoreline, Seppo and Rose can do the middle, and Diaval can check the back." I tried to make my voice command-like, similar to the surety that both Diaval and Soren had in their voices when they told everyone what to do, but it lacked something and I tensed in frustration. I kept feeling like I was lacking so many things that I should have known or been able to do, and yet here I was, floundering along like a half-drowned rat trying to swim against the current. The excess energy made my fingers curl into a fist and had me looking angrily for something to punch.

Soren put a hand on my shoulder, and I forced myself to relax. "It's okay," he said softly, so the others couldn't hear as we began our search. "No one expects you to be perfect."

No one except for myself, at least. But I tried to break away from the poisonous useless thoughts as we walked down the shore of corpses. I kept my eyes glued to the sand, worried every time it rippled of what was lurking under it. Once or twice I swore I caught sight of a flicking forked tongue or a disappearing tail, but the Nidhogg didn't bother us as long as we didn't touch those condemned on the shore.

I wasn't sure what acts one had to do to get put on the shore of corpses—nothing good considering this was Lydian's current resting place—but even the knowledge that these men and women might be murderers or rapists or something worse didn't sit well with me as I watched vultures peck out their eyes, only for them to grow painfully back in, or for odd, scaled crustaceans to gnaw at their exposed feet and rip away chunk by chunk which again respawned in painful rejuvenation. Their screams alone had me gripping tightly to Soren's hand. The screams of dying, tortured men who knew that they would never get the relief they sought wasn't as terrifying as the men and women and other creatures who'd been on the shore long enough and had a dead, blank stare to their faces like their spirits had been completely severed from their bodies.

My stomach twisted as the tide receded and a horrible, rotting smell permeated the air. There'd been bodies lying under the water bloated and completely unrecognizable as to who they could've been or what they might've been when they were alive.

I cast a glance at Soren, nearly fooled by the stoic expression on his face, until I noticed a muscle in his jaw twitching. This close, our bond ran deep, and his discomfort and distress at the horrifying sights might've been easier for him to hide, but it was there like a building storm.

"Does it make me odd if I say that Lydian was a terrible person, but nobody deserves this?" I asked him.

"No," he said. "It makes you compassionate and a better person than I am. If I could watch vultures pick out Lydian's liver, I'd enjoy every second of it. But you're far kinder than I. But this sight *does* unnerve me."

His eyes showed nothing as another shriek pierced through the air and another person was swallowed by the massive snake creature, blood pooling around where the person once was chained. I winced at the crunching and crushing of bones; the sound sending chills up my spine and I feared I was gripping Soren's hand so tight that I was cutting off his circulation.

Then the tortured body that had been swallowed whole and crushed was back upon the rocks, waiting for the tide once more.

Maybe it was my own experience with torment but there was a pulling in my gut that told me no living creature, no matter how evil, deserved something as brutal as this. I tried to picture Lydian, bound to the rocks, regenerating whenever birds picked out his eyeballs or other animals took out chunks of his flesh. I imagined being swallowed and crushed by the Nidhogg's powerful muscles. Even then, my stomach could barely handle the imagery, and the deep sense of *this is wrong* still lingered inside of me.

"I hope we find him and get out quick," I muttered, eyes darting around. The longer I spent on this shore, the more my own sanity slipped.

"We should've asked Diaval to do a spell," Soren replied. "Locating him or something. She could've probably done it." He shook his head in disgust. "Doesn't matter now. Let's keep looking."

Staring at bloated body after bloated body, I knew that for a long time after today, I would be having nightmares. "This doesn't bother you?" I asked.

Soren shook his head. "Not that way. I mean, it's disgusting and that bothers me, but emotionally? Not really. It could, I guess, if I wanted it to. It'd bother me if it were you or someone else I cared about. But I don't know these people, so I don't really care about them. It's horrific in an objective sense but subjectively . . ." He shrugged. "I feel emotions, we've crossed that bridge before, but I still process them differently. And I guess I process this in a way that it doesn't bother me."

Yes, I had to remember that. While we'd established that yes, his kind could definitely feel emotions long ago, there was still a difference in the way we processed our emotions. Either entwined with them or detached from them depending on who we cared about and why we were feeling the way we were. I knew if Soren saw *me* being hurt like this, he would tear the world apart to free me, but strangers? They meant nothing to him. He tore into other goblins during fights with brutal efficiency, not holding back, no room for mercy. If I looked inside of myself, there were reasons I didn't care either, buried under a hundred years of human emotion.

They should've meant nothing to me. This was their punishment, as said so by the cosmos, but I still couldn't shake the humanity that remained inside me and told me that any type of suffering was wrong.

It was in this time that I wished I had more control over the impartial calmness of the stag's powers. When it came over me, everything felt all right, everything felt like it was the way it was supposed to be. It was an alien feeling but a good one all the same.

A piercing whistle broke me out of my thoughts, and I brought my hands to my ears, wincing as blood dribbled out of them. Some of the older, rusted chains cracked and rattled, stones broke apart with their prisoners still on them. Soren, too, winced from beside me and brought a hand up to wipe away the blood. There was only one goblin we knew of who could whistle sharply enough to make stones break and ears bleed. Seppo was calling us.

We spotted him and Rose standing next to a dead driftwood log where a limp body was tied and chained. Even from far away, there was no mistaking the agony. They had found him. Picking our way over to where they stood, a hand grasped my ankle as a condemned man looked me in the eyes, pleading for me to kill him in hopes death by my hands would stop his regeneration. I shook myself and tore my foot away; there was no way I was going to be able to help him, and my ankle was now marked from the blood and dirt of his touch.

"Are you ready?" Soren asked me, a strong presence by my side.

"As ready as I'll ever be," I said quietly, taking a moment to close my eyes and breathe in through my nose and out through my mouth until I calmed my rapidly beating heart. I'd faced Lydian before and come out victorious. He couldn't hurt me anymore. All that could hurt me was the memory that he left behind, and I had other, better memories to think of now. He would not see me stumble or shake. I could do this.

Opening my eyes, I approached where Seppo and Rose were with Soren at my side. Diaval had arrived before us, her eyes flickering around the shore in the way they did when she couldn't lower her defenses and when magic was brewing beneath her fingertips. Hopefully, there'd be no reason for her to use it.

"Nephew," Lydian said in greeting toward Soren. His yellow hair was matted and tangled, full of seaweed and brine, his nails had grown jaggedly long, and his face and once-smooth skin were weathered by the harsh sand and winds. His body was bruised from where the water beat him, and there were thick dark rings around his neck as if something or someone had tried to choke the life out of him multiple times. His clothes—the very same clothes he died in—were torn and soaked and bloody, and yet he still had that look on his face like he was king of it all.

"We have to hurry," Rose said, his eyes taking on a bit of a sheen. "I'm trying to watch to see if Hel knows where we are—if she knows we survived, but I'm not really good at concentrating with this seer ability yet. So, let's get in and get out as fast as we can."

"Sounds good to me," I said, hearing the others also agree.

Soren trudged over to Lydian and crossed his arms, staring down at his uncle for a long moment.

"Are you going to scold me?" Lydian said, a slick smirk on his face.

Soren drove his boot into his uncle's ribs. Once, and then again, and then again twice more until Lydian was left curled to one side as much as his bonds would allow and breathing heavily.

"You know it'll take longer to escape if you break my ribs," he said.

"I don't particularly care," Soren replied, driving his boot into the soft flesh of his uncle's stomach, causing him to cough. "I don't know when the next time I'll have an opportunity like this again, and I figured I better make the best of it."

He bent down and punched Lydian in the jaw hard enough that the goblin spat two teeth out. "You punch like your mother," he said, then his eyes landed on Rosamund's. "I wonder if you punch like yours."

Rose turned sharply, but before he could land a blow on him, Seppo pulled him back. "It's not worth it," he said.

"What he did to her—" Rose began but was interrupted.

"If I was punished by you five for what I did to everyone's loved ones, I would remain chained to this rock forever while you beat me into a bloody pulp," Lydian said.

"That can be arranged," Soren muttered.

"No," I sighed. "It can't. We need to get him and get out."

"You *don't* want to beat him up?" Soren asked me incredulously.

"Did I say that? Once we get out of here and are tracking Fjalar, we can do whatever we want. But I'd rather not stay in Hel longer than necessary."

"The girl has a point," Lydian said.

I kicked Lydian in the hip, causing him to gasp in pain. "Shut up. I said we shouldn't beat you to a bloody pulp *yet*. Not that I was averse to it or disagreed with the idea as a whole."

"All right, all right, kicks for everyone when we get out of here," Lydian said. "Let's get *out* of here."

Soren shook his head in disgust as he bent down to look at Lydian's restraints. They'd deeply burned and bruised his skin due to their tightness and the heat they absorbed, and

Soren turned his head to the side to get a better view. "He's stretched out pretty good on the driftwood," he said. "Might be better if we turn him over."

Before Lydian could protest, Soren started moving the log and continued even when Lydian made a pained sound, now being semi-crushed by his own prison.

He pulled at the chains keeping Lydian together and hissed in pain when they stung his hands. Iron, of course. Still, it was old and rusted, and Soren took out one of his many blades and began to pry the chain links open at their weak spots. His muscles strained from working at the chains, but if anyone else stepped in to help, he waved them away, saying it was his uncle and his problem.

I watched impassively as he did his work. It was nothing different than getting an animal out of a particularly tangled snare.

Finally, with a grunt, the chain that kept one of his arms in place came undone and Lydian stretched his arm, hissing in pain as the damaged muscle moved. He could only continue to lay there though as Soren worked on the other chain, having switched sides of the log to easier reach the restraints. The sand shifted as once again Soren finally managed to bend the metal links enough for Lydian's other arm to come free.

Lydian sat up, pulling at the chains around his feet despite the burns they created on his fingers. "Come on," he said, eyeing the shifting sand. "We need to hurry."

Soren continued to try to pry the metal apart, but the process remained slow and painful for both of them. Now Diaval was looking around with darting eyes, same as Rosamund.

Seppo and I casually reached for our weapons, knowing the tells of our friends when they showed them.

Soren had almost finished prying Lydian's legs free when, from below the sand, the Nidhogg slowly raised his head, his tongue flicking in the air, his cold reptilian eyes watching us with displeasure.

"Bollocks," Soren cussed, putting more force behind his movements until the metal snapped open. Lydian toppled off the log, and Soren was faced with the angry Nidhogg staring at him.

"Don't look away from him," Lydian advised, and for once, Soren listened to his uncle, locking eyes with the angry serpent.

The stare down continued for an eternity with me and the others tensed and ready to fight as soon as the snake made its first move. Soren became unnaturally still, his eyes locked on the serpent's while he slowly slid out one of the other longer daggers he'd kept in his sleeve.

The Nidhogg slowly began to lower its head back down into the sand as Soren breathed in relief. That is, until his dagger clinked against another weapon, and the Nidhogg shot forward, jaws open, and sank its fangs into Soren's face.

The scream that came from Soren caused my insides to turn as all at once we sprang into action. My axe went down heavy on the Nidhogg's side but it's armor-like scales kept it from any injury the sharpened blades might've created. Seppo's and Rose's weapons were also of little use as blood gushed from Soren's face. Lydian and Diaval met eyes and nodded once, an unspoken communication going through the two as Diaval started to chant in the ancient magical tongue while Lydian lunged at the Nidhogg, wrestling the snake away from his nephew and tearing its fangs out from his face.

Soren looked a bloody mess, and he held his hand over where one eye was, gasping in pain as a black, wispy circle formed around the six of us. The black wisps swirled around faster and faster, creating a dome that the Nidhogg couldn't get through, I assumed from its frustrated sounds. Diaval clasped her hands together and yelled out a single word, and the shores fell away in the blink of an eye. Then we were falling and falling and falling.

We landed in a world shrouded entirely in mist with the ground already darkening from Soren's blood.

PART THREE

THE IN-BETWEEN

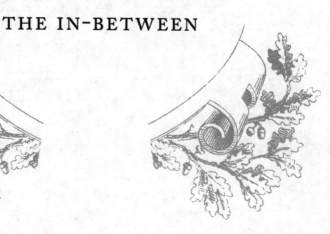

17

AS ABOVE, SO BELOW

THERE WAS SILENCE on the frozen ground as we all lay in shock from the portal. Only Soren's aching moans broke the eerie quiet that was the world of mist, Niflheim. It was a dangerous place, connected to Hel, and monsters and lost souls wandered around growing more and more unhinged at the darkness and mist. My father told me breathing in the mist of Niflheim would take all of your sanity if you did it for too long.

Finally, I managed to unfreeze and rushed over to Soren. He was clutching his right eye and baring his teeth, trying to stay silent throughout the pain. But the right side of his face was bloodied and warped, and the eyeball had been completely detached from the socket. Some vomit rose in my throat, and I forced myself to swallow it down so I wouldn't upset him as he lay curled in a tense ball. His hand clutched the right side of his face where the Nidhogg's fangs had run down creating two deep and bloody crevices in the skin. His blood formed in a pool underneath him, and I knew I had to do something. I was the stag, and I couldn't let this kill my Erlking.

I removed his hand from where he was clutching the wound and placed my own hands on top of it. Before I started, I sent a small prayer to the gods that this would work and I would be able to grasp onto the stag's power enough to heal him. Anxiety and doubt rose in my throat, but I forced them back down like I had the vomit and got to work.

Focused on the wound, the position of his body, feeling his blood pulse like it was my own. There was a strong connection vibrating between us like the strings of a lute that had always been out of reach whenever I tried to touch them. But now? I grasped on the cords, and whiteness burst behind my eyelids as I took in all of Soren's pain. The burning, the stinging, the aching, the throbbing, everything that was stormy inside him hit me like a brick wall, and for a moment, my connection wavered.

Please come back, I called to the link the stag had created in me. *I must heal my Erlking. It's not time for him to die.*

My bond with the cords connecting us tightened, and while still in pain and with my eyes closed, I somehow knew if I opened my eyes, they would be bathed in golden light. Soren's wounds were closing up; each sinew and muscle and cut slowly closed and leeched away the pain. I did not see it, but I knew what was happening all the same as the connection to his body deepened, and finally I pulled away from Soren and opened my eyes.

There were three new scars over his right eye, freshly pink, but healed, but his eyeball was completely gone, leaving an empty socket that was gruesome to look at. Even with all that effort, I couldn't regenerate his eye. I didn't have to be linked to him to know he would take this very poorly.

"Janneka," he said softly, "I can't see out of one eye."

"I'm so sorry, Soren. I managed to nearly completely heal your face, but you have three scars now. And I couldn't save your eye. I'm so sorry, I swear I tried, I—"

"You did excellent work for someone with your skill set," another voice broke into the conversation.

"Leave us alone, Lydian, we're having a moment," I snarled in the nastiest way I could manage.

"I'm not dead or bleeding out," Soren said. "So while I hate to say this on principle, my uncle is right. I'll get on, Janneke. It'll take me a while to adjust, that's all." A lesser skilled person couldn't properly make out the bravado in his voice and the fear and anxiety that leaked from under it. But I was his second half, and in that moment, his pain and despair crashed down on the both of us like waves.

I kissed him softly on the forehead and then looked in his remaining lilac eye. "I understand, Soren." I hoped he understood the message in my voice. Soren wasn't the first one in this group to lose a body part. I had made an oath to Tanya that I would keep him safe and was already failing.

"You look terrible," Lydian said, staring at Soren's face. "The luck you've had with ladies is completely gone now."

"Good thing I have my lady already, then," Soren coughed out in a dry, scratchy voice.

"Shut up, Lydian." I grabbed the bigger goblin and shoved him hard enough for him to fall back five feet. "Does anyone have a cloth we can use?"

Seppo dug in his packed knapsack and came out with a long cloth bandage and threw it over to me. "This is not because your eye is terrible to look at," I said firmly to Soren. "It's because the socket still needs more healing, and we don't want to get any infections in it. You understand?"

Soren gritted his teeth but nodded as I tied the bandage around his eye.

An uneasiness hung in the air after that. No one knew exactly what to do or say, but we couldn't keep ourselves here. Sooner or later, Hel would be after us for stealing Lydian from her kingdom, and staying too long in one place in the mists of Niflheim without a purpose would make the mist affect us even more.

"Where exactly did you take us, Diaval?" I said to the still-panting she-goblin. Blue sparks shot from her fingertips, and her body was drawn in together like the cold particularly affected her.

She turned her head to look at me and I was shocked by the electric blue that colored streaks in her otherwise dark irises. "Niflheim, we're in Niflheim."

"We know that bit already," Rose said, groaning in pain as he straightened out his body. Gods, if he'd broken a bone, we'd be completely fucked. "Where are we in Niflheim?"

Diaval shook her head, her eyes still blazing electric blue. "I'm not sure. It takes time and ritual to create a traditional portal that will take you exactly where you want to be. We didn't have that. I had to do something quick and hope it turned out okay. I'm sorry."

"You don't need to apologize, Diaval," I said. "We all understand."

Seppo, Rose, and Soren agreed, though Soren's was more of a low grunt than any words.

Lydian sat looking in the distance with his eyes squinted. "It seems congratulations are in order. You might not have known where we were going, but it's in the right direction." He pointed slightly right in the distance. "There's a line there, a boundary. If we follow it, it should take us to the liminal entrance of Muspelheim. Fjalar lives there. We have to walk to it, and I have to lead. If any of you try to, you won't reach it; it's between space and time, and other than Janneke, who doesn't know how, I'm the only liminal thing here."

"Never thought this day would come," I muttered under my breath. The absurdity of being led anywhere by Lydian was almost enough to make me laugh. But it wasn't like we had much of a choice, anyway. We were little, blind rabbits led on by a wolf we could only pray wouldn't eat us.

"Can Soren stand?" came the reply.

"Of course I can." Soren stood, staggering to his feet. He swayed back and forth, and when he walked, he couldn't manage a straight line. A sinking feeling struck me as he tried to clumsily straighten the quiver that made a mess when we fell, missing the opening each time. Soren was good at archery enough when he could use it to save his life, but the skill quickly diminished due to not being able to take in much light through his lilac eye. Functional archery, hunting with a bow and arrow rather than a spear would be near impossible now that he only had one eye left.

No one brought it up because it angered him so badly in the first place, and now the sinking feeling told me he would probably never shoot a good arrow again. For anyone, that would be a big blow, but for Soren? His skill at hunting and fighting was his life, and losing the advantage of two eyes instead of one would fiddle with his depth perception until he got used to it.

"I can help you if you want," I suggested.

Soren shook his head. "Janneke, we're over one foot apart in height. It would be physically impossible for you to help with."

"Good thing Rose and I are here, then. We can split the duty so we don't get overly tired with you leaning against us," Seppo said.

Soren sighed as his dignity and pride fought against the feelings of uselessness. I tasted it on my tongue as we spoke. So far the link to each other hadn't been severed, at least emotionally, since I could feel his pain.

Focusing on the bond, I tried to send him waves of comfort, waves of peace, but if they worked, he didn't seem to react at all. There was a certain dullness in his eyes—eye—that lay heavy in his face, and it made my heart hurt to see it.

When we had a moment together, we would need to speak, alone.

With Rose and Seppo helping Soren stay steady, and with Diaval close to my side, we braced ourselves for the unthinkable—being led by Lydian. My stomach clenched at the thought of it, and I forced myself to think of something else because otherwise I was sure I'd get sick.

"We need to leave," Seppo said, "before Hel catches up to us."

Diaval snorted by my side. "Hel won't dirty herself with hunting us; she will send something. It will be horrible but it won't be her."

"The witch is right," Lydian said. "But so is the jester. We need to leave as fast as we can. Remember that the mists of Niflheim will mess with your head eventually. Don't, for Odin's sake, leave the path that I create. If there's one thing I ask of you, it is to please trust me about this. Niflheim is dangerous."

And so, with no other choice, we trudged along after Lydian. Icy wind sprayed on our faces from all directions, and we huddled in our parkas the best we could to hide against the blasts. I pulled my hood up immediately and pulled the mask up that covered the bottom half of my face, so only my eyes peeked out from underneath. Even then, the blasts of cold and mist made me squint.

One by one, everyone copied me, feeling the cold as well as I had. Even Lydian pulled up his hood, despite showing no signs of being bothered by the weather. I'd been sympathetic enough to pack him clothes before we journeyed to Hel, knowing that his were most likely ragged and full of gore. Other than the practical reasons why I did it, I hadn't wanted to smell that rotten *stink* for days. When he originally appeared in Hel, I was glad of my decision.

In the cry of the wind, voices called out to me in the echo of my family, the people I loved who were dead. It brought back memories of the last trial, and my chest squeezed until it hurt. People sprung up in the misty air, not that I could recognize any of them, but I knew they were lost, wandering souls that took the wrong pathway to Hel and ended up in this desolate place.

Someone's hand caught my wrist. I tore it away when I found out who it belonged to.

"Don't get distracted and stay on the path." Lydian thumped his boot on the ground and swept aside some of the ice and snow. It was barely a flash in my eyes before I noticed it—the red tinge of the ice.

"I see it," I said, rubbing my wrist like I could rid myself of his touch.

"Good, you might actually be good for something as the stag after all," Lydian said.

"Don't you dare talk to her that way," Soren growled from where Rose was supporting him. "I may have one eye but I'll kill you just the same."

Lydian huffed and turned back onto the path. Diaval placed a hand on my shoulder. "Are you all right? You're shaking."

I took a second to compose myself enough to speak coherently before I nodded. "Oh, yeah, I'm okay. Just some jitters."

I didn't have more time to ponder what it meant as Lydian stopped and put his spear down to mark the point on the ground. "All right, as Janneke has wonderfully shown us, the effects of the mist can be lethal to even a strong goblin or the stag. Time for a few rules. Do *not* ever look behind you. Whatever you hear, whatever drips down your neck, *don't* look at it. You may see people who look similar to others you've known, friends, family, enemies, both dead and alive. Do not talk to or interact with them. If the person looks like one of us, check to see if it has a shadow. If it has a shadow, it isn't us. Niflheim doesn't have enough sunlight to make actual shadows. Last, but most important rule—sleep. You're going to need it these next few days. We'll all sleep for an allotted time in a place that's safe from the mist. I'll point them out, but soon you'll know as well where to find them. You may feel the urge to wake up and stay awake all night due to anxiety, dread, fear of someone watching you, voices you keep hearing, etcetera. You *must* sleep. It's the first defense we have in the mist. A tired mind is a vulnerable mind. If it's *not* time or if it is time to sleep, I'll say so, but assume if I don't mention sleep, then you're probably gonna have to stay awake. Do anything you can to help you stay awake, got it?"

Soren scowled, and I was sure I had a similarly displeased look on my face. Diaval nodded silently, and Rosamund grunted his response. Seppo cheerfully took the advice, gave Lydian a thumbs-up, and said "Got it!" in his usually chipper voice. Part of me wanted to hit him.

As we walked farther into Niflheim, the breeze got colder but luckily, less loud, and we were able to talk to one another if we raised our voices almost to a shout. But everyone was too tired, stumbling along with sleep in their eyes despite not getting very far at all; the cold itself tried to lull us into its warming open arms. Tempting us to stop and sit for one moment in its embrace as it curled around us tighter and tighter like a snake until it squeezed the life from us.

Everyone, but Seppo. Who, true to form, was making it

a requirement to annoy the piss out of Lydian as much as he could without the spectral goblin lord killing him.

"Hey, so you know my mom's with child again, right?" he called, as if he were speaking to all of us and not the goblin he wanted to torment.

"Everyone knows your mom's with child again," Soren growled. With his teeth gritted into a terrible snarl and his single eye shining from both pain and humiliation one might mistake him for an incredibly pissed-off cat.

"Not Lydian!" Seppo said cheerfully.

Lydian winced. "I must have missed the memo."

"Well, yeah, with you being in Hel and all," he said, beaming. "It's with a guy she's been with before. First kid turned out human, but we think this one is going to be a halfling."

"Pass along my congratulations," Lydian said, "in case I don't survive this journey."

"Yeah, I guess one kid is enough for some people, huh?" He shot a look at Rosamund who gave him the finger in return. "Why did you hide that tidbit, anyway, Rose?"

"I thought I made it clear that I desire no contact with him, deny any relationship with him, and all he is to me and my mother is an unwanted sperm donor. If I didn't consider him my father and wasn't raised by him, he's not anything but someone who happens to share blood with me," Rosamund said, green eyes glaring. "The only good thing about this is that I have a cousin."

Soren half smiled at that, and my heart warmed at the sight. "It was a shock, but you're really not so bad," he said. "Your taste in males is questionable, though."

There was a long beat before Seppo got the joke and gave an undignified "Hey!"

Lydian simmered by my side. "I'm finding it really hard to be calm right now," he said. "I would very much like to rip his throat out, and I can't imagine saying this, but thank the *gods* I never got with Satu."

"Everyone thanks the gods you didn't partner with Satu," Soren said. "And welcome to the group, if you're calm and not about to pull someone's intestines out, something's very, very wrong."

THE SKY OF Niflheim neither got darker or brighter as we moved on, only an endless gray sea of mist that rose into the sky, going on forever into the void of space. We could've been walking in this silent realm of cold and mist forever until Lydian stopped us and pointed out a shelter we could sleep in.

It wasn't anything special, a snow burrow that stood frozen as ice.

"Looks a bit small," Soren commented, eyeing the burrow.

"It's bigger on the inside," Lydian said.

And so, on the words of a murderer, we slowly slid into the den, and to my surprise, it *was* a lot bigger on the inside. Big enough for all of our group to fit, plus one or two bodies. We set our packs down and began to get into a tight formation that would hopefully keep us all warm enough over all our clothing and the furs we'd brought with us. Except, of course, for Lydian, who was sleeping on the other side, away from everyone else. No one dared ask him to come near the huddle and he never demanded it.

I had my head on Soren's chest, listening to his slow heartbeat and he had an arm wrapped around me, pulling until not just my head but half my body covered him. Behind me was Diaval, whose back was pressed to me and whose head was cradled into Rose's shoulder, while Rose lay with his back to her, his legs and arms tangling with Seppo's.

When the sounds of sleep came from everyone but us, I turned to Soren. "I love you, you know."

He smiled, though winced in pain when the movement affected the muscles around his lost eye. "Do you think I'm beautiful even with one eye?"

"You're gorgeous," I said, kissing the tip of his nose. "Now go to sleep."

NOT LONG LATER, I woke up while everyone else lay in the huddle around me. Unsure, I looked around, but there was nothing other than the snow den and the icy air outside. I put my head back down on Soren's chest and closed my eyes, but there was something itching in my head and I needed to clear it out. Slowly, I climbed out of the pile and crawled out of the den, making sure not to wake anyone else. I stood with shaking legs as I stared into the distance. The ice particles in the air were swimming, dancing, twirling around and around in a series of colors; bright blues, dark reds, purples from soft lilac to dark indigo and even darker still as they meshed with the grayness of the mist.

I took a step forward; there was something glowing golden in the distance and it sang to me. Want filled me and I took another step, trying to find where the glow was in the mist and hearing it sing out to me in response. The mystical tune got louder and louder as I stumbled in the darkness. Something shimmered in the air around me as I reached out to the golden light, *knowing* in my gut it was the source of all my questions about the stag's powers, that if I could find it and hold onto it, I'd finally feel what I'd been missing.

The shimmering lines around me became like an upside down whale carcass, like the ribs we used back in my old village in many ways so there wasn't waste. A little part inside of me was screaming, but I ignored the screaming, knowing the light would have every answer possible.

"Janneke!" a voice yelled, followed by another. I turned as the monster closed its trap, encaging me in its long, bone-like fingers.

I ran to the sound of the others calling me as quickly as I could, hoping the fingers had a weak spot or an empty place somewhere I could get free. The warm, calm feeling in my chest turned into an icy fire in my lungs as I ran toward Soren's and Lydian's voices and as Lydian told Soren exactly where to strike. Meeting him somewhere between the tips of the fingers, I screamed out, "I'm here! I'm here!" and thumped on the wall of bone.

Soren turned immediately in the direction Lydian pointed and brought out his swords. Unsteady and shaking in his grip, fighting against a monster no one but Lydian and I (to a lesser extent) could see, he lunged, and the goblin-forged steel cut through the bones like sliced cheese. I burst out of the opening he made for me and into his arms.

The monster that got to me was wailing in pain and the ground shook as it stomped away to look for another meal. Lydian nodded. "And this is why you don't leave the path."

Shaking and out of breath, I took a moment to respond. "What—What was that?"

Soren shrugged. "Most likely some type of lure for a giant or something equally as chaotic. Let's hope we scared it away and it's not coming back with more friends."

"You could see it, couldn't you, Janneke?" Lydian asked. "Not well enough to avoid walking into its trap, but well enough to direct us to where you were stuck."

"I didn't see anything but shimmers," I said. "Just outlines shimmering that something was there. Otherwise, like Soren, I didn't see it at all."

Lydian shook his head. "No, it's something. Your use of your stag powers earlier are probably breaking down whatever is covering your third eye and taking down the wall between you and the stag until you're one being. Your powers are coming in."

18

THE GAUNTLET

"HOW DO YOU know so much about the stag?" I asked as Soren led me back into the snow den and back into a warm position. My body trembled and shook even though it was nearly entwined with Soren.

"Because I know everything," Lydian said.

"That's a shit answer," I muttered. "I want you to tell me what's going on with me."

"Tomorrow," he said. "There's still a few hours of sleep we can reach if we want."

"Tomorrow, then," I said, as I buried my head into Soren's chest, hoping for sleep to come.

It did, agitated and broken, but it did come, and I woke up last that morning with Soren handing me a bowl of pemmican. I had to hold back a sigh. The pastelike combo of seeds, plants, and berries always stuck to the roof of my mouth. The taste was terrible—bitter and chalky—and lingered in my mouth all day long, no matter how much I tried to rid myself of it.

But it was travel food because none of us would be able

to hunt or gather in Niflheim, and other than pemmican and strips of sun-dried meat and assorted types of salted jerky, we had no food. It wasn't very appealing as a meal, but it would keep us going and give us energy through the day.

That didn't mean I didn't have a grossed-out face when trying to stomach the first spoonful, though. I shook my head and winced. "Bleh, that's terrible." I barely stopped myself from wiping my tongue on my sleeve to get rid of the flavor. Someone tried to put more fruit in the mixture to counteract the bitterness, but instead, it tasted bitter with a sickly sweet aftertaste.

Soren smirked at me, his remaining eye shining with fondness. "I can't get over how cute that is," he said. "Over a hundred years and you still make the exact same face."

I was still trying to get the taste out of my mouth and unstick my tongue from the roof of it. "I don't understand how you can get that to move from your mouth to your throat, much less swallow it completely. It has to be some goblin thing," I said when I got my tongue free.

"Technically," Rose butted in, "it's a human creation that we've adopted for situations, well, not *like* this but similar."

I rolled my eyes. "And I hated it back when I lived in my home village too. I'd even take raw meat over this."

There was a snicker from the corner. Diaval, who somehow supernaturally had almost finished her bowl, said, "I've seen your attempts at raw meat, Janneke. You're good for many things, but not for that."

"It looks like trying to feed a small, alive cat to a fussy yearling," Seppo said, "and believe me, I have experience with this. Half of my siblings are younger than me and I have to help feed them."

"It is pretty funny," Rose said.

"She once cried when I fed her balut," Soren said, lips twitching. "Which was probably my fault because you can't throw balut at someone who's only been in the Permafrost for a few months."

"You fed me an egg with a dead duckling fetus in it and said it was a luxury food," I said dryly. "How did you possibly think I'd take that well?"

"To be honest I probably wasn't thinking," Soren said.

Lydian shrugged. "It's okay, Janneke. I don't have a taste for raw meat either."

An awkward silence cast over us like a raincloud. Other than Lydian, who didn't seem to see anything wrong with the comment, the others had dark looks on their faces at the casual comment. As if he were part of our friend group and could join in the conversation, especially when it was targeted at *me*.

"Let's get going," I said, scooping the uneaten pemmican back into the bowl I got it from. With a quiet click, the lid was closed and I shoved it into my knapsack.

It was silent then, except for the noise that came with shoving things back into jars or other containers, organizing the knapsacks so they could hold more without being overbearing. Seppo and I switched knapsacks—his had been considerably lighter than mine. I frowned, slightly offended. Did he think I was too weak to hold a regular bag? I shot him a sharp look.

"You're more important than I am in this mission. So, you should have the lighter bag in case we need to run," he explained, rubbing the back of his neck.

"I appreciate the thought, Seppo," I said, "but you're just as important as I am. However, if it keeps you asleep at night, I'll use the lighter one."

When we finally climbed out of the den, Lydian was standing there glaring at us. I rolled my eyes, not particularly caring if we abided by his personal schedule, and asked, "So, where to next?"

Lydian pointed north. "The line goes that way. Be careful, there's a certain stretch of ice that's impossibly thin. I'll point it out because otherwise we'll all drown."

A roll of hostility went over me. Lydian managed to say these things in the voice of trail guider—informational, conversational, pleasant—as if he were any of those things for real. I knew by now, not all monsters wore ugly skin and the most terrible creature could look beautiful, but it still made my stomach clench at the way Lydian spoke and moved; everything about him that came off as *normal* made it feel like bugs were crawling all over my skin. But if you knew nothing about him and just looked at him, you'd see a normal goblin. I didn't want to see a normal goblin.

Soren's hand found mine. "You okay?" he said. "After last night?"

"Yeah," I said, breath creating a cloud of frost in the air. "I'm not hurt. I guess it goes to prove that it's dangerous out here."

"I'm sorry I couldn't help more," he spoke quietly.

I turned to fully face him and knocked him gently on the

uninjured portion of his head. "You literally carved the hole I escaped from. I'm pretty sure you couldn't have done more to help." Gods, it hurt my heart to see Soren so resigned. Over the past hundred years I'd gotten to know Soren very well, and never once in the cacophony of behaviors and actions from him had he been like this. Silent, frustrated, in pain that wasn't just physical. I placed my hand over his heart, letting it glow for a minute like I'd done on his face, but nothing happened.

"I don't think you fix this type of feeling that way," Soren said, offering a smile.

"It'll pass, Soren. I promise it will." The others began their trek back into the ice and mist. "Let's go," I said.

Soren made a few uneasy steps forward until he found his center of balance once more and then continued behind me toward the line of single-file travelers that we created. When rejoining, I noticed Rose offering his help to Soren once more, but Soren shook his head, prepared to walk alone. And he did, and though his step was a bit heavy and lumbering, he managed to keep himself on his own two feet.

"He'll be fine," Lydian said. "He's stronger than his insecurities."

I nearly jumped from the unexpected voice at my side. "No one asked you. No one wants your opinion on anything other than how to get from here to wherever we need to go. You don't get to judge any of us or act friendly like nothing ever happened."

"You did ask me a question though, about the stag. And I'm assuming I'm the only one who can answer it, unless someone else here has been cursed with infinite, insanity-driven

knowledge that they have a smidge more control of now."
Gods, the cockiness in his voice made me want to strike him.
The thing that got me was how much he sounded like *Soren*
when he was trying to annoy me. I quickly swallowed the bile
that came up with the thought of Soren and Lydian having
anything to do with each other.

"So, answer me, then. Stop messing around with my emotions and stop trying to get me to go into a rage."

"But it's so very fun," he complained. Lydian sighed. "It's
simple. Like my current form, you're a liminal creature. When
your body was infused with the stag's essence, it acted like it
was a foreign entity and built a wall to create a way to separate you and the stag. The more time you spend practicing, the
more you connect your spirit to other things or go into other
places as a liminal being, you make the wall thinner, more
transparent. That's why you can see the marks now and the
outlines of some of the creatures here."

"Until what, the wall goes away until I become wholly the
stag?" That drop of fear had my heart turn colder than the ice
I was trekking through. One day there would be me, a body,
but not me, Janneke, inside it.

"Usually a thin film remains to keep your personality and
human spirit in check. But don't see it as the stag taking over
you. See it as the stag becoming one with you. You won't be
Janneke the stag and Janneke the human, you'll be a mix of
the two. Janneke of the in-between."

I eyed him suspiciously, unsure if I should completely trust
the words that came out of his mouth, but knowing I had no
better option.

The hair on the back of my neck prickled, and I turned to see Soren glaring holes into Lydian's—and maybe my—neck. I raised an eyebrow at him, confused, trying to send across the message that this wasn't the conversation I truly wanted to be having right now and that I'd rather keep to the end of the line with him. But he still frowned and a fang appeared slightly over his lip like a snaggletooth, his features merging to his other form from his agitation. There wasn't anything I could do about it, knowing what was churning inside of him. He'd just have to get over it. He *knew* I was his and no one else's. He knew I loved him. He knew I didn't enjoy being three paces behind the person who caused me nightmares for the last hundred years.

Before I could say anything to him about it, though, Lydian called for a halt. We stopped, bumbling into one another and crowding up so we could hear better what our next step was.

Lydian pointed to a long strip of clear ice. The mist had abandoned the place, the wind blew around it as if it didn't exist. It shone in an almost rainbow color of lights in its icy sheen, like what had lured me outside into danger. Even now, the magic pulled on me like it had a hook around my belly button, almost forcing me forward. I gritted my teeth and stayed in place.

"This is the gauntlet. It's different from the ice in the other areas. It's easy to shatter and falling on or through it is about akin to a death sentence." Lydian turned back to look at the ice again. "Sometimes you may hear voices or urges to go under. If you do, avoid those, or else you'll end up like Janneke almost did last night."

Diaval frowned. "What happened to Janneke?"

"I got lured outside and almost eaten by a giant thing formed from ice and mist," I said quickly, unwilling to let the other two men tell anyone about what happened while the feud was still strong. "I'm okay, though. Soren saved me."

Lydian rolled his eyes as Soren's lips twitched into a hint of a smile.

"Anyway," Lydian said, voice overtaking ours. "We go through single file. No running. Careful steps. Judge the ice with your foot or something before you actually press your full weight on it."

With that, he started across the gauntlet. I watched intently as he slowly lowered a foot down, pressed some weight on it, and then when the ice didn't crack, pressed his full weight on it. Then he did so again and again with a pace as slow as a cat's stalk.

Rose went after him, looking uncertain about the ice shimmering at his feet as he placed his steps slowly like Lydian did. When Rose was a few feet out, Diaval came, then it was Seppo's turn, then mine, then Soren. I looked over my shoulder at Soren, fearful of his heavy, unsteady steps and what they might do, but for the moment the ice appeared strong enough around them.

Lydian never said how long this field of ice was, but my anxiety spiked even higher with every step onto the rainbow-glimmering surface. I put a prayer out there to every deity I could think of to keep the ice steady as we walked and walked and walked.

Up above, my heart jumped into my throat when Diaval

stumbled in a misstep but managed to catch herself before she'd fallen completely over. Everyone froze for a full minute, listening for the faint sound of ice cracking or making spidery webs across the top surface. Time passed with all of us as frozen tableaus in the clear, non-misty air until Lydian signed a thumbs-up that got passed all the way down to the end of the line, and we continued our deadly walk across the gauntlet.

I tried to look at each step before I placed it, but it was hard when the rainbow-shimmering ice kept twisting and turning before my eyes. Sometimes, like last night, it called out to me, telling me I'd have all the answers I ever needed if I sank into its grasp. It showed me visions of events that happened long, long ago with my family, enticing me by whispering *don't you want that* in my brain, though I shook the thought out thoroughly. Images of me and Soren spending peaceful moments together for the past year came as swiftly as the visions of my family went. *Don't you want this? The peace and comfort? Don't you want to sink back into a happier place?* It could never happen. Family was gone, in a better place, and I was here. While I may not have had the time of my life since entering the Permafrost, there were times when I was wholly content among the danger that the Norns, the masters of our fate, set out for us.

But still, my heart was hungry for those images as the ones I had of my family rapidly faded away in my memory. I lifted my chin and turned my gaze to right in front of me, looking at Seppo's back and focusing on his easy movements through the ice.

The lure, the tug that pulled from behind my belly button,

disappeared, and I continued forward with less of an urge to fall into the icy prison. I scanned the field in front of me, happy to know everyone else was managing to do the same . . . except . . . Soren had stopped in his tracks and stared at the ice with his eye vacant of any emotion or thought.

"Soren!" I cried out. Our eyes met and I recoiled: his eye was dull with an unseeing gaze before looking back down at the translucent ice. He began to step forward off the path that Lydian had traced.

"Fuck," I said to no one in particular but started to trace my steps back to where Soren stayed frozen.

The sound made everyone else turn and look at the scene. Someone screamed our names, something about too much tension on the ice. But I knew whatever the ice made him see, it would keep him trapped there forever until he eventually fell through and was embraced by the freezing water.

And I couldn't let that happen, not to him.

I stepped forward on the treacherous ice, off the path myself. No longer was it clear and spiderweb-free but clouded, and the little fissures in the ice ran from every direction at some points. I steeled my courage and continued on, close enough that I could speak to Soren.

"Soren," I said, "we need to follow the path."

"Don't need the path, my other eye is here," he mumbled. "Don't need the path."

"Soren, you do need the path. It won't give you your eye back. It won't give us anything it tells us."

"Why should I trust you?" he said in the same half-coherent tone. "Friends with traitors, I'm worthless, get rid of me, but instead, you rub it in, oh look at this new friend I found," he growled, "as if you forgot what he's done."

Okay, that was it. No more being nice. For Soren to be dealing with emotional issues due to his lack of an eye, that was one thing. For him to be blaming me in any way for Lydian being here, to claim that I'd forgotten what he had done to my body, that was something else entirely.

I grabbed him by the arm, and with sharp reflexes, he threw my grip off and pushed me onto the icy floor. The horror in his eye returned from the dullness as I fell and hit the ice with a hard crack, and the little spiderweb lines of already-broken ice cracked quicker and louder. Before he even had a chance to lunge for me, I fell into a cold so intense that my limbs were like twigs about to snap. Colder than even the river we had to cross to get into Niflheim, cold enough that my blood froze in my body with so much pain that I screamed out, cold water forced into my lungs as I screamed again and tried to take in a breath of air. Cold so bad that unconsciousness, death even, would be a better replacement from what I was feeling right now.

No sounds came beneath the surface, and I opened my eyes, still barely able to move through the cold. I stared in shock and began to sink, then something gentle embraced my waist. A woman, smiling? No, not a woman—or well, not a human woman. Her scaly fingers stroked my cheeks as she slipped around me, her grasp ever changing so I couldn't move. Her touches were kind and tender, like tending to a new baby.

She made an echoing sound across the ocean and more and more of her kind, the margygur, came. So much like the tales of the sirens and mermaids who came up from the coasts told, but also so much different; the human eye couldn't appreciate their beauty, the human skin couldn't completely process their touch, and I could barely process it now as they swam and spoke around me.

I struggled to get out of her grasp before I was crowded by them, but I couldn't break free. She had me where she wanted and finally released my wrist from her clawed grip. Little beads of blood floated away in the water.

The surface was getting farther and farther away from me, but every time I tried to push up, the margygur pulled me back down and whispered to one another, stroking my face and belly and waist, my sides and my legs, the outline of my lips. Their burbling talk came through as words.

Beautiful child.

Neglected child. No more.

Pain-filled child. No more.

Confused child. No more.

No more. No more. No more blame. No more pain. No more confusion.

We take it all away. No more stone sinking on your chest.

Beautiful child. We feed you bits of seaweed and the flesh of the great big fish that traps those two-legged, mouth breathers who stay on its back too long. You become happy. Memories and pain gone. Become our water sister, you will. Happy, you will be.

My eyes grew tired as I listened to their silky, song-like voices, and my body weakened until they lifted me up into their scale-patched arms, murmuring sweet things inside my ears. Staring up, the patch of broken ice had disappeared, and no longer led me back to the surface.

All I had to do was sink down and down, and let them weave seaweed into my hair and feast on the flesh of the great big fish, and wait as they wrapped my legs together with an unbreakable cloth until they could feed me the mixture that would make me like them.

No pain. No pain with the cloth. No pain to transform. All your pain seeps into the ocean and is eaten by the one who no more eats his tail. A hand brushed over my temple. *Close eyes, land sister, be with us, forever.*

My eyes shut.

19

LIFE BOAT

SOMETHING WAS WHISPERING to me. Not the silky voices of the merfolk pulling me down, but something warmer, came from inside me.

Wake up, the voice said. *Wake up and swim. This is not your destiny.*

My eyes shot back open as I was being bound in seaweed and decorated by mud from the sea floor. I struggled, unable to grab any of my weapons before another feeling of calm flooded me.

You can do this. You defy space, you defy time, you are liminal.

I focused on the axe off my right hip and somehow the seaweed binding that area fell away, as if it were never there at all. I took the axe and hacked at the stem of the plant keeping me in place, and it fell back into the muddy water of the ground of the lake.

My lungs ached painfully, but with how long I'd been down here, they should've shut down at least when I was bound, and yet when I breathed in, I breathed air, not water.

Your body will make the plane of existence to keep you alive. Until then, swim! This is not how the great stag ends.

I ignored the aching feeling and breathed in and out as normally as I could with the salt stinging my sinuses and the taste of it in the back of my throat. The mermaids were already crying out as I started to make the swim back to the top of the ocean, and once again their soothing melodies began. But this time they morphed into mutated cries.

Drown her.

Bind her!

She is ours!

Pretty child cannot escape her fate!

Well, whatever my fate was; two different entities disagreed.

I kicked up to the surface, finally finding the light that indicated the hole I fell through—I hoped. And with waning strength, I swam hard to the hole, noticing the mermaids stayed back and out of the light that was pouring from it.

Soren was out of my reach to truly contact, though I could feel his blistering pain, and I couldn't send out a mental message to anyone else, so I prayed they hadn't gone too far from where I'd fallen as I broke through the surface that already started to thinly ice over and gasped in the freezing air.

Someone rushed for me and pulled me up and out of the water completely, but it wasn't Soren. Diaval was staring at me with light in her dark eyes, then embracing me with all she could. "Thank the gods. I don't know what happened to you, but thank the gods it did."

My body was already shivering, ice was forming on my clothes, my eyelashes, my parka.

"Come on," Rose butt in between us. "She needs warm clothing. Please tell me someone packed a spare."

"I-I-I have a spare parka in my bag," I said.

"Okay, that's good," Rosamund said. "We need other things. Socks, pants, a shirt, an overshirt. Come on, I know you all like to get pretty. Soren, do you have anything?"

Soren turned sharply from where he was still staring in the water, his features twisted from guilt. "Yeah," he coughed. "Let me grab my bag." He slung the bag off his shoulder and quickly pulled out an undershirt and a few overshirts as Diaval handed me a pair of fur-lined pants.

The clothes I was wearing had turned to ice, and Diaval had to quickly help me pry them off, before handing me whichever piece of clothing to replace it fast enough so the cold couldn't set into my skin and bones and turn them black. Out of the five of them, only Lydian turned away fully as I dressed—I was grateful for that. More of a spiteful grateful because I had a hunch that my disfigurements by him made him uncomfortable, and I wouldn't pass up a chance to remind him in any way what he did to me. He deserved to feel awful toward me.

The second the cold hit my naked skin, my body nearly doubled over, but I was quickly covered by the clothing donations from the others. I was swimming in them; even Diaval's, who was short like me, hung from my body and sagged. But they were warm, and truly that was all that mattered.

"Are you okay, Janneke?" Seppo asked, concern filling his voice.

"Yeah," I said, "I'm fine. I don't exactly know how I'm fine, but I'm fine."

I turned to Soren, but he wouldn't face me. His shoulders sagged forward, and he was muttering a string of curses under his breath. When I reached for the usual golden strings that tied us together in my mind, I found they had turned a dark, almost black, blue. I could barely breathe through the despair and loathing sitting on my chest as the scene of me falling in the ice went along over and over again in his head. His thoughts went past in a stream too fast for me to fully read—but I got the gist anyway. All insults. All directed toward himself.

I ached to talk to him, but we couldn't do it on the gauntlet.

"We should start up again," I said.

"You sure?" Diaval said. "You're feeling up to it?"

"Doesn't matter if she is," Lydian said. "We can't stay on this path. No shelter. We don't want to be out in the open when it gets dark."

With that, he began his delicate walk across the thin ice, and I followed with the others behind me. Soren was at the end of the train, almost dragging himself along. I winced at the sight.

"So, can you see them?" Lydian asked, not looking at me.

"See what?"

"Look at the ground."

Scowling at his tone, I did as he said and looked at the

ground. The icy ground and the wind blowing the frost around distracted me as it hid what looked like an invisible dome around us and anything blown by the wind redirected to above us and the other side below.

But that wasn't what caught my eye. What caught my eye was the bloodred stain on the ground. Like someone had taken a paintbrush covered in blood and quickly applied it in a long line going forward, twisting and bending, until it was out of my sight.

"Those are the pathways you see," I said to Lydian.

"And now you see them too," he said. "If you look closely, you'll see thousands of little lines coming out of everything, you, all the people around you, every tree, shrub, stone, and twig."

"We don't have stones, trees, shrubs, and twigs," I responded, mainly to antagonize him.

"You get my point. You see the lines. Each individual string is a path, a destiny that may or may not happen. You can't follow them unless they cross your own, love. You won't know what happens unless your path intertwines. Or, unless you're me." Lydian sighed, shaking his head. "And I'd rather not know either, but that arrow's already been fired."

It was quiet, and I fumed slightly as we slowly completed the gauntlet. Ice and mist began to blow in the air, their swirls blocking our vision again. The once-clear ice had the ice dust drifting off its surface and into the air, twinkling with the colors of the rainbow. The sun lowered in the sky as we took each step as carefully as we would enter a sleeping lindworm's cave, and the slow pace may have been making my muscles ache to move faster and sprint across the ice, but walking with careful steps proved to be what kept us afloat on the thin, breakable ice.

Finally, when Lydian stopped and turned back around, I breathed a sigh of relief. "This is where the gauntlet ends. The rest will be mostly regular ice, some may have thin patches but that's more of a problem with ice in general." He shielded his gaze with his hand as he looked behind us into the distance. "We've been moving quickly. That's good."

"What about Hel? Won't she be sending monsters?" Diaval asked.

"Most likely. She could also wait for us to die. We're still in a very dangerous place and she knows that. If she thinks we're going to fail, the safer we'll be. Even if she sent anyone out to hunt us down, they probably won't reach us for another day or so. Maybe less due to the time we passed waiting for Janneke to surface. It depends on who she sends."

"Don't say that like it's *my* fault," I growled.

"You're right. If anything, it's my fault," Soren said. "I'm making us lag behind. I should stay here, offer myself as bait. Maybe catch up to you, maybe not."

The urge to slap him was particularly overwhelming. "You are the fucking Erlking, Soren. So what? You lost part of your face. I lost part of my chest. I'm full of scars, you're full of scars. We both have bad memories to conquer." I stepped toward him and gave him a light shove on the chest. "I know it's hard and I know it's emasculating. I'm not a newcomer to goblin culture. I know you feel desperate and worthless, and I know you don't understand the point of why you're still alive as if the point isn't standing in front of you and all around you, listening to you mope like a child. You lost your eye. So what? You can relearn to fight. I fell in the water. So what? I'm fine." I took a breath, so I would stop shouting at him. "You are more than your goddamn eye. I wish I could get that through to you. I know it's hard. But we don't have time for an identity crisis right now."

I was being harsh, and I knew it. If someone had come at me like I was going at Soren, a mere day after Lydian had destroyed parts of my body, I would have raged and raged until there was nothing left inside of me. I was being a hypocrite to try to force Soren to get over his lost eye even a little bit, but it was true—we had no time for him to fall away into a dark space of his mind. It wasn't safe, not for him, not for the mission, not for everyone else. It stung to be so tough on him, knowing that I went through something so similar and how long it took until the pain eventually ebbed for me, but I didn't think I had a choice.

He still was unable to meet my gaze.

"I'm trying to softly encourage you and give you space to process, but I'm not going to let these suicidal thoughts rule over your head. I'm not going to let you wallow in self-pity until you drown. You're the Erlking, Soren. After all that's happened, you're still the Erlking. That should at least tell you something." My voice was halfway between a beg and a command. The pain in his heart was like nails lodged into an already-broken chest, pushed through the ribcage, and into his heart, his lungs, into his very spine. I knew that hurt, and I knew how tough it was to let it go, and I couldn't judge him for it nor how severely he acted toward it because once upon a time, I was there too.

I took two steps forward and pressed my palms gently to his cheeks before raising his head so he could look me in the eyes. I stared into his remaining eye, still so beautiful, and I slowly took off the bandage that hid his socket, and then gazed upon both sides of his face, never flinching from the now-healed, dry wound.

There was no lying that it was a serious wound. I could see where the fangs had entered through the deep marks on his forehead and follow the carved flesh as it went through his eye socket and out of his cheek. It was angry still and pink, and I had no doubt that it hurt so badly.

"I know you may not hear this from me, it might go in one ear and out the other," I said, "but you're beautiful and handsome and fierce to me, and one day you're going to think that again and I'm going to be there because I will always be there. It may take a month, a year, a hundred, or even a thousand." I dropped my hand to his and squeezed tight. "But I will be with you."

Soren took another moment before he said something. His eye flickered above my head to the others watching, and I could feel the glare as they all took a step back with boots crunching in the ice. "I feel like a child. I'm being a brat, I know. I just . . . feel helpless and that's never been a feeling before. I've known since I was six that I could knock down a grown goblin standing, and now I can barely use a sword, much less my bow and arrows. I became the Erlking, but how can I be the strongest goblin in the Permafrost if I can't even fight?"

"You don't need to fight to be strong," I told him. "Sometimes the strongest thing we do all day is wake up and get out of bed and continue living and figuring out new ways to do the things we once did." I held out a hand. "Walk with me, please."

He nodded warily and grasped my hand with his as we walked back toward the group who all were doing their best not to pay us any extra attention. I had a feeling goblins didn't normally have heart-to-hearts regarding weakness and strength and the meaning behind it all.

The day continued the same as it had yesterday, cold, irritating, but thankfully boring. My insides warmed when Soren and I caught up to Rosamund, and they began questioning each other about where they lived before court. From side by side, there were definitely similarities. Both had sharp jawlines and thick hair, though very different shades, both had eyes slightly tilted upward at the back corner, giving an odd feline-predator expression to their faces. But Soren had a widow's peak where Rose did not, and Rose's cheeks were much fuller than Soren's nearly gaunt-looking cheekbones.

"You said you grew up near White Fang River?" Soren asked.

"Yeah, close enough to walk to it and back without wasting much time."

"Tanya told me my mother used to have a small house there, not a manor or anything, and she liked to visit that part of the woods."

"*My* mother raised me in a little house."

"Made by wood and stone? Fire-warmed?" Soren asked.

Rosamund nodded.

"Guess that means I'm older than you."

"Yeah, yeah. Don't get too cocky, *cousin*."

I snickered at the two of them. When they weren't at each other's throats due to some insignificant thing, they actually got on quite well together. Behind us, Seppo happily bit his lip while trying to keep from splitting his face open from smiling; any outward acceptance of Rosamund also meant outward acceptance of the red-haired goblin's and his relationship. For now, the weight pressing down on my chest had lifted slightly, and I could breathe easier than I could in days. I had no doubt I'd have to speak to Soren again, this stuff didn't exactly stick around the first time you heard it, but I understood because I'd been there, and thinking back over the many times he'd been there for me—even if I hadn't recognized it in my blind pain and hatred—I now knew the lengths he'd gone to keep me sane after my trauma. I would do the same for him.

Lydian had us stop when the sun was more than three quarters of the way down, pointing out another well-built snow den. "We stay here until first light. If we're lucky, we could be able to cross the void into the two worlds by two more days." He pointed to a dark, thickened bloodred line that only he and I could see.

"I have a feeling we won't get there undisturbed," Diaval said, having chosen a space to sit, and was now crosslegged with her eyes closed, palms up. Little bits of electric blue crackled from her fingertips.

"I'm not magical or anything, but Diaval's probably right."

Seppo raised his voice in agreement. "Hope this time it's a person and not a giant animal."

I raised my eyebrows toward him and he shrugged back. "I don't know what *you* think," he said, "but I prefer to fight things of the humanoid variety. It's a lot easier to tell where you need to stab."

I gave him that.

WE'D ONLY BEEN walking the path for a few hours the next day when there was a piercing cry overhead. Everyone ducked as a winged monster swooped down at us with its sharp, bloody talons. The overgrown bird landed on the air like it was a tree branch and cawed at us with a shriek so shrill blood trickled down my ears. They rang, and for a minute all I could hear was the loud piercing ring. I'd never understood why they called it deafening silence before, but as my head vibrated from the sound yet refused any new sound in, I thought I now knew.

"Fuck," Soren muttered from beside me. "That's Hraesvelg." The mighty corpse-eating eagle flapped its wings, and we all flew back from the wind it created.

Hraesvelg. The giant eagle who ate the dead who escaped from Hel. Whose wings were so fierce, they caused the very winds to blow. Couldn't Hel send some nice, happy draugrs at us instead? Maybe a giant wolf or two? Something that stayed on the *ground*?

Eagle was a generous term for it. It had a massive wingspan, almost as large as a common dragon, and a cruel pointed beak from where rotting viscera hung. Its feathers were full of the arrows and spear tips of people who had tried to kill it before and failed. Both of its eyes were bloodshot with clear liquid running from the corner down its sharp beak.

I groaned and took a few arrows into my fingers, holding the extras in between my non-shooting fingers. We all backed up into a fighting stance, everyone's backs touching one another's to make sure that every spot was covered as the giant eagle's wings caused the mist and ice dust to swirl in the air like a storm so thick I could hardly see the enemy above.

Then the thing swooped down upon us, breaking our circle moments after we made it, each of us blown in different directions by powerful wings.

I let loose an arrow and it sank into the monster's chest but had no signs of slowing it down. I muttered a swear under my breath. Soren and I were the only bow users here, and Soren couldn't even use his. Unless Rose, Seppo, or Lydian developed a startling ability to walk on air, they were all useless.

A wave of blue magic swept past my face, hitting the eagle in the eye. It shrieked and lunged blindly down, and I got another arrow in its stomach but it still wasn't enough to fell it.

"I've got your back," Diaval called out.

Somehow I managed to forget—Diaval didn't use any weapons other than her magic and whatever rituals and divinations it came with—I wasn't as alone as I'd thought.

We kept moving, Diaval and I, one of us shooting, arrow or magic, it didn't matter which, while the other one ran to the open space the last shot created and made our own mark, dancing around the eagle like two smaller, pissed-off birds.

At one point Diaval winced as a talon tore into her thick pants but shook it off and continued the fight.

The idea was working as the eagle was beginning to flap slower, its bursts of wind losing the strength to blow us down. But when I aimed another arrow at it, I was shocked to see a different arrow fly into the air. It didn't hit the eagle at all, and I mentally swore as the eagle began to dive bomb the new target: Soren.

I raced across the ice and knocked Soren to the ground in time for us to miss a swoop of its mighty talons.

"What were you thinking?" I shouted, nearly out of breath.

"I can help. I have arrows," Soren said.

"You can't shoot! You have no depth perception! You nearly killed yourself!" I shouted back, desperation in my voice. The thought of having lost him burned in the back of my throat. "Give me those arrows and go over to the others who can't do anything this time around. I've got enough to worry about without worrying you'll be dead!"

He grunted and shoved his quiver in my arm. I laced it across my back, looking toward the count of arrows in my own quiver. Damn. If felling the eagle took all my arrows and the corpse wasn't close enough to the path, I'd be screwed.

"Stupid single-use projectiles," I muttered as Diaval gave the eagle another blast of magic.

I had to make a decision quickly. Diaval had a limit to her magic, and sooner or later I'd run out of arrows. We needed to take this thing down, *now.*

"Diaval," I shouted, "get it to show me its face, the eyes, I need its eyes."

She grunted and nodded, springing up again and blasting the eagle toward my direction. I held my arrow strong and tight, waiting for the exact moment when the eagle would fall backward before regaining its notion of gravity. Waiting until one of its beady eyes opened . . . and there.

I released the arrow and it soared straight across the sky into the eagle's eye and nearly through the other side. The giant bird fell with a heavy thump, and Diaval ran up to it, making sure it had truly died.

When she did, I went through the gruesome task of pulling all the unbroken arrows from its body and cleaning them with a stray cloth. Not just mine either. If any of the older arrows still had any kick to them, I scavenged them too. You could never have too many arrows. Steam rose from its guts and the smell was rank, but the warmth sure made up for it.

———— ••• ————

WHEN WE BEDDED down for the night, I held Soren close to me, his head this time on my chest, and stroked his cheek. "I'm sorry," I started, "if what I said during the battle hurt you. I know it was insensitive of me. I . . . I was concentrating on so many things, and I couldn't stand to have you hurt."

Soren nodded. "I understand," he said, hot breath against my chest. "I should have gone with the others. I didn't want to be a . . . didn't want to be a liability."

"You're not a liability," I said, my thumb brushing his pallid cheek.

"No, you were right before. I need to accept this is how I am right now, and one day it will get better. But I have to go at my own pace and wait for myself to heal." He added, "Otherwise I'm putting everyone else at risk."

I bent my head to kiss him, and we shared a small, sweet kiss, unable to do more because of our exhausted bodies and the people we were bunking down with.

That night, I went to sleep with warmth in my heart, for me, for Soren, which is why it was so painful when I woke that morning to find Soren and all his belongings gone.

20

THE STAG AND THE ERLKING

THERE WAS NO heaviness on my chest, one that suggested a head was lying on it. My body had grown stiff in the cold without the warmth of the other body that had been beside it. I lay there and stared at the slightly darkened spot where Soren should have been lying, but all that was there was his bow and quiver of arrows. My brain struggled with a number of thoughts, but none louder than *Why?*

A tidal wave of emotion was crashing through a very weak wall, and in a few seconds I knew I was going to lose it completely. I couldn't do that out here. So, I stared at the spot where Soren was supposed to be and closed my eyes tight, willing some type of connection to the bond but . . . no. Nothing. Nothing in the air, nothing in the wind, there weren't a thousand heartbeats of all the little creatures, and when I finally, ashamed, crawled outside the snow den, there were no more little lines of color either. The stag had left me, like Soren, in this cruel place. Left me to most likely die at the claws of Fjalar. A tear slipped from my eye and down my cheek.

The rest of the group didn't say anything to me and lingered in the presence of my pain. I was glad for that. I couldn't bear to let them see me like this. My guts hurt so bad, I wanted to throw up, even though I'd had nothing yet this morning and had since digested the food I ate last.

Was this how it felt to break again? To hold yourself together by your arms in fear that the break in your chest would make you fall to pieces? I made a pitiful noise in the back of my throat. This was what happened when you trusted someone. Sooner or later, they broke it, in some horrible way, and left you to pick up the pieces of yourself like glass. I thought I *knew* Soren. At least, I thought I knew him enough to know he'd never run away from a challenge.

I thought he'd been okay. He was struggling with his disability, and I couldn't blame him considering the culture he came from. Fighting was an identifying characteristic of a strong goblin, and if he could fight, then why was the stag still by his side? Not just fighting, but it came to my attention I'd never seen a goblin with a physical disability before.

He'd always been protective. But I liked to think of it as a good type of protective. He'd taken care of me at my worst for years. But now, I could hold my own, I could protect him back. And me protecting him without him being able to protect me must've dug deep into the cultural viewpoint embedded into his brain.

Despite everything I said, I couldn't fight this for him. I could try to say words to break through the self-hatred, but I couldn't get it to go away on my own. It was something you did yourself with the support of people who loved you. Even that wasn't enough, sometimes.

Disappearance or not, I knew he loved me. The feeling in my chest that swelled up whenever we were alone together was all I needed to know to deduce that. He didn't leave because he didn't love me, he left because he loved me and couldn't stand putting me in harm's way for him. Or something like that. Anything other than not loving me.

But now the bond was broken. It wasn't like I was no longer the stag. I felt nothing like the stag. Just like plain old Janneke the human, outsider to everything. Broken. Worthless.

"He left most of his things here," Seppo murmured, going through the packs. "Though no weapons other than his bow and arrows. But he didn't take much food or water or anything else." He frowned. "Why?"

"Many goblins," Lydian said softly, "especially the males once they reach past their prime and know they can't survive on their own anymore or run a manor without people trying to usurp them decide to go out into the cold. They walk until they freeze and die. They usually leave behind something as a note, a testament, for who they want their lordship to go to, and seal it with the remains of their magic so no one can change their choice. It's a noble death."

Something like poison and fire filled my veins, and I tackled Lydian to the ground with a force and speed I didn't know I possessed. I gripped the front of his parka.

"Take that back!" I yelled in his face, teeth bared. "Take those words back, you filthy monster! Soren's not dead! He's not dead! I don't know where he is, but he's not dead, so take it back!"

Lydian's eyes widened in surprise by my reaction, and using one hip, he knocked me off the top of him. When before, this would be the beginnings of a bloody fight, now, he calmly waited for me to sit back up and gain awareness again.

"But you can still feel him, right?" Rose said.

I shook my head and fought valiantly to hold my tears back so they wouldn't freeze on my face. "I can't feel anything. I can't see anything. There's no bond. There's no lines on the ground. There's no ever-present beat of the world. It's all gone." I wiped my eyes. "Maybe that means I'm useless too. That I need to go into the snow and die. Because I can't feel the stag's power in me anymore."

"Well, we're certainly not letting you do that," Diaval said, wincing as she stood. She took her share of the stuff to carry now that Soren was gone and slung it on her back. Once again, she winced.

"Are you all right, Diaval?" I asked.

"Fine, I reopened a scratch last night," she said.

"Why didn't you say something?" My mind turned directly to Diaval's situation. One of the few things I could do as the stag was heal. Now I didn't have that power. But if a scratch was causing her to show physical pain—something both humans, goblins, and probably all humanoid creatures tried to hide—then I wasn't completely sold on Diaval being "fine."

"I didn't want to be a bother," she said. "It'll heal. It's not like Hraesvelg is venomous or has poison on his talons or anything."

"Well, it's obviously not healing right now," I said.

"I'll go easy on it," Diaval said, barely containing an eye roll. "Just for you, I promise."

With nothing and everything left to say, I turned to Lydian. "Should we head out?"

"We can probably make it by tonight if we're fast enough, and we'll be able to move faster now." I caught the unsaid words in that sentence. *Now that Soren isn't here, we have less of a burden holding us down.* No one else caught the meaning unspoken, or if they did, they were pretending not to. Gods, Soren was already swirling with pain when I could feel his own emotions. He'd *lost an eye* for gods' sake. But with this type of commentary and unsaid words . . . I'd been used to people joking about my disfigurement. Not Soren, of course, but all the others around me had been merciless. Those who were in thralldom didn't, and Soren gave very angry looks and possibly more to goblins in his manor who said anything but . . . everyone else in the Permafrost? The mocking and whispers dredged up the pain inside of me every time I meant to soothe it, and being the victim of a brutal assault didn't make it any better. Few had any pity for that type of thing here.

I'd had years to get used to it, but Soren only had a few stress-filled days where events over and over proved to him— no matter how shaky or situational the proof was—that he was weak, useless, and other words that reminded him that suddenly he was *different* and not in a way his culture believed to be good.

A sharp bead of pain ran through my chest. Could I have helped him more? Found the right things to say? Or was I always fighting a battle on the losing side? I pictured thousands of years with Soren when I became the stag, but as the lines on the ground had told me, there were a million different fates for even the smallest thing and even the tiniest nudge in one direction would throw you onto another path.

"Yeah," I said. "We should go." I picked up Soren's bow and quiver and tied the quiver to my belt next to the other one. Unfortunately, I couldn't sling the bow across my back.

"I'll take it," Rosamund said, appearing by my side.

"I can manage." The words came out in a predatory snarl.

"Janneke, as much confidence as you have in yourself, Soren was more than a foot taller than you, and the bow is also nearly as tall as you."

I narrowed my eyes, gripping Soren's elaborate carved weapon. White bark streaked with dried red sap for color. The top of one side featured a roaring white wolf and the design on the sides was a twining snake.

What happens when the serpent stops eating his tail? I must've been going off-kilter because that riddle had been solved already, and there was no more reason for it to bounce around in my mind like an angry hornet.

"Janneke." Rose's voice was soft. "You can carry the quiver and I'll carry the bow, just so it doesn't get injured before Soren comes back, okay?"

I nodded, throat clenched, and handed him the bow, which he strung across his back.

Despite the burning in my chest and tears starting to freeze on my eyelashes, I wiped my face, and turned back to our guide. *How could Soren leave me alone with him? How could he even think I'd possibly feel safe around Lydian without him?* Despite our somewhat civil conversations, looking at him made me want to retch and tied my guts up like string.

But there was nothing I could do about it, other than mourn, other than hope he found us again and came back from whatever he was trying to prove. He couldn't be dead yet. Stag powers or not, I'd *know*.

"Let's go, then," I said. "We don't want to lose daylight."

Seppo peered behind his boyfriend's shoulder. "Are you sure you're okay?"

I shook my head. "No, I'm definitely not okay, but for the sake of the nine worlds and the Permafrost, it doesn't matter how I feel. We have to do this. We have to complete our mission here, whether or not Soren is with us." I thought the words would burn my very tongue when they came out of me, but all I heard was quiet resolution. I was getting better at faking my emotions and responses.

Lydian nodded and began to lead the way again, and for the fourth or fifth day in a row, we trailed behind him through the thick and icy wind and the frost burnt air. All of us sucking down breaths and cringing as the very air itself burned our lungs with the coldness of it.

Out of the corner of my eye, the dancing multicolored frost blew, and I straightened my head, knowing from my experience last time that those beautiful shards of frost could be incredibly deadly.

Seppo followed my gaze and sighed. "Why is everything

beautiful so deadly here? Sometimes I wish I could wake up in the Permafrost and like . . . paint a picture of the landscape without burning my hands."

"I'll get you someone to paint you as many pictures as you want, dear," Rose said from behind us with humor in his voice.

"But it's not the *same*. I want to be able to do it," he fake-whined.

I smiled slightly at the two of them. "I didn't even know if halflings were inflicted with the curse that causes goblins not to be able to create."

"It's a coin toss," Seppo said. "I landed on the wrong side of it."

"Besides," Rose said, "some of us can do it. Some of us can touch iron and not be bothered by running waters. The only problem is that person has the temper of a five-foot-three raging bull and is named Diaval."

There was a growl from behind us where Diaval lagged, limping ever so slightly. "I could turn you into a frog, you know. Not a very good frog, it would probably still have humanoid teeth and shocks of red hair and maybe an arm coming out of its guts, but I could do it."

"You're absolutely terrifying," Rose said, not a note of sarcasm in his voice. "How did so much chaos get into such a small woman?"

She gave a devilish smile as she went for a comeback only to stop and fall to her knees, groaning. One hand reached out toward the wound she said was a scratch on her thigh. Everyone but Lydian ran over to her, a desperate murmur filling up the air.

"I don't think that's a scratch, Diaval," I said, narrowing my eyes in an attempt to guilt her for her lie. Sometimes it was cool that Diaval didn't have the limitations normal goblins had due to her ability to use magic; now was not one of those times. Whereas the others would probably be healed by now, Diaval wasn't.

She hissed in pain as she slowly lowered the fabric to show the top of her thigh. It was red and swollen with a thick deep red gash going from her hip to halfway down her thigh. Inflamed and angry, it oozed redness, and pus was starting to form in little pockets in the wound.

"That's not from the eagle," Rose said.

That must have caught Lydian's attention because he finally turned around and looked at Diaval's wound. Diaval growled at him as if she were a dog telling him to back off.

"That's *definitely* not from Hraesvelg," he responded.

With the eyes of three very concerned friends and one mildly concerned monster all giving her different versions of the same look, she gritted her teeth in pain before admitting the truth. "Fine, I got a scratch from that invisible dog thing. Garm. I didn't think much of it. I did a spell, and it worked until the last two days. I'll be fine. An infection's not going to be the death of me."

While I appreciated the faith Diaval had in herself, I wasn't sure that was going to happen. The wound smelled rancid and black necrotic tissue surrounded it. It was amazing she'd been walking for so long without being healed, if not incredibly stupid and risky.

And, of course, it came during the time where I couldn't

access any of the stag inside of me and couldn't heal any of her wounds with anything that I had physically on me.

"Do you have any physical magical power left?" Lydian asked, shoving between Rosamund and Seppo. Each gave him an angry look.

"Not enough to heal the wound—if I had that power, I'd have healed it in the first place."

Lydian scouted the area for a moment, knees in the snow as he dug in with uncovered hands. Blood soon streaked through the snow from the cuts of the ice on his fingers, and he clenched his teeth but dug on until there was an impressively deep hole in the ground. When we went to look, he held us back at arm's length. "You can't see this," he said. "You don't want to."

Squishing sounds came from the hole as he dug his hands around in it, and the squelching made me want to puke. From behind me, Seppo was puking and Rose's voice rose to comfort him.

Finally, he found whatever he was digging for and pulled it up from the ground. His hand was covered in red all the way up to the elbow, and his furs were drenched in what I could only think was blood. I frowned at the object in his hand. It was nothing but a little root.

He pushed the snow pile back into the hole. "Don't mind my hand. It'll heal itself. Not the first time I've dug into the world's guts. Blood isn't mine for the most part." He shifted over to Diaval once more and held the root out to her. "Do you think you can do a simple transformation?"

"How simple are we talking here?" she said.

"Root to maggot."

Maggot? Why in Hel would she need a maggot?

She nodded, swallowing deeply, then closed her eyes and whispered something we couldn't hear. The root transformed slowly from top to bottom, the bark becoming pale and fleshy before the creature squirmed around blindly.

Diaval took a deep breath, covering her nose and mouth with her non-maggot-holding hand, and dropped the creature onto the wound. She then accepted a strip of the bandage cloth that Rosamund offered to her and tied it around her thigh before pulling her pants back up. When she was finally free of her duty, her hands shook rapidly.

"The maggot will eat the dead skin but leave the living. We'll need to check it out in case it tries to breed, but at least it won't let necrosis settle in," Lydian said. "Also someone needs to carry her. She can't walk on the leg, and maybe once we get there, she'll have more energy for magic, but she'll still be scooting on her arse all during the fight."

I was cold all over. If I lost Diaval—I couldn't lose Diaval. Not her too. Not my best friend. The weight of a ton of boulders sat on my chest—a feeling I'd been having often lately—I couldn't protect my partner, I couldn't protect my friend. It was pathetic.

Please, let her be okay. I prayed to whatever deity might hear me and dare to care.

Rose nodded and gently picked both Diaval and her pack up, positioning her so that she clung to his shoulders, reminiscent of the piggyback rides my father gave me as a kid. He took a strap of the bag and looped it around the arm opposite to her injured flesh before he hooked her damaged leg into his arm so that it neither hung free nor bore any weight.

Then, much like all the other delays, we continued on until the horizon turned into a swirl of red and white, and Lydian declared we were finally there.

***

WITH THIS ONE night between us and battle, sleep was crucial, but even curled up together, no one managed any shuteye. There were the sharp gasps of pain from Diaval, and Lydian's clockwork-like checking of her wound every hour. Seppo hung onto Rose, and I turned my head away to give them privacy when things between them got a little too hot. I lay alone, staring at the quiver and bow Soren left behind and wishing it were really him and his large, warm body that I could cry into.

Our fighting force had gone from six to four. I didn't possess any of the stag's powers, our Erlking was missing, my friend was sick, and to top it all off, there was a sinking feeling in my gut that told me none of this would be enough. We would fail and die. The world would end despite our attempts to stop it. The feeling hurt so bad, I wanted to scream and rage and cry. If I ever saw Soren again in this world or the next, I would bang on his chest and scream to his face, why did he have to leave, what had been so important to leave us to die? His crippled pride? His sense of superiority? His inability to accept that he didn't need to be the strongest or the fastest? I wanted to shout at him, repeat the words he'd said back to me a long time ago about love and hate and trauma, and

I wanted to screech and know why I wasn't good enough for him to stay. Why we weren't good enough to die with. My tears flowed like the sea, and this time I did nothing to stop it and let the pain flow out of me in a rushing river of tears and sobs and curses.

After a quarter hour, I dried my tears; all they were doing was distracting me from the precious sleep I needed. Diaval wouldn't want me to cry; she'd want me to fight with twice the strength so she could fight alongside me in spirit. She wouldn't want me to grieve; she would want me to kill the thing that did her in, and if I couldn't kill it, she would want me to face it, never fear it, and spit in its metaphorical face.

I had to do that now, for Diaval.

When I did finally fall asleep, I dreamt of the world on fire.

21

WE ALL FALL DOWN

IT WASN'T SURPRISING to find myself wide awake in the early hours of the morning, watching patches of red break through the misty sky. There was too much going on, too much to think about, and in a few hours, we had to fight a monster, stronger than anything we'd been up against before, and our forces were decimated with Diaval sick and Soren gone.

Usually someone had some lucky, harebrained plan that ended up working, but no one here was inspired at all. It was like we were all resigned to this fight somehow leading to our deaths, to Diaval's death, to Soren's death. What would happen to the stag's power if I died? I still couldn't reach it, not even when I stretched my mind to the farthest corners I could. Maybe it had already been drained from me and passed on to another person, someone who may not be in intimate danger of dying.

Sometime, still before everyone else was awake, Rose came and sat outside with me.

"I'm sorry, by the way," he said. "About Soren. I don't know why he did what he did, but leaving you high and dry like that . . . asshole could've wrote a note or something."

I *hmm*ed in response. Soren wasn't really a note type of person; then again, he also never struck me as the type to leave in the middle of a crisis either. He was good, but he had his faults. So did I. But I thought that our ability to openly speak with each other had changed for the better in the last year. Maybe I didn't know him as well as I thought I did.

But none of that speculation would do us any good now. We had an enemy, we had to kill it, our odds were low but they weren't zero. Whatever Soren's motives were, they didn't matter. He was gone and lingering on whys and other questions wouldn't ever make me feel any better. Despite the pain in my chest, I needed to get on with this.

"How's Diaval?" I asked after a moment of quiet.

Rose shook his head. "The trick with the maggot saved her life, probably. It ate all the necrotic tissue and left the healthy parts alone, so we were able to remove it. The wound doesn't have much pus in it anymore, but it's still really red and angry inside and on the skin around it." He sighed. "Maybe it's the best thing Lydian's ever done for us."

"I don't like thinking of 'Lydian' and 'best' in the same sentence. He's here for his own survival. He was willing to unbalance the entire Permafrost and assaulted and disfigured innocent people." A bad taste formed in my mouth. "I try not to judge as much as I used to, but some things you can't forgive. But you're right. It's odd to say, but I'm grateful Lydian knew what to do."

"At least he's not an incoherent mess anymore," Rosamund said.

I snorted. "Small miracles."

"Diaval isn't waking up, though," he said, tone switching to become more serious. "She's not dead, but . . . she's not asleep in the regular way. I can't rouse her. I don't know how long she'll be that way or what we can do."

"She has to wake up. Even if she can't fight. She's the strongest out of all of us and the only thing keeping us together," I said. "Never mind the Erlking and the stag and Lydian as a liminal being, if we didn't have Diaval smash our heads together every time we argued, we'd be dead already."

Rose's lips quirked up. "You're not wrong about that."

I opened the pack beside me as well as my jar of pemmican, eating the last spoonfuls before there was none left. The paste was thick and hard to swallow, even with water, and once again I found myself making a face at the taste of the food. Somehow it managed to taste worse than usual.

"Disgusting," I finally said once I could unstick my tongue from the roof of my mouth.

Rose chuckled at the sight, and I rolled my eyes and said, "Did Seppo ever tell you how we met?"

"He mentioned it before. Something about dragons and nökkens and annoying Lydian, and you threatening him with physical actions every time he annoyed you."

"Yeah, that's basically it." The sky was turning beyond the thick mist, and soon those sleeping would be woken so we could examine Fjalar's lair and maybe think of a plan before we went in with weapons raised. Or, at least, Lydian and Seppo would wake. I wasn't sure what would happen with Diaval.

Closing my eyes, I sent out a prayer to Freya, among other things the goddess of magic users, and begged for her to save Diaval's life. I couldn't lose her yet. She was a light in my darkness, the snarky voice when all the guys did something dumb, and the first person who'd sought me out after the coronation, practically forcing her magic lessons onto me with dark sparkling eyes.

Now all I saw when I shut my eyes was her on the ground, rolled up with her knees to her chest, shivering but never waking. The life drained from her—unable to make any movements, let alone comments. Terror built up in me at the thought of her dying. At anyone here dying. Okay, maybe not Lydian, but everyone else.

WHEN THE REST of the group woke, they ate the final portions of their meals and sat soberly with the two of us as the day finally peeked into existence. Even Seppo, never without a joke, was somber as he stared back into the burrow we'd been sleeping in. Diaval lay in there, covered with every fur and blanket imaginable, with supply bags left for her so she knew she wouldn't starve, and a note in case she woke up but we failed in our battle.

Without so much as a word, we grabbed our weapons and followed Lydian. The snow and ice beneath us was stained black as if it were burned, and heat began to fizzle in the air, making the ice specks melt in mid-swirl until they were replaced by ash.

We approached a giant fjord, standing at the edge of the left fork where there was still snow and ice. On the other side, hot lava ran through and dripped down stone that fissured the earth there. For the first time in days, my eyes lay on a landscape other than snow and ice—trees and large boulders and a giant cave that rested in the middle of the fork and looked like it went deep down into the ground, farther than the eye could see.

The ground shook suddenly, and I fell over as the others scrambled to hang onto their balance. My elbow hit something hard; wincing at the sharp pain, I scurried toward the others as they dove behind a boulder.

"This is it," Lydian hissed. "If you have any prayers, say them now."

I tensed with my bow already in position and three arrows in my hand, two tucked away in my back fingers until I could use them. With my heart beating in my throat, I wouldn't have time to keep reaching back for every single arrow.

The ground continued to quake as Fjalar continued toward the entrance of his lair. Did he know we were out here? Could he smell our blood? Did it smell *good* to him? I wasn't sure I wanted to know.

"How big is Fjalar, anyway?" Seppo asked quietly. "Like, I know it's basically a giant rooster but roosters are pretty small, so how much of a threat could it be?"

"Does the fact that it could end the world mean nothing to you?" Rose said. "I'm very sure it's big and deadly."

"The books describe it as bigger than a small mountain, but they tend to overexaggerate," Lydian said. "They like doing that with the godly creatures of the nine realms wherever they lurk. But I have a feeling that my son is right, if less verbose, regarding the rooster being 'very big and deadly.'"

"Don't call me your son," Rose growled but earned a shush from Lydian as the giant creature ambled out of its home, dragging a chain that was attached to one scaly leg—probably the only thing keeping it from going on a killing rampage.

My breath was stolen from my lungs as I finally saw the monster in full. I knew it was supposed to essentially be a giant rooster, but whoever had written that description was being incredibly generous.

Fjalar's beak was impossibly sharp, and he had black gums that created a stain around his mouth. His feathers—if you could call them that—started out on his skin as scaly appendages before turning into feathers with razor sharp edges, and each wing had a vicious claw. But even more vicious were his scaly, disfigured feet with their wide talons that gleamed in the sunlight—less like the feet of a bird and more like the feet of a dragon.

Seppo sucked in a breath. "That is a monster cock."

"Honestly, Seppo? Timing," Rose said as he tracked the beast with his eyes.

"I feel like we should attack from different spots. Janneke in the front, Seppo and I will take the sides. Lydian, you dive in wherever someone is struggling." Rose continued, "That's our best shot at this."

"Wait," I said. "That thing's taller than all of us. Other than me, how are we supposed to even hit it?"

Rose frowned, taking that into consideration. "Aim for the underbelly if you don't have the reach. Seppo might be able to stab at the wings. You'll be our main source of power, Janneke, so that whole arrow-in-the-eye trick would do well right now." He looked at Lydian. "Do you even *have* a weapon?"

"You think these fine people"—he motioned toward me and an empty spot which I assumed represented Soren—"let me carry a weapon?"

I sighed and pulled out the two axes stashed on my hips. "These are mine, and I want them back."

"How good are you at throwing axes?" Rose asked Lydian.

"Better than Soren back when he had two eyes," Lydian said.

I clenched my fist at the joke but didn't say anything. We couldn't divide ourselves anymore.

Seppo was still staring at the "monster cock" as he called it. "Let's go do this before my rational mind finally kicks in and I flee in terror."

We all glanced toward one another, nodding our agreement, and then rose from behind the boulder. We barely got a chance to get away before Fjalar's great beak smashed down where we had been hiding, cracking the boulder open and turning it into a pile of little rocks with the strength of the strike. The groove in the earth where we'd been sitting was massive, enough for a fully grown person to be able to stand inside and not see over the top of the hole.

It took everything inside of me not to freeze in shock and

horror at the destruction one peck from Fjalar's beak caused. But the claw of the massive beast came down right before me and ripped my clothing as I rolled away just in time.

Rose, Seppo, and even Lydian had varying looks of shock on their faces, eyes wide and their jaws dropped slightly open. But they followed Rose's orders as their shock began to wear off.

Seppo had his featherstaff out and was quickly rushing in and out from underneath the bird, avoiding the legs as much as he could as they swatted at him and made large craters in the ground while doing so. Every so often, he got a hit and the bird would shriek but thankfully not the shriek we were fighting to keep it away from. The shrieks to start Fimbulwinter were alleged to shake the very ground and make all living creatures fall to their knees in pain. The first shriek released the army of the dead all by itself, while the second broke Fenrir's—the giant wolf whose children would eat the sun and moon and turn the world dark and silent—chains, the third woke the angry giants from their sleep, and all together the battle for the end of the world would begin.

I took a defensive position, lined up a shot, and scowled when my arrows did nothing against the scale-like skin of the creature, only ripping through the feathered part. Once again, I would have to aim for the eye or maybe the throat and chest where the skin might be weaker.

Rose had gotten creative and tied his axes to the end of two ropes and swung them around individually before aiming for the giant rooster. One swing missed but the other lodged in the non-scaly part of the wing, and Fjalar screamed in pain and lashed out with a mighty swing of his wing and knocked Rose clear across the battleground and into another boulder. The force caused the boulder to crack like a spiderweb and crumple over, some falling backward and some hitting Rosamund. Blood streaked his body, and he didn't move from where he'd been thrown. He gave a painstaking groan.

"Rose!" Seppo cried out in anguish, and from his very face, it was easy to see he was fighting internally whether he should continue to fight or run to his lover. His eyes became set hard in his face in an expression I'd barely ever seen on him, and he turned on his heel to face Fjalar.

"I will gut you for that," he growled. "Cover your ears!"

Lydian and I both had the sense to retreat with our ears covered as Seppo let out a mighty whistle causing the oversized bird to drop to its knees, screaming in pain. Seppo himself had his fists clenched so hard that blood began to pour from the marks of his nails and dribbled down his nose, ears, and eyes.

Fjalar bled out of the same orifices, and Seppo increased the pitch of his whistle as the blood came more freely from his face, and he himself became pale and shaking. His whistle also filled his mouth with blood and it dripped down his chin.

Eyes, ears, nose, mouth, all openings in the face bleeding as his face became pale and drawn, his cheekbones hollowed out, his eyes bulging and bloodshot—fear flashed like lightning in my body. In my brain Seppo was safe, he was kind, he couldn't harm me. Now with his bloody, emaciated body and the fire in his eyes, he was like a demon straight out of Hel.

The bird lay its head down and used its wings to cover

its face from the infernal noise, and Seppo began his charge. Quickly at first, but the toll of his power was taking from him too, and as he rose in pitch, the skin of his arms began to split open in vertical cuts. Blood ran down and darkened his clothing before he was halfway there. The tiny wounds we all received—scratches and stings and regular wear and tear—opened all over his body like blood eyes, weeping with rage.

Lydian and I exchanged a look, and we nodded toward each other as he bolted forward to grab Seppo and throw him out of the way, breaking his magic whistle. The cuts on his arms didn't close up, though the blood on Seppo's face continued to trickle to a stop while the freshly opened wounds slowly returned to their normal forms. He turned his rage onto his savior.

"Why did you do that?" he shouted. "I was about to kill it!"

"You were about to kill *yourself*," Lydian said.

As if to prove his point, Seppo suddenly gasped and fell to his knees, coughing up blood as he did so. Lydian grabbed the back of his hood and hauled him over to where Rosamund lay, and with a growl on his lips, he told him to stay right there. The growl probably wasn't needed as Seppo could barely keep his eyes open and blood still fell from the orifices in his face.

Which left the fight to me and Lydian. For once, fighting together to help each other instead of kill each other. Somewhere, the gods were laughing at the irony of me defending my most-hated enemy.

I managed to get an arrow in one of Fjalar's eyes. Remembering what my father taught me. Breathe, nock your arrow, breathe, draw back your bowstring, breathe, catch sight of your target, then release as you expel the air inside of you. The arrow soared true and landed the hit, but either it wasn't sharp enough or wasn't deep enough because the beast still lived, and the arrow only made a superficial wound.

Again and again I shot until I realized I was running low on arrows in my own quiver and soon would have to switch to Soren's. Some of the arrows stuck out of Fjalar in an awkward angle, but mostly they only mildly bothered him, as he shook off most of the projectiles with little to no care.

Lydian took a stance beside me. "We're not going to win this fight," he said emotionlessly.

"We have to try, at least!" I argued.

"Look around you. What do you think we've been doing?" Lydian motioned toward the blood-splattered ground and the two fallen bodies of our friends. "We're lucky they still are alive," he said.

"We have to do this. We can't let the end of the world happen!" I shouted.

He shook his head. "I appreciate your determination. It has always impressed me, in fact. But we're not going to win this battle. We'll die."

"We need one last chance! We need to try!" My face was hot and desperate; my clothes clung to my skin with either sweat or blood. Deep down in my body, my muscles screamed and my bones ached, and the world was fuzzy in my eyes. I leaned dangerously on my bow, breathing heavy and fast.

From beside me, Lydian didn't look much better, and the two others fighting with us lay in a pile, alive but unconscious.

Lydian was right. We would die out here fighting a battle that we couldn't have won in the first place. Fjalar made a run for us, but the chain around his ankle kept him from actually catching up to us, and for that I was thankful, as the two of us backed off and ran to the unconscious bodies of our friend. Seppo moaned when I checked over him and I mouthed, *I tried.* I brushed his hair back and told him he was a hero while Lydian was looking at Rosamund with something bordering on sentimentality in his eyes. Like it was the first time he was actually viewing his son in depth. He heaved Rose over his shoulder, and I put Seppo's arm around mine as we stumbled back in retreat.

Back in the burrow, someone checked on Diaval, whose state had stayed the same. We laid Rose next to her as they were both unconscious and maybe could share warmth with each other. Seppo fought his way to Rose's other side before he passed out as well.

My own body ached so badly, it was all I could do to lay a fur on the ground so I wasn't sleeping on the ice before I fell over and started to quiver. My eyelids fought to stay open despite feeling like someone had tied sandbags to them. Try as I might, I couldn't stop shaking. The battle had sapped energy from me even without serious wounds.

Lydian peered out of the burrow, looking for what, I didn't know. He closed his eyes and sighed in defeat before climbing back into the burrow. I made it a point to be as far away on the opposite side as possible from him. The entire trip I'd had a buffer between us with my other friends and comrades, and now I was alone with the goblin who not only admitted to torturing me due to his wrongful interpretation of a vision, but stated without any doubt or waver in his voice that he would do it again if he had to. I wouldn't lie about how uncomfortable that made me, but I had to remember that he couldn't do anything now. If anything, I was more afraid for my friends than Lydian's shade.

But the fear for them didn't have time to penetrate my mind fully as the ground started to rumble again, the little ice chunks and rocks shaking madly. The scent of something burning filled the air, and for a moment, all noise stopped from the tiniest of insects to the largest of monsters.

Fjalar cried out from his domain, just once, but once was enough to have the entire ground shake, to burn the air around us, and to take away our hearing, leaving us with ears ringing and bleeding from the loud shrillness of it all. It was like a combination of all the worst sounds—nails on a chalkboard, the shriek of a dying sow, the dying moans of the men on the shore of corpses, the battle cries of a team of goblin raiders as they tore about my home, the first time Lydian truly snarled when I was his captive, the anguished cries of Soren as his eye was ripped from his face—all of that and much, much more. All there was and all there had been was this sound, this deathly, shrill sound that shook the ground and broke the world around it.

When it stopped, all I could do was lie there in shock; from across the burrow, Lydian was also in the same pose.

"Two more cries," he murmured to himself. "One for the dead, one for the chained, and one for the sleeping."

But as our ears stopped ringing and began to pick up actual

sound again, there was no second or third cry. We still had a chance to stop Fimbulwinter . . . except, did we really? Four out of six of us were majorly injured, and Lydian and I couldn't kill it alone.

The sandbags pulling on my eyelids finally did the trick and my eyes closed. But instead of blackness, there was a white piercing light. It whispered to me as I fell into unconsciousness and told me what to do. My last thought before I drifted into sleep was if it would hurt very much to be eaten alive.

22

ODIN'S OTHER EYE

I T WAS A feeling I had deep down inside of me. Not like the way the stag's abilities or my connection to Soren felt. It was 100 percent my own—not tainted or touched by anything. It frightened me, but it also hardened the resolve around me. That I didn't need the stag's power or any magic or weapons to do this.

I didn't know *why* it was that way, just that I did, and I knew to trust it.

I left the burrow early, before the dawn's light began to brighten the sky. My only weapons were my bow and one arrow, the tip soaked in flammable fabric that I managed to find. A piece of flint and steel. Other than this, I was going in empty.

Praying to myself that my intuition was true, I stroked the stone until it sparked and until that spark caught the edge of the flammable fabric and burst into flames. Standing, I notched the arrow and with one more silent thought—*please see this, please come to me*—I let the arrow soar through the sky like a comet, farther and farther away until I could no longer see its light.

Heading to the mouth of the cave of Fjalar, I found a safe spot to sit and wait until morning light came. For the moment when the gray sky turned pink with dawn just as Soren liked.

I wouldn't risk any more friends' (and enemies') lives during this fight. A hardened ball of resolve was in my stomach. Somehow I *knew* the way we approached it—all of us together—was wrong. There was some sort of spiritual residue I couldn't pin down that came from Fjalar, and if I was right about my feelings, if I could trust them, this would work.

It had to. There were no other options.

I breathed in and out. Calm, like Diaval had taught me. Clearing my mind of all my fear and anxiety, all my doubts and worries, until the calmness flowed through my body like clear water, washing away everything. I knew what I had to do, and for once, neither doubt nor fear lingered with my knowledge, only surety and focus.

The sky began to turn a pale gray ever so slowly, and with each dark shade that faded into brighter ones, my stomach clenched with doubt. I forced myself to swallow it down and go back to my breathing. Even if my gut feeling was wrong, this was still how I chose to go out.

Fingering a piece of Diaval's ritual chalk, I began to draw a large circle around the area. From as far as behind the boulders near the burrow the others rested in and as close to Fjalar's lair as I dared without getting close enough so that the rooster itself couldn't step into the circle. My hand drew like it wasn't a part of my own body. Something inside me filled me up as I took each symbol and each line and chanted words unfamiliar to me. A brilliant type of floating feeling in my body seeped out with every type of symbol I drew. Magic leaked out of me and coated the symbols with invisible color and invisible power and something else that I couldn't grasp yet.

When I finished drawing and chanting, I went back by the boulders to wait. The sun was beginning to rise, and for the first time in Niflheim, it looked like a clear, non-misty day. Coincidence or an omen? I hoped for the latter but steeled myself for it to be the former.

But then he came. Walking out of the dissipating mist with a slight limp but still holding himself up with no need for anyone's help. He didn't stumble or veer off in a random direction or snake-like line, but walked straight toward me until I was staring at him, drinking in his features since I'd seen him last.

Much was the same. Soren's hair was still short and braided across his scalp. His skin was still the pale blue-gray color of the sky right before the dawn truly hit, and his eye was still lilac. But he stood with confidence once more, and the bandage over his eye had gone, leaving a clean if not new and pink scar across his permanently closed eyelid.

He took a long breath before speaking. "Hi."

I slapped him across the face as a response.

"Yeah, I guess I deserved that."

"Do you know how upset you made me?" I whisper-shouted, trying to keep my voice down not to wake Fjalar but also unable to contain all my rage.

"I'm going to assume a lot," he said hesitantly.

"A lot!" It was getting hard to keep my voice from rising as it collected all the emotion and heartache I'd suffered the past two days. "Cutting off contact, disappearing in the middle of the night. I thought you *left* us, left *me*, I thought you were going to kill yourself from exposure. And now you see my flaming arrow, and you come back like everything is fine? Explain yourself."

Soren bowed his head. "Something happened to me when the Nidhogg ripped my eye out. I don't know if it was venom or because of where we were or what, but I . . . It felt like this thing wiggling in my brain. A shadow I couldn't get away from." He clenched his hands and the hard muscles in his arms stood out. "And you're right. I felt sorry for myself. I felt like I was no longer worthy of anything. I grew up mastering swords and daggers, and while I'm not the archer you are, I could do it fine too. I grew up being told that was my worth, my strength. And then suddenly, I couldn't wield any weapon or even walk straight, and the whispers that slithered around in my head got darker and darker."

He sat and I sat beside him, backs against the boulders. "They told me to hurt you, Janneke. They told me I needed to kill you in order to get my strength back, and the worst part is some primal part of me craved strength at whatever the cost, and the moment I entertained it for even half a second, I knew I needed to leave. I couldn't bear to say what was happening to me."

Some of the fire that filled my body burned away as I

clasped his hands. "You would never hurt me. I know that more than anything else in the world. You should have told me about it, told one of us."

Soren made a pained sound. "I was going to, but then . . ." He shook his head. "I can't believe I'm actually saying this, but I got *jealous*. I was in the back of the line needing Seppo and Rose to help support me, and meanwhile you were by Lydian's side, and I *know* it didn't mean anything. I *know* the pain he caused you. But that vicious little voice kept pushing the idea further and further to the surface."

Maybe some part of me should've felt offended or disgusted by that insinuation. But if Soren was right about the voice inside his head and knowing it was wrong but not being able to change his thoughts no matter how he tried, I could bring myself to a cold understanding.

"And so you left?" I asked.

"I left. I felt like I had to. Something was lingering in my gut, there were the worms in my head, and I was useless. It was like watching myself slowly decay. So, I got up and followed the urge to walk."

"And?" I asked.

"Yggdrasil," he said. "I don't know what or who exactly was leading me there, but that's where I arrived and then passed out on the roots and bark, and when I woke, my mind was clear again, my scar stopped hurting, and I felt amazingly stupid for everything I did."

I nodded in agreement. "Good, you should feel that way." I looked at the sky to check the time. There was some gray among the red light of dawn, so there was still time to talk, but as soon as the red came, I would need to begin my plan.

My heart ached at the same time that my blood still boiled over Soren's choices and his inability to communicate. I loved him, but . . .

"Soren, I want you to know I love you. I'm terribly mad at you. I wish you could communicate better, and I wish you had more faith in me." I took a breath. "But I do still love you. And as the stag to Erlking, I trust you. But as Janneke to Soren, I need you to give me my space to get over this. I don't want you trying to convince me or beg for forgiveness. I'll come around. But I need to regrow my trust in you, on a personal level."

He nodded, eye looking down at his feet. "That makes sense."

The sky was now streaked with red, and I needed to get a move on. "Come on, I need you to help me move everyone." I began walking to the burrow with Soren catching up behind me.

"Wait, what's wrong?" he asked.

I served him a glare. "We tried to fight Fjalar yesterday. I'm the only one still conscious. I don't think anyone died, but Diaval won't wake up, Rose got smashed into rocks, Seppo nearly killed himself with his magic, and Lydian didn't wake up this morning either."

Soren ran a hand across the horrified expression on his face. "That's my fault too, then."

"I'll give you fifty-fifty. We chose to fight. But having you would've made a difference. It still wouldn't have worked, but it would have made a difference." I ducked into the burrow and found the four others still sleeping. One by one, I wriggled their bodies out from their curled-up positions and managed to get them to Soren, who dragged them out of the burrow completely.

"I need you to set them inside the circle I created. Doesn't have to be super deep in. Make sure they're far enough away from the mouth of the cave but set them inside and all together."

He nodded, and with more gentleness than I'd ever seen from him before, he cradled Seppo's body as he turned away.

Why is everyone so much bigger than me, I thought as I began to work on Rosamund with gentle fingers, terrified of breaking anything after he got slammed into the rocks. Soren was there to take his body, and I went down next to Lydian, managing to pull him out with a little less gentle of a grip because out of the four of them, he was easily the least injured.

My eyes got wet when I turned to Diaval. She lay still with only the faint rise and fall of her chest to indicate she was still alive. Her wound had grown infected again, and I prayed Tanya would be able to do something when I saw the small streaks of red on her skin, emerging from her wound.

She didn't struggle or cry out when I grabbed her and dragged her outside as best I could without bothering her leg, but that didn't make me feel any better. It meant she was too far gone to even feel the pain in her own body.

With Soren's help, we gently laid her beside the others. He stood in front of the four bodies and murmured something to them, but I was too far away to hear. It was showtime.

"Come on, we need to get ready."

"Where are the weapons?" Soren inquired.

"Worthless and we're not using them." I must've sounded completely out of my wits, but I continued on anyway. "You know how you had a feeling? Well, I've been dealing with my own, and it finally fixed itself when the cut off of the contact between the stag and the Erlking happened." I swept my foot across the icy ground and stared at the colored lines leading every which direction on the ice. "I can see it now. I think I understood after the first fight. There are only two people combined who can stop the end of the world, and those two are us. That thing"—I pointed to Fjalar's cave—"won't fall to weapons. It'll fall to us. If we can combine our power and unite, we can do it."

His brows furrowed in confusion. "I'm not sure what you mean, but I trust you on this."

"Good," I said, looking over my shoulder at the reddening sky. It was almost time. I checked everyone once again. Everyone was inside the circle, the chalk marks hadn't been scratched or wiped away, and in a few seconds, we would have to fight.

Now, I stood in front of the entrance with Soren a few paces behind me, took a deep breath, and let out a scream.

The winds blew from the force of the sound, and the clouds of dust and ice and snow made the once-clear air nearly impossible to see through. Soren jolted in surprise next to me but did nothing as the unhuman scream came out of my mouth. I dropped to my knees, feeling my vocal cords strain as I stretched out my arms.

The ground shook with the arrival of Fjalar, but he was invisible in the mist; though from behind me, Soren swore under his breath at the sight of the liminal monster.

My scream continued, pushing back the animal until I felt the next step of my plan come and bury itself bone-deep inside of me. I stood and dropped my head until the crown faced the ground, and I thought of that wall inside my body and the thin ice of the gauntlet, and like an actual stag, something inside me crashed through the wall and continued to run through my body. My veins, my muscles, my skin, every part of me was filled with a fiery sensation—not painful—as the power danced around my body, and as stag me and human me merged together in a beautiful storm of ice and fire.

I took a step up into the air, and it formed like a step from the ice under my feet. Turning, I reached a hand to Soren, who while thoroughly terrified—I knew his every thought and emotion now, no need to reach, no need to dig—accepted my hand as I pulled him up with me.

The inferno of ice that surrounded my body quickly climbed across our linked hands and circled his body too, his remaining eye turning the color of frost, and the scar where his eye should've been *shone* in the same bright color.

When I spoke, the wind spoke with me, and my voice boomed over the flat icy plain that was Niflheim.

"I am ash and I am elm," my voice boomed over the wind. "I am Frigga and Freya, Skadi and Gefion, Idun and Sif. I am Sigyn, Eir, Fulla, Gna, and Hlin. I am Ilmr and I am Hel. Every goddess throughout time, named and unnamed, flows through me. Everything that is or ever has been is in me. I know without knowing. I see without seeing. I am the beginning and the end and the time in between." My words lashed out at Fjalar like the swing of a sword, and the rooster shrieked in pain as it bled.

Soren clutched my hand and said, "I am the hunter. I am death. I am the brutality of nature at its fiercest and its protector at its weakest. Through me flows the blood of the Ancient One, the first Erlking, and through blood and sweat, I claimed the throne and I will rule. I am Odin's Other Eye and to slay you is my destiny."

Another shot of icy fire hit the bird, and it stumbled, bleeding from two very deep cuts in its chest.

The thing inside of me that told me to speak, gave me and Soren the words to say, pressed on.

"I am life, I am the cycle, and I forbid you from my realms," I shouted. The swirling of dust, ice, snow, and mist made it almost impossible to see what was happening to our enemy, but I could *feel* it in my very bones as Soren continued the chant.

"I am death. I am the pile of bones and the skeleton with a crown, and I will drag you down to your end," Soren snarled.

"We are one," we said together. "We are many. Bow to us and perish."

The ground started to rumble again as Fjalar gave out another deafening cry—not one of its magical cries—a cry of pain and agony as the world mist swirled around it closer and closer, the ice cutting deeper and deeper, until the liminal creature was no more.

I fell to the ground, landing on my knees. The earth was still shaking and a crevice was cracking open the ice where the cave and Fjalar had stood. The cave crashed into the next world, the fires of Muspellheim and the hot lava burned underneath me, rising up from the ice. I scrambled back from the lava as quick as I could, only for the plate of ice I was on to break. But before I could plunge into the heat below, Soren had me by the hand and pulled me to safety.

"Okay, now what?" he asked, panic creeping into his voice at the incoming heat.

"Trust me," I said and took out Diaval's chalk, drawing a marking on the palm of my hand and another on Soren's. Clasping them together, I shouted. Not a word I knew or a word I didn't; no one had taught me it and it sounded foreign to my ears, but I knew what I'd be able to do when I said it and that was enough to trust it.

Slamming our clasped hands to the ground, the snow began to dance around Soren and me, around Diaval and Lydian, Rose and Seppo, faster and faster and faster until I had to close my eyes before I threw up. I held on to Soren as tightly as my muscles allowed.

Then suddenly it stopped, and we were all spewed out back into the courtyard of the Erlking's palace, exactly where Diaval had created her original portal. From there, a bunch of people, goblin and human, rushed up to us as Tanya called everything to order.

Soren was lying on the ground with his face toward me, and he had a bloody grin from where he split his lip on the landing. His eye shone. "How did you know how to do that?" he asked, nearly giddy.

"Around the time you left, after the first fight with Fjalar, it hit me. Suddenly I felt everything. There were no more walls. I think—I think it has to do with you lying on the roots of Yggdrasil, if I'm honest. Because all of a sudden, I knew—I was forcing myself to keep each part of me separate. But there is no separation. There is no Janneke the stag and Janneke the human. There's *Janneke*." I gave him a goofy smile back, blood pumping through my veins fast as I realized I finally did it.

I crawled forward to embrace him, but someone grabbed the back of my hood. "You're hereby forbidden to move until I give the say so. All of you." Tanya's eyes swept over the group and scowled a bit at Lydian's flickering body. Back in Midgard, him sustaining a corporeal form wasn't as easy.

After trying to convince Tanya twice of my health but only hearing jumbled words come out, I succumbed to her and her healers.

IT TOOK THREE days of nearly nonstop healing sessions before Tanya declared me fit for the world again, and the moment she said it, I was out of my sickbed like a wildfire and running to Soren, who'd been actually the best off out of all of us if you didn't count losing an eye, as he gazed at the sleeping figures of our friends. Tanya had moved all of them into one room so she could keep an eye on them all together.

"Janneke," Soren said happily, and I got the feeling he'd rush over to grab me if it wouldn't jostle the cot Diaval was sleeping on.

"How are they?" It hurt to see the three of them in such broken states after all they'd done for us. Whether or not they survived, I would never be able to pay them back for the help they gave us, the loyalty they showed. I never thought I'd have actual friends in the Permafrost, but I did, and anxiety churned in my stomach at them lying in front of me, injured and powerless.

"Seppo is mainly fine. Some wounds but he used too much power when fighting Fjalar—the whistle attack you mentioned—and he should be awake in four, maybe five days, but he will spend a month or two needing to build back his ability." He paused before continuing. "I can't tell if Satu is proud of him or furious at him, or if it's some odd mixture of both."

I nodded. "Sounds like her to me." Seppo looked so peaceful. It would be good when he woke up again. I was going to yell at him for being so stupid and trying to sacrifice himself, but that was kind of how my relationship with Seppo went. He annoyed me, I yelled, he continued to annoy me because he found my yelling hilarious.

"And Diaval and Rosamund?"

"Diaval's the worst," Soren said, casting a soft look at the magic-wielding goblin. "She's lucky she didn't lose her leg, let alone die. If the infection had lingered any longer . . ." He trailed off. "Anyway, Tanya says it's just a matter of time until she wakes up. She'll wake up. We just don't know when.

"I really hate having to say this, but we were lucky Lydian was there. He saved her life, most likely, with the maggot thing he did. But I guess I have to give credit where credit is due. I'm grateful for him in that aspect, anyway," Soren continued.

I nodded. "I feel the same. It's conflicting. What about Rose?"

"Rose is very lucky his spine and skull aren't broken, and managed to get out of the entire fight with a few broken ribs and a broken leg," Soren said. "I'm glad. I'm starting to like the idea of having blood relatives who aren't always trying to kill or torment me."

"Speaking of blood relatives . . ." the voice that came from the corner of the room hoarsely spoke. Lydian.

"I thought you were asleep," Soren said. "Or whatever shades do to rest."

"You thought wrong. And to answer your question, shades who are corporeal can sleep."

I crossed my arms. "What do you want?" I asked. "Not that I'm unappreciative of your help, but it still doesn't change much."

He made a sound almost like a chuckle. "I didn't expect it to. No, Hel will still be after me. I'm technically a runaway soul. All I ask is you burn my heart and whatever pieces of me are left over and give the ashes a proper burial, so I can truly reside in Hel's realm. It might calm her."

"You want us . . . to kill you?" Soren said. "And make sure you get proper rest?"

"I know what you two are going to say. I don't deserve it. And you're right, I don't. But Hel still needs my soul, and well, I doubt she's going to make my afterlife any fun. You don't need her breathing down your neck with a war going on."

War. Gods, we set out to kill Fjalar before its three world-ending shrieks but failed to stop the first. Somewhere, the ship of the dead was being readied to turn to the unholy sea.

"Your request is accepted," I said. "We'll hold the burning later tonight."

He nodded and coughed, wincing in pain as he did so.

Soren looked at me. "Do you think we're prepared for it? War?"

"We have to be," I said. "Look on the bright side, it's the *Naglafar*. Everyone will be undead, and how much can a ship made of nails hold, anyway?"

Lydian raised his eyebrows and gave the two of us a glance that could only be read as exasperated. "The world is doomed."

"Right, onto burning your heart and ending both of our miseries," Soren said with a matching expression.

THE FIRE BURNED low in the coals, barely lighting the brazier, but the heat danced on my skin like the warmest sun. I couldn't take a proper breath, not with my chest this tight and my head this full of air. In truth, I could barely believe what was happening. That someone who'd tormented me for years, even after death, would finally be silent. *Finally*.

I wasn't unaware the memories I had would still return at random. I wasn't deluded into thinking that my nights would forever feel peaceful or that I would end up never again flinching at fast movements or that I'd ever love the feel of someone's skin on my skin. But it was a step forward. Maybe tiny, but all steps were good steps.

My heart was high in my throat as I waited for Soren. I'd refused to actually carry the still-beating heart. A part of me couldn't take it. It may have been the last of Lydian, but I still couldn't touch it, didn't want to be near it at all.

Whatever I had been through with him in the past few days, Lydian was still a demon who lurked in my nightmares. And at first seeing him in pain brought up a wicked feeling of vengeance, but it slowly wiled away down to nothing. This man was nothing to me. Alive, dead, half-dead. Now, with his entire physical form burned away from the world, he was truly, truly nothing.

The doors to the burial room creaked open; they were brass and heavy with carvings of runes all around them. I still couldn't read most of them, but I had the sense they spoke of the afterlives. With Hel, Freya, and Odin. I didn't need to vote on who I thought was taking Lydian away.

Soren carried the plate the heart had been placed on. In all my imaginings, it looked giant, but in reality it was slightly smaller than a fully grown, human male heart. That was interesting—for creatures who hovered above humans in every way, from ability, to speed, to fighting, to biological features, the small heart broke some illusion of their superiority.

Finally, he came to me and offered me a part of the plate. I swallowed my disgust and took the plate by the ends of my fingertips where no blood nor flesh could reach. Together, we dumped Lydian's heart into the coals and watched as it crackled and blistered as the flames took over.

The lump in my throat was now gone, and a weight lifted off my chest and shoulders like thousands of boulders rising up and away from my body. There was a soreness in my heart, a bruising where I'd been forced to carry that weight—forcing *myself* to carry it for my own undeserved penance.

It all rose up into smoke as the heart burned to ashes and finally, *finally*, standing by Soren's side, despite what was coming for us, I was completely, fully safe.

Epilogue

THE NAIL SHIP

SOMEWHERE IN THE deep bowels of Hel, there was a deafening crack of iron and rust and a chain unrooted from the earth. Thousands upon thousands of men, corpses filled with holes and half-eaten bodies and maggot-covered faces, those made up solely of bone and those so new that the skin had barely broken, they all pushed the sharp ship made from their nails into the sea of the dead. A serpent's head rose up to meet them, before moving on through the waters of life and shaking every world above him as he did.

The ship floated in the water as corpses rushed inside, and it held together despite the capacity of dead compared to its size. Because what was size when it came to the wicked, and what could they do other than sail for days and nights on end without tiring.

The *Naglafar* was coming and spreading its oily darkness into the water and sky where it passed. For every world, every realm, it would spread darkness like an endless night until they were all full of coldness and despair.

Acknowledgments

There are so many people to thank for getting this book out. First, I wanted to thank the lovely Caitlin and equally loved Kat, who really helped when I was approaching the deadline and having problems with the writing. You guys helped save this book.

Obviously, Eileen, my editor, deserves a huge thank-you as well for all she does and how hard she works. I wouldn't be here without her.

I'd like to thank the other important staff at Wattpad and Wednesday Books who've helped so far, Aron and Tiffany and many others whose names I can't recall because my memory is worse than Soren's ego. But just know, you all rock and I'm so very grateful.

Katherine, you're also mentioned in the dedication, but you're such an amazing friend and I love speaking to you whether it's about politics or writing or our fur babies, and I'm so glad I met such a wonderful person like you. You add so much to my life.

The same goes for Erika, or as I know her, Xenoclea, from Wattpad. She's *White Stag*'s first major fan and has been waving the encouragement flag for me ever since. The fact that you're willing to talk to me for two hours in the middle of the night about Permafrost is not something I haven't noticed. I'm very lucky to have your friendship.

Of course there are also many other users on Wattpad who I have to thank. Just to name a few: Saintc, Mal, Absent-minded_Artist, Kyle, DracoNako, CholorplasticCandence, FantasybkLover, Delia, Elle, astrophile, and many other members too numerous to name. Your love and support and enthusiasm for my writing is why I'm where I am, and I hope *Goblin King* impresses you the same way *White Stag* did.

Of course, I must thank my doctors and therapists for keeping me sane and healthy during hard times, especially during the pandemic. I'd also love to thank all my friends from Twitter who amuse me and make my life fuller every day and sometimes teach me things I had no idea about.

I can't not thank my family for putting up with me while writing *Goblin King*. Thank you, Mom, for allowing me to take over your house for two months, and Elaina for understanding I was on a deadline and couldn't do some of the things we wanted to do together. Thanks to Chris, my mom's partner, for being chill with me working in the basement at two a.m. with the lights on while he tries to sleep in another room. Also for being an excellent cook.

Special shout-out to Lady, my kitty I adopted in September after my old kitty, Kanu, died. You're such a sweet thing when you want to be and an absolute hellcat when not. I love your cuddles and kisses, and I'm glad you came into my life so soon after my old buddy left. You're wonderful even if you bite all my toes.

And of course, the best for last, thank you all, readers and supporters of the Permafrost series. You guys are wonderful and make it possible for me to do what I do, and I can never express the amount of gratitude that I have for you all. I love reading your tweets and seeing your images and thoughts about the book whether positive or negative and finding a community of fellow trauma survivors doing what it takes every day to get out of bed. You all are champions.